TUI DELIGHT

An Anthology from the
Michael Terence Publishing Short Story Competition

December 2017

Michael Terence
Publishing

First published in paperback by
Michael Terence Publishing in 2017
www.mtp.agency

Copyright © 2017 Michael Terence Publishing and Authors

Each author has asserted the right to be identified as the author of their work in accordance with the Copyright, Designs and Patents Act 1988

ISBN 9781973554240

All rights reserved. No part of this publication may be reproduced, stored in a retrieval system, or transmitted, in any form or by any means, electronic, mechanical, photocopying, recording or otherwise, without the prior permission of the publishers

Cover image
Copyright © Pavlo Syvak

Cover design
Copyright © 2017 Michael Terence Publishing

To writers and readers everywhere.

TURKISH DELIGHT

An Anthology from the
Michael Terence Publishing
Short Story Competition

December 2017

INTRODUCTION

This collection of short stories is taken from the Michael Terence Publishing Short Story Competition, December 2017.

Entries were received from across the world including the UK, USA, Canada, South Africa, Australia and Finland – which perhaps helps to explain the wide and stimulating range of subjects covered.

We extended our sincere thanks to the judges for their hard work and diligence. The panel was truly impressed by the overall high standard of the submissions – so it's big thankyou to all of the authors.

Here we publish the three prize-winning stories plus a selection of works that were highly commended by the judges.

Each has been published as it was received, without further editing. We hope you will enjoy reading them all.

ABOUT MICHAEL TERENCE PUBLISHING

In the past, the founders of MTP experienced the frustration of having a great manuscript but meeting a brick wall when trying to find a traditional agent/publisher. Quite simply, MTP was founded to give worthy authors a platform to publish their works, earn maximum royalties, gain the best online sales for print books and eBooks and then, based on that success, give them the option to find a traditional publisher.

Today, submissions of new works in all genres are being gratefully received via our website www.mtp.agency.

CONTENTS

Turkish Delight – Owen O'Hagan 1

Days – Liza Kocsis 9

The Wish Carver – Hannah Contois 19

Homage to Chagall – Diana Brighouse....................................... 28

Rope – Michael Thompson 37

Voices and Songs – Edward Sergeant 43

Standing Awkwardly in Rooms – Francesca Casilli 52

In Wolf's Clothing – Celia Law 57

More Than Life – Pete Pitman 62

Take the Gamble – John Bunting 70

The Last Voyage of Ferrywoman Katherine Marshall – John Bunting 78

Angels with Razor Wings – Laure Van Rensburg 86

Zig Zag – Charles Osborne.. 96

Busting a Rhyme or Two on a Lovely Spring Morning – Sean Crawley.. 101

Aspirational – Jennifer Hayashi Danns 107

The Nervous Bread Van – Michael Demus Hanson 116

Five Pound Notes and Fluffy Bunnies – Mary Charnley......... 125

How to Commit a Perfect Murder – John Notley 134

1½ Minutes. (Approx.) – Lee Wadmore 143

Stalking the Muse – Steve Wade 149

Lucky Number Seven – N.B. Cara 157

Heart of Gold – Wanda Dakin 160

The Kite – Hannah Van-de-Peer 168

The Cold Records – Dan Patton 176

Sonata for Sausage Roll and Exploding Foam – Richard Salsbury 186

Starving – Yvonne Popplewell 194

Consequences – Sen Jayaprakasam 202

Valentine's Day – Jordan Ryder 210

Blind Date – Philip Pendered 216

Cleaning Up – Sandra Howell 226

FIRST PRIZE
Turkish Delight – Owen O'Hagan

Two shots of Aldi peach schnapps and an amaretto is not enough to get me drunk, I realise, standing in the Northern Quarter amongst what seems like the entire of Manchester.

I open the notes on my phone pretending to be busy because then surely no one will notice me. I'm early even though I tried my hardest to be late. I walked slowly to the metro, walked slowly to the restaurant, even though walking slowly is something my long legs never really do. And yet, I'm still five minutes early.

There are two muscly bouncers next to me – it's as if they were employed only because they look like stereotypical bouncers. They're laughing and joking, chatting about a woman they both seem far too familiar with. Then a taxi pulls up and two girls in short skirts jump out.

I don't want them to see us kiss. I walk a little bit down the street. Just because the first date ends in a kiss, doesn't mean the second has to begin with one, does it?

Then there he is, crossing the road, maybe wearing the same black clothes from Sunday night. The same *hype* backpack over his shoulders. The same bouncy walk that reminds me of my best friend from school.

Do we hug? Do we kiss? Do we do nothing?

He hugs me, *how are you doing* he asks, kissing me on the cheek. We pull away and there's this second of silence so I ramble about how loud it is in the street. Apparently I'm eighty years old.

We shuffle towards the entrance, uncomfortable with each other, neither willing to take the lead. Climbing the stairs we get the *how was your week* awkwardness out of the way.

Then we're told there's an hour wait for the table. *Fuck*. The waitress takes my number and says she'll text me when the table is available. I play it cool, ramble like an old person again about how modern this is, as if I'm trying to convince him I'm not nine years younger than him.

As we're waiting at the bar I'm playing back everything we spoke about on our first date so I don't fuck up and ask him the same questions, tell him the same stories. At least there's a cocktail menu to steal our attention away from each other. Strawberry daiquiri. O*oooh* we both say almost simultaneously and then laugh nervously. Long island ice tea. I want to say *ooooh* again but resist.

I'll pay, I insist. I don't want him to think I'm letting him buy everything because he's older. He refuses until he has to agree because I'm not giving in. He goes to find us place to sit and I wonder whether it's his breath that smells or mine. I overdosed on mouthwash so it can't be me. It better fucking not be me.

He gets a tequila and absinthe concoction. Possibly the worst combination in the world. Mine is vodka-y and bright blue with a cola ice-pop sticking out the top. Things are improving.

Now we're sitting face to face and I have no fucking clue what to say. The first date didn't feel like this, did it? I sip out of my funky straw and smile. He smiles back. Then I check my phone to see if the table is ready. It's not. I ask him about work and conversation starts to flow. *Phew*. He made a mistake today that cost his company at least 50,000 pounds. I don't really understand what he does but at least we're talking. A song comes on that I recognise, and he says he'll *Goggle* it, smiling, reminding me about how much we *googled* on the first date. Somehow we already have an *in* joke after only one meeting.

He asks my favourite TV show. I say *Six Feet Under*. He says how much he loves it too. He really wants to re-watch it soon. *Hint hint*. His drink tastes shit. No one's surprised but him. He tells me to try it and yes, it's disgusting. But I volunteer to have it anyway because I need to be drunk. I mix it with my blue drink to make an extra special cocktail. At first he's laughing but then I spill some and the crushed ice skids across the table towards another couple.

He tuts. A disapproving *'I can't believe you just did that'* tut that makes me feel shitty about something that I really don't think I should feel shitty about. And then he apologises to the couple at the end of the table, twice, even though they barely noticed. I take a drink from my new cocktail, almost a little ashamed, avoiding his eye contact. Still no text from the waitress. *Hurry up.*

What am I supposed to be feeling for him?

He goes to get a merlot, I say I'm fine. *Who the hell drinks merlot?* I check my phone a few dozen times until finally, just as he's back with his goblet of wine, the waitress texts.

There's two tables we can choose from; one out in the open, the other in a dimly lit corner. I know which one I want to choose but he picks the corner and we're sitting down. I change my mind about the drink and order a vodka and coke. I need to loosen up.

The menu is like all menus in the world to me; pointless because I already know what I want. A burger. He *ums* and *ahs* and keeps saying *trailer trash fries* in an American accent as if it's meant be funny. So I laugh.

When we order I don't ask for no salad on my burger even though that's as natural to me as chewing on the food. I drink the vodka as quickly as possible. It doesn't seem to be helping. I'm fine, I'm confident. I'm telling stories and listening and laughing but I just don't feel anything. *A spark.* I am putting on this act but I can't stop myself, like a rocket already set off.

I take the lettuce and tomato out of my burger, hope he doesn't notice. We talk through full mouths, say how good all the food is, especially the *trailer trash fries* he says, laughing at himself again. I laugh a little quieter this time. Another song comes on and he *googles* it and we laugh. *Hahaha.* He asks why I don't eat salad and puts it on his plate.

I don't think I fancy him. I do not fancy him. I definitely don't fancy him.

Then he asks if I'd like to go somewhere else after the meal. My stomach sinks, if only I could squeeze my eyes shut, open them again and wake up at home. No I don't want to go somewhere else.

Yeah sure, I say.

We go back to where we had our first date. But instead of an acoustic indie band playing quietly in the corner you can barely hear anything but the beats of the R&B DJ. I order him another merlot, thinking I'll likely never order this drink at a bar ever again. I get a double vodka this time. *Can you get a triple?*

We sit in the dark bar, underneath an unusually large plastic red lampshade, barely able to hear each other. Occasionally one of us lean over and bitch about the music. *This music's shit. What? The music, it's shit. Yeah, it is.* It doesn't seem to be bothering anyone else. They're having fun. Maybe they're not listening so intently.

We down our drinks and move on. Yet again I want to squeeze my eyes and disappear. I want the night to be over. I want to go home. But I keep going, rocket flying high.

This next place is better. *Musically.* But I'm flagging, my false enthusiasm dying slowly. I can't think of anything else to say and so let the silences hang in the air. We watch some rowdy drunks throw their coats in the middle of the bar and start dancing around them. I wish I was out with them.

Suddenly, I feel him stroking my thigh. I ignore it.

I go to the toilet, even though I don't need to go. I stand at the urinal, nothing happening, wondering how I can escape. I realise I need to leave before I look strange.

Same hanging silences, same dancing drunks, same attempt at thigh stroking. So I go to the toilet again, ramble about how alcohol makes me pee too much. I want to ask someone to save me, get me out of here, bump into someone I know. I don't.

So what do you think of me, he says when I get back, closer to me now. *Do you see me as more of a friend or do you fancy me? Do you fancy me?*

Is this a normal question to ask? Isn't that what you leave for the polite but slightly rude text when you've both gone your separate ways? *Uhhhhhhhh* is all that comes out. I should tell the truth. But I do *want* to fancy him. Why don't I fucking fancy him?

I say something about how it takes me time to see someone in that way and ask him what he thinks. He fancies me, he says. How is that possible? How can we not be feeling the same things? Then, suddenly, he asks if I want to go back to his house.

Maybe it's the bar. I'm self-conscious. I'm not used to this. Maybe it will be better when we're alone. So I say yes. And somehow, it's better. It's night and it's rowdy in the streets and I'm following him in a direction I've never been to before. Conversation flows so easily as if all we needed was some fresh air.

He tells me about watching *Queer As Folk* and how it helped him come out. And I agree. I totally agree. He's going to make me a hot chocolate. We'll watch the first episode of Six Feet Under. This is good. This is fun. Maybe I could fancy him. Maybe I do.

There's this little petrol station that's open and he asks if I want some chocolate. Of course I do. It's like I'm high all of a sudden. Or maybe the vodka's finally kicked in. I'm giggling trying to choose a chocolate bar. He's laughing too, indecisive. He picks a fruit and nut bar which I only judge internally. Then I see these Turkish Delight bars I used to get at home in Ireland. *Oh my god,* I gleam. I pay for the bars because he hasn't got any change. We agree to eat them at his.

Finally we're at his apartment block and it reminds me of the last time I went home with a guy way back in university. I was drunk then too. He keeps apologising about how untidy it's going to be. We get in the lift and there's a giant mirror at the back of it but I don't want to look into it.

The flat's not messy, it's nice and modern. *It's lovely,* I say, again and again. A word I've barely used in my life. I don't even sound like me anymore. He shows me the balcony. It's the most amazing view of Manchester. How can this be his flat? How can he own all of this? If there was ever going to be a *moment* this would be it. I sense it in the air. But I pretend not to notice.

I'm not relaxed. It's not better. I don't fancy him.

But he has sensed the moment too and definitely does not ignore it and suddenly he's kissing me. I close my eyes and kiss back even though I'm not sure I want to or if I'm any good. Finally, I pull away and laugh, more nervously than intended.

Sorry, he says. *You're not,* I think.

He's making me the hot chocolate he promised me, *Six Feet Under* ready on the TV. What the hell am I doing here? What the fuck have I done? He asks if I want my Turkish delight but I say no. I can't stomach it. So we watch *Six Feet Under.* I'm sipping the luke warm hot chocolate, him another glass of merlot. I don't look away from the screen until half-way through when he stares at me and asks if I'm alright. I look at him and smile politely. *Yeah.*

Five minutes later, my favourite programme on in front of me, his legs near mine, I realise I need to leave. I cannot stay here after this episode ends. The decision is made. It might be the worst thing I've ever done. It will be awkward. But I am going home tonight.

The credits roll, *shit.* He gets up to take the DVD out. And then I do it.

I think I have to leave, I say. I can't stay there tonight. He's defensive, arms folded, saying *that's fine that's fine.* I keep saying *sorry* and putting my hands in my head. He says *don't be silly* and I say *I'm sorry* again.

He's older than me, he says. He knows what he wants. He wants a relationship. He didn't drag me there. *I know,* I say. *I'm taking the blame. I shouldn't have come back with you. No,* he says. *You shouldn't have.*

He's right.

I don't think I understood awkward until now. I used the word a lot, felt it maybe, but now I really and truly know what it means. He edges to the end of the sofa, offers to call me a taxi but I say I'll do it myself. I dial and realise I need his address. *Fuck.* I ask him and he tells me.

Thirty fucking minutes away.

He says he needs to sleep and somehow I find myself washing the hot chocolate mug. He tells me to leave it and I feel just like I did in the bar when I spilt the cocktail. *You can wait here until your taxi comes,* he says. I lie and tell him it's outside.

Do you know how to get downstairs, he asks.

Yeah, I say, lying again

He opens the door for me and gives me directions I try to listen to. I step outside into the hallway and he tells me to message him when I'm home. I turn to him in the doorway, wonder whether we should hug, or shake hands, or acknowledge each other in some way. But instead I just say *bye,* almost laughing to myself. I am the arsehole here. I am the one messing him about. He doesn't want to hug me.

The door closes. *Down to floor 2, cross the garden, down to floor 0.* Somehow I find my way out first time around. It's dark, eerily quiet except for the occasional revving car. I have no fucking idea where I am. It's cold. It's 2am. And the taxi won't be here for twenty-five minutes.

What if it doesn't come? I call three other companies just in case, all of them are too busy. So I just wait, walk out of sight of his window so he thinks I'm gone. Thirty minutes later, still no taxi. Drunks walk by, coming home, barely noticing me. Other taxi's pull in and out but none of them are for me. *Shit, shit, shit. This is the stupidest thing you have ever done.* Who can I call at this time? They'll all be asleep. And this is embarrassing. I don't know what to do. Should I start walking?

Then my taxi pulls up. I run over desperately and climb

inside. It smells stale, like old men, but I don't care. This is best taxi in the world.

Why so far from home, he asks.

Bad date, I say, thinking over the night now as if it never happened.

He gets embarrassed himself, tells me I don't have to talk about my personal life. We don't talk anymore, sit in comfortable silence. *I'm going home.* I need to get cash out so he stops half-way to Didsbury, tells me it's better if I have money before he drops me off so I don't run off without paying.

I almost don't want to leave him. From the cash point I keep turning to make sure he's not left me, pretending the drunks all around me don't exist. Nothing *really* happened to me. I wasn't hurt. I'm okay. And yet I can't help but feel unsafe now, wounded maybe. My pride. His pride. I'm not sure. I climb back in the taxi and eventually recognise somewhere near home. I get out and probably tip him too much but I don't care because to me he just saved my night.

I walk home, arms folded and shivering, head heavy and drunk.

I don't take off my clothes or brush my teeth, just lie on the floor and stare at the ceiling, the room spinning. I look at my phone; 3.30am. I message him to tell him I'm home, adding a final *sorry* because I can't resist. Maybe he didn't actually want me to message him. But then maybe he did because he's clearly a better person than me.

I type *why don't I fancy people into Google*, laughing to myself. Then I take the *'Am I sociopath?'* quiz and it tells me I'm 76% not a sociopath. That's okay then.

Finally I take off my clothes, wash the night off my face and gurgle some mouthwash. My head finally on the pillow, the room still spinning, I suddenly remember the Turkish delight I've left at his flat.

Damn it. I really wanted that.

SECOND PRIZE
Days – Liza Kocsis

Day 1

06:59 *Good morning everybody, you are listening to Sunshine FM, the time is 7am, it's shaping up to be a beautiful day in March, with the temperatures reaching up to twenty degrees, rain is not forecasted anywhere in the UK...*

Glass breaking. The radio stops. Silence for a while.
-What on earth did you break again?
-A wine bottle. Why are you leaving it in the way?
-It was empty anyway.
-Sure. You won't be the one cutting their feet open.
The girl sits at the edge of the bed for a little while. She takes a deep breath and jumps over the broken wine bottle. She digs her coffee stained, pink dressing gown out of a pile of dirty laundry sitting on a chair and puts it on. She walks to the small kitchen that's only a couple of metres away from their bed in the studio apartment. She slowly opens the fridge, stands there for a couple of seconds, then takes out an empty milk bottle.
-Can you tell me why you always have to leave the empty bottle in the fridge? Is it so difficult to chuck it in the bin?
-The bin was full. It didn't fit. Do we have to have the same conversation every single morning?
-I'm asking the same thing! Do you want coffee?
She rinses two dirty mugs under cold water, and makes a coffee using whipped cream that was left over from Christmas, instead of milk. She opens the balcony door, warm spring breeze sneaks into the room. She is observing the still sleepy and quiet city, the old ladies rushing to the market, the pigeons mating dance. She lights a cigarette and takes a sip of her coffee. She suddenly spits it out.
-Don't drink it. The whipped cream is off.
The doorbell rings. She freezes and looks at her dirty dressing

gown.
-Could you get that please?
-Nope, I'm sleeping.
-Thanks.
 She opens the front door, the postman looks up and down on her hungrily, until his eyes finally settle on her tights.
-I'm delivering a last warning from the gas company. You need to sign here and here please.
She turns the letter in her hand, contemplating whether or not she should open it, but in the end she just throws it on the table on top of the other unopened post and empty pizza boxes. She goes back to the room and stands around for a while aimlessly.
-You need to wake up or you will be late for your interview.
The boy moans and turns on his side. The strong sun is burning his eyelids, he is hot. He kicks the duvet on the floor. She gets dressed, brushes her teeth and shouts back from the door one last time:
-I'm going to work. Please get up, I don't want to listen to your annoying dad again for two weeks. I will call you in 10 minutes to make sure you are up.
She slams the door hard. Flakes of paint crumble of the walls. The loud bang echoes in the silence for a long time, it broke the peace of the morning, gave a sign to the city to start the day. A bus rushes through the wide road, two homeless men argue over a secure sleeping spot, a little bee hides away, trembling. The city life doesn't suit it.

16:39

As the girl gets home the boy is sitting on the edge of the bed, smoking a cigarette. The girl stops in front of him and runs her fingers through his hair.
- How did it go? I asked you not to smoke inside.
-It wasn't bad. They asked a bunch of questions about my dad. I think I got it because of him, but only so he can keep an eye on me.
The boy's phone starts to buzz. He runs out to the balcony and shuts the door behind him. He comes back 5 minutes later.

-Who was that?
-Father...To see if I went. He said if I don't get it he won't send any more money, he won't pay for my weed, bills and the rent...
The rest of the day goes as normal. The afternoon light paints the walls a different colour, the heat bounces back from the ceiling and splashed on the floor. The girl takes down the rubbish in the evening, her lung squeaks on her way up the stairs, the old lady on the second floor doesn't return her smile. The city doesn't want to go to sleep for a long time, there is something in the air. The wind carries dirt around. Then everything goes quiet.

Day 2
06:59 *Good morning everybody, you are listening to Sunshine FM, the time is 7am, it's shaping up to be a beautiful day in March, with the temperatures reaching up to twenty degrees, rain is not forecasted anywhere in the UK...*
Glass breaking. The radio stops. Silence for a while.
-Not again?!
-Why are you leaving it right next to the alarm?
-I didn't put it there this time.
-Whatever, I don't want to argue.
The girl gets up, jumps over the shards on her way to the fridge. Takes out the empty milk bottle.
- How can you drink so much milk? Now I won't have any for my coffee again.
-I don't know what you are talking about, are you drunk?
-Shut up.
The girl puts on her slippers and goes out to the balcony. The doorbell rings.
-Who the hell is that now?
She opens the door, the postman is standing there, his eyes settle on her black bra peeking through her dressing gown.
-I've brought a final warning from the gas company, please sign here.

-I've already signed for this yesterday.
-Not possible. It has today's date on it.
She is rummaging through the mess on the table. A pizza box falls on the floor, but no letter is found.
- Never mind, I sign again, why not.
She stares at the envelope for a while, then chucks it on the table. She gets dressed quickly, kisses the forehead of the boy who is still lying in bed and goes to work. She leaves the balcony door open, two homeless men are arguing on the street. A bus stops with a huge sight. A little bee flies through the open windows and happily ventures between dirty dishes. It found what it was looking for.

16.56

The door opens, the girl walks in. The boy is pacing up and down the door angrily in his sweatpants. A cigarette is burning away between his fingers.
-So father just called. Asking why I didn't go to the interview. Telling me he is going to cut me off, that I am a druggy, who doesn't know what to do with himself. I tried to tell him the interview was yesterday but he was having none of it. He is gone crazy...
-Everyone was really weird at work today too. They gave me the same numbers to process as yesterday.
They stare at each other for a while, then the girl turns around and runs down to the street. She returns with the newspaper under her arm.
-It says it's the 21st of March. I thought it was the 22nd.
The rest of the day goes on as normal. They order a pizza and smoke some weed. The sun finally goes down at 6pm, leaving a slight scent of cut grass in the air. There is not a single cloud in the sky, it's a fine spring evening.

Day 3
06:59 *Good morning everybody, you are listening to Sunshine FM, the time is 7am, it's shaping up to be a beautiful day in March, with the temperatures reaching up to twenty degrees, rain is not forecasted anywhere in*

the UK...
Glass breaking. The radio stops. Silence for a while. The girl turns around in bed, they are looking at each other, frightened.
-Did you..?
-No!
They jump out of bed at the same time. The girl gets dressed straight away, and when she turns around she notices the boy standing in front of the fridge, staring at the empty milk bottle in his hands. They both have their coffees on the balcony, black. The doorbell rings. The boy goes to answer it. When the postman sees him the smile disappears from his face.
-I brought a final warning from the gas company sir. Please sign here.
-Could you tell me today's date please?
-It's the 21st of March, sir.
She leaves for work, meanwhile two homeless men start a fight on the street, bus 96 suddenly comes to a halt while smoke pours out of the engine. The city is having a difficult start.

Day 5
06:59 *Good morning everybody, you are listening to Sunshine FM, the time is 7am, it's shaping up to be a beautiful day in March, with the temperatures reaching up to twenty degrees, rain is not forecasted anywhere in the UK...*
Glass breaking. The radio stops. Silence for a while.
-You know what? Don't go to work today. What's the point?
She makes a cup of tea. They are drinking it slowly, sitting by the kitchen table, when the doorbell rings.
-Don't open it! Or open it, but naked! Imagine the old perverts face when he sees you!
They watch the letter fall through the post box. They laugh. The boy leans over and kisses her neck, then lifts her up with one smooth motion and takes her out to the balcony.
-What are you doing? People can see us!
-So what?
-There could be children around.

-They will forget it by tomorrow...

Day 22
15.13

They are sitting on a bench in the park. There are lots a people running on the grass, enjoying the early spring heat.

-Why do you think we are the only ones? Who noticed about the time...repeating?

- Look at these people. They were living the same day even before it happened. They have the same past, the same future. Look at those kids smoking by those bushes. They think when they finish college they will be free. They don't know they won't have jobs, houses, pensions. And the ones that will have these things... Well what's the point? Family, crying baby, fat wife. It's better for them like this. They are not going anywhere, like they weren't before.

-Why not us though? We haven't got a flat, or money. You have no job. We are running the same circles too!

-Maybe somebody wanted us to see them. And us. I don't know. Look on the bright side. We will never have to pay bills again. Even if we wanted to, we couldn't clean the apartment. It's paradise!

-We could rob a bank and be rich for a day. I can eat whatever I want and I will never get fat. I won't have to work with those idiots again.

Day 37
21:49

The couple is out dancing. Their pulsating, overheated bodies move to the rhythm of the music. He gets too wasted and throws up on the middle of the dance floor. She carries him home.

A lot of people are getting drunk tonight. They are trying to forget yesterday. Little do they know that they are locked in today. The city wants to rest for the night, but they won't let it. A rat finds a whole slice of bread on the street, drags it into its hiding place and peacefully munches on it, when a loud noise scares it away, leaving more than half behind.

Day 55
06:59 *Good morning everybody, you are listening to Sunshine FM, the time is 7am, it's shaping up to be a beautiful day in March, with the temperatures reaching up to twenty degrees, rain is not forecasted anywhere in the UK...*
Glass breaking. The radio stops. Silence for a while.
-Could you be more careful? You know that goddamn bottle is right there, would it be so difficult not to break it?
The girl jumps out of bed angrily, accidentally stands on a shard, cuts her foot deeply, the dirty white tiles are painted red in the kitchen. She suddenly starts crying, not from the pain, she shrugs down, hugs her knees and weeps.
-I'm sorry, I didn't mean it. Come here, you won't feel it tomorrow.
She frees herself from his hug, puts on a dress and storms out, banging the door behind her. Yellow paint crumbles off the walls. Its 7:22am, a warm March morning, the old ladies left for the market early. A girl is running on the street, not knowing where to, not caring who she pushes out the way. She runs past a homeless man sleeping, past a broken down bus. A little bee flies next to her persistently, it's drawn to her yellow dress, it's hungry and thirsty.

Day 79
10.12
The couple is sitting at the corner pub. They are stirring coffee in silence; she is deep in thought.
-Do you think if we went away it would be the same? Maybe we were meant to do something good with this extra time, other than shagging and getting stuff for free.
- I don't know. I don't think so. Where would you go anyway? It's shit everywhere, not just here. Look at that miserable waitress, look how useless she is. She dropped something again.

-Do you have to be so negative? I can't take it anymore. I can't even look at you. You know why we are the only ones knowing about the time? So I can see what a miserable bastard you are! I never noticed it before. You think we are better than everyone else, the chosen ones. We are not. I wish we didn't know about anything. It was fun at first, but not anymore. Maybe we didn't have a future but at least we moved from A to B.
-Are you going crazy or something?
She jumps up and rushes out the door. People are staring at her leaving, then throw murderous looks into his direction. He shrugs his shoulders. Maybe he would care if they remembered this the next day.

Day 104
They haven't spoken to each other in three days. The silence is cutting through the room like a knife. She gets out of bed, gets dressed and leaves. She buys a coffee and flirts with the barista for a while. She is looking at the kids at the playground with pity and some jealousy. She could do anything a child can now, without consequences. But no, she knows too much of life. She couldn't laugh or love like a child can. Can she love at all? Does she love the boy she's been living with the past 10 years? The boy who doesn't want marriage or children. She gets an ice-cream and runs away without paying.
14:11
When she gets home she finds the boy in bed with another woman. She turns out the door and gets lunch somewhere. She doesn't get home until late evening.
19:29
-Fantastic. You found a woman willing to sleep with you in three hours. Bravo.
-Listen, I'm sorry, you know I love you. The world is our oyster, baby. She won't even remember me. Come on, I was bored without you here.
-I hate you. If everything was normal, would you not be bored then? Our life wasn't much more exciting before either. You just had to cheat on me, didn't you? If you loved me you

wouldn't be bored. No, leave me alone. Don't touch me! Leave me alone!

23:33
The city is trying to sleep, but keeps getting woken up. The rat couldn't finish his dinner again. A rotten smell pours out of the drains. The girl is standing on the balcony, smoking her fifths cigarette in a row. Her hair is messy, there is a strange light in her eyes . She bit her lips bloody. She is flicking the ashes on the street below, watching them drifting in the moonlight. She moves slowly and quietly closes the balcony door behind her. She purposefully makes her way to the kitchen, where she fumbles around for a while in the dark. She stands by the bed, looking down on her boyfriend's sleeping body. She is looking at his stomach pouring out of his t-shirt. His thinning hair, his yellowing teeth in his open mouth. His arms she used to love, big hands covered in veins. She is not thinking, she is not feeling. She grips the kitchen knife and strikes him in the chest, in the stomach, in the leg, once, twice, a hundred times. While she is working she is thinking about empty milk bottles, yellow walls, mouldy pizza slices, bills piling on the table. He doesn't even have a chance to wake up. When she finishes she wraps the body in the sheet and rolls it off the bed. Thick, dark blood spreads quickly, and seeps through the gaps of the wooden floor. Suddenly she feels tired like never before. She lies in the bed that is still warm from his body. She falls asleep immediately.

It's a strange night. Clouds are gathering in the sky, growing ever so bigger. The air is filled with electricity. The bugs and animals seek shelter somewhere safe. The moon can't be seen anymore. The city can't wait for the rain to ease the abnormal heat and to settle the heavy dust.

Day 105
06:59 *Good morning everyone, you are listening to Sunshine FM, I am sad to report that the heat did not last long, temperatures dropped more than 10 degrees over night, rain is forecasted all over the UK. Now let's*

listen to Creep by Radiohead, I would like to address this song for all of those who struggled to get up this morning. Let's get to work, people!

THIRD PRIZE
The Wish Carver – Hannah Contois

I never woke up. There was no gradual increase in awareness. There were no flickering eyes or twitching fingers. Everything was black, empty and blank, up until the moment it wasn't. A flash of lightning that lights up the night's sky, I suddenly existed once more in the inside of bolt of electricity.

I had no concept of time in the white. Hours, days, years. Any amount of time could have passed. I only knew the piercing light and the vast, sucking emptiness of my existence. I only knew the ache of a memory of a warm palm in mine. I only knew the stifling silence without my daughters' chatter and the pressure in my ears as I tried to listen for them.

"Are you willing to pay the price?" A young man's voice slipped into the space that I wandered around, the first sound other than my own voice in this shrieking silence.

I whirled and there was a boy. No older than 13 or 14, he rocked back on his heels, hands in jean pockets, watching me. While his face appeared young in the long but soft way of young men's faces, his eyes were ancient, timeless. Black as night. Black as the darkest part of the ocean. Absorbing without a speck of light in their depths. Shark eyes.

Surprised, I stumbled back and he watched me fall without the slightest sign of reaching out to help me. The smallest hint of a smile played with his lips, pitying and yet self-satisfied. Unruly black curls puffed away from his forehead like dark rainclouds under his hood.

"Tell me," he said, tone sardonic and cynical, like he already knew what my response would be. "Are you willing to pay the price?"

I swallowed hard, thinking that it should hurt to swallow around the lump in my throat. "Price? What price? Who are you?"

He untucked his hands from his pockets, bowing like a

jester. "I'm the Wish Carver. For a price, I will grant you a wish." He glanced up at me from his bow, eyes glistening from below the edge of this hood.

"What's your name?"

"I don't have one. Or if I did, I've long since forgotten it in the eons that I have been here serving the souls who cry out for change. For a wish."

"A wish?" I breathed, my family filling my thoughts; my daughters' shining blue eyes, my husband's smile that could fix even the darkest of my days. "Any wish?"

The Carver shrugged lean shoulders. "If you're willing to pay, there is no end to what you could have." He swaggered in a circle around me. "Fame. Riches. The list goes on."

I shook my head. "I want my family. Are they okay? Are they alive?"

He nodded in the impetuous fashion of teenagers, indicating over my shoulder. I turned, fearing the worst. Fearing that my family was here in this void without me. That thought was almost worse than having them live without me. They didn't stand there but a TV did, conjured out of thin air by the Carver, resting on an old fashion AV cart like the ones from my high school. I held my breath.

Playing on the screen was a video and in a rush, like water from a dam, memories plowed into me, playing in synchronicity with the video.

It had been muggy, typical for a Florida morning. My husband was driving our minivan, his shaggy oil slick hair mussed from the wind. I leaned across the center console and whispered something into his ear and the ghost of the words hung on my lips.

Come on, Mav. Do some of that pilot shit.

Behind his favorite Aviators, I knew his blue eyes had twinkled like blue flames. He'd pulled me in close so that his lips had brushed against the apple of my cheek.

Have you lost that loving feeling?

I remembered his voice with stunning lucidity, like a nightmare that never left. The eerie clarity of the words was carved into my bones. Etched into my soul. The piercing stare and butterfly swarm that his words had induced and the sappy, sweet smile we'd shared. Then his swearing as he had veered across the road, broad hands yanking the wheel. There was a flash of light on the screen, the reflection of the sun off the hood of the oncoming car, and then sparks as our minivan skid on the asphalt. The scream of metal assaulted me in the silence of the void and the ghosts of the sparks hitting my skin popped along my arm and neck.

An image of Michael holding our daughters on our couch flickered across the aged screen and I fell to my knees. This was not part of my memory. This was their reality. They were curled into his chest like sleepy kittens with brows knitted like they were having nightmares. I coughed lightly, choking without knowing it, without feeling it. My husband looked empty, drawn. Not a smile in his eyes or on his face. He looked in so much pain that I crawled on hands and knees towards the TV before I knew what I was doing. The screen snapped at my touch as I traced over his downturned mouth, wishing beyond anything that I could take it away. On the table at his side, tucked into the picture frame that held an image of us laughing at our wedding, was a strip of newspaper. My obituary.

"I'm dead?" My voice was empty, flat. Surprising given the turmoil that blanked my brain.

"Of course," the Carver snapped, as if my question was the stupidest thing he had ever heard. "How did you think you got here?"

"I don't know," I mumbled, sounding small and broken. I felt small and broken.

He smiled that cynical, satirical smile at me. "You wanted something so badly that your soul cried out loud enough that I was summoned to offer you a deal."

"What deal?"

"A second chance for a price."

"What's your price?"

Clucking his tongue, the Carver wagged a finger in my face. "I can't tell you. You have to make the deal without me telling you the cost."

Again, I spoke rashly. "I need them. They need me. I wish to go back. I'll pay. I'll pay whatever it is."

Shark eyes pinned me in place and I wobbled on my feet. He shook his head. "You souls are always the same. Disappointing and predictable, thinking only of yourselves. I was hoping that you would be different but if that is what you really want, your wish is my command. I'll send you back to your precious family," he said, tone impudent and irreverent.

"What is it like?" I asked.

"Just like hitting the reset button." He snapped his fingers with a shark's smile and all went dark.

"Have you lost that loving feeling?"

I smiled into Michael's face and then hiccupped back into my seat. Something was off, an itching sense of wrongness, but I couldn't pinpoint it. A pain lanced my collarbone, distracting me. I sat forward, reaching to pull the vanity mirror down but movement in the road up ahead caught my eye. A car, careening across the median and into our oncoming traffic.

"Michael!" I screamed, throwing my hand out to catch his arm. He cursed and veered, slamming on the brakes as the front of the car just kissed the nose of the mini-van, and sent us into a spin. The girls screamed behind me, with me, until we finally stopped. In a cloud of burnt rubber and dust, we stopped.

"Everyone okay?" Michael's normally steady voice, shook. His hands white-knuckled the steering wheel as he glanced in the rearview mirror, at our daughters, and then at me.

"I think we're okay," I managed to whisper.

"That was close," he breathed, arching around the edge of his seat so that he could see the girls. Both their small faces were pale, tears welling. My own eyes burned. We were alive.

All of us. I unbuckled from my seat and jumped in the back, wrapped my arms around my children and hugged them close. A broad hand landed on my back, warming my frigid bones.

A tow truck came and hauled away our car, stuffing all four of us into the cab that smelled of cigarette smoke and fear sweat, the latter of which came from me. I had one of the girls in my lap while Michael held the other. Neither of us were letting them go.

Years passed by. I watched my children grow, my husband age like a sunset over mountains; beautifully. My girls went away to college, bold and brave, ready to take on the world. Ready to change the world.

I got the call no parent wants.

My daughters. My beautiful, intelligent young women, were dead. Caught in an accident on the highway.

It was like no pain I had ever experienced. Like jumping into a frozen lake, the shock took the very air from my lungs and left me dry heaving on my living room floor as Michael asked the officers for details. I begged for it not to be true, clutching at Michael's pant leg and felt only agony. Consuming and choking agony.

Michael carried me from the room while I thrashed and sobbed; ripped apart, decimated, never to be put back together again.

I dreamed that night. Trapped in a white void that hurt my eyes and burned my skin like the sun on a hot summer day. Chest aching, I'd spun in circles trying to place why it felt so familiar.

"I've been here before," I had muttered to myself, spinning in circles.

"You have."

Startled, I turned and saw a young man with unruly black curls in a hooded sweatshirt and baggy jeans slouched against an unseen wall. "Who are you?"

He had shrugged away from the wall. "I'm the Wish

Carver."

I got a flash of memory; a shark smile and snapping fingers. "How do I know you?"

"You've been here before. Years ago." He walks a small circle around me and I turn to keep sight of him.

"I don't remember," I said though bits and pieces were starting to float into my mind.

"Let me help you then."

He stepped up close and pressed a thumb to the center of my forehead. It was like a jolt of lightning through me, shocking the breath from my lungs. It all came back to me. The car accident. The same white void. The emptiness and sorrow. The wish.

"I made a deal with you," I breathed. "I made a deal and you sent me back."

He hummed. "I did."

"Why did you take them from me?" I had screamed, voice ripping into my throat like the devil's talons, hard and hot. "Why?"

"I didn't take them from you. You took them from you!" He had screamed back, face reddening. "Did you think of no one but yourself when you cast your first wish?"

Taken aback, I'd fought back tears of anger. "I thought of my family."

"Oh, yes," he sneered. "Your family. But why did you think of them? Because you missed them? Because you needed them? You, you, you, you, you!" He quieted but looked no less angry. "Your children should have grown up to be leaders, strong in remembrance of their mother. In time, your memory would have softened in your husband's mind and he would have been happy again and changed the life of a woman and her son, who would grow to do great things in his time. But because of your selfishness," he spat the word, "you created a ripple in time and space that caused the death of your daughters."

Shocked, I'd choked. "I did this?"

"You did this," he'd hissed at me. "Because you changed the course of time and lived that day, another car was hit. In that car was a young man. In the first reality, that young man watched a paramedic try to save your life and was so inspired by his efforts, that he grew up to be one. When your daughters got into the car accident, he was the one who saved them. In the altered reality, he died. You killed an innocent boy. You took away someone's opportunity to make a difference in the world and changed the lives of more than just yourself."

The weight of his words nearly took me off my feet. "But I said I was willing to pay. Me."

"And so you did. In turn and in time. But you dropped a stone in a lake of time and caused a wave on the other side. Everything you have ever done has an effect, even if you don't see it."

"Fix this!" I'd snapped, tears searing my cheeks like acid. "I didn't ask for this!"

"You asked me violate your justice," he boomed in a voice that was stronger and more commanding that his teenage body should be able to produce. "You asked me desecrate the flow of time and space. You asked me to penetrate your very soul. You think you can be free? Think again." He turned another circle around me and stared me up and down.

"Honestly, why are you fighting against the very thing that you created?" The Carver whispered in my ear, so close I could feel his lips graze the shell and I repressed a shudder. The words were damp and heavy, a summer storm with none of the relief in the aftermath. He pulled back ever so slowly, his young face creeping into my periphery and I'm struck again by the stark difference between his flushed cheeks, youthful and smiling, and the darkness in his eyes. Opal and deep, cynical and jaded. Old eyes. Soulless eyes.

"So," his Cheshire cat smile appeared once more and I had to bear down on my knees with my fists to keep from clawing at his mocking stare, my anger replacing the cold dread his declaration had doused me in. "What will you do?" Hands stacked on his hips he leaned back, towering over me with that damned smile on his face, daring me to make my choice.

Potentials and consequences were a flock of screaming crows in my mind. Pecking at my conscience.

"Tell me!" He demands, voice going diamond hard and I flinch in my skin, shutting my eyes tight. "What will you do?!"

I shut my eyes, blacking out the view of him and remembered that last hug I gave my children. I remembered the proud smile my husband gave me when they walked out the door for college and the glow in my chest when I knew, without a doubt, that they could change the world for the better.

"I want to reset the clock. One more time."

He'd hummed, interested. "Are you willing to pay the price?"

The question shook my bones, piercing into my chest where the mark had been burned into my breast. "What is the price?"

"You know that I shouldn't tell you but this is special case. No one has ever come back to fix what they broke." His head had turned, a snake staring down a curious mouse before striking. "You would have to become the next Carver, as I did eons ago. Take my place here and I will fix all."

I'd thought of all the things that I had done, my purpose in the world. I had been a passionate woman who loved deeply and raised my children to be the same, but better. Where I was happy with my small, perfect world, they were the ones that saw the bigger picture. They had goals to perfect the world outside of our small one. They saw the potential and were determined where I was happy to be in my happy bubble.

"Yes." If it meant that my daughters, my brilliant world-changers, would be alive, there was nothing that I wouldn't give up.

Something other than irony sharpened his eyes. "That was the right answer." He stepped up close. "Are you ready?"

I didn't want to but I hesitated, scared of the unknown.

"What is dying like?"

The Carver shrugged. "Like falling asleep. Don't you remember?" His thumb pressed deep into my forehead as he shoved me and out of the light.

I knew what was coming this time so I left the vanity mirror down so I could stare into my daughters' happy, brilliant eyes a little longer. This time, when I leaned over to whisper in Michael's ear I told him that I would love him until time itself ends. He looked at me curiously but told me he loved me, too. Rather than release his hand, I held onto it tight. I held onto it until the very last second. I felt the warmth of his palms in mine until he let go to crank the wheel and steer them into safety and me into the void.

And all was right with the world.

I blinked as movement from the corner of my eye cleared away the memory. A crying, sputtering soul tripped towards me with a red nose dripping snot, and tear chapped cheeks.

He was young and told me his story, declaring injustice. Why did he have to die? He wished with every breath for things to be different. I said nothing until he finally fell into a hiccupping silence and stared at me, all wide swollen eyes and heaving chest. When I moved, it was with the same timeless grace that Carver had when he first slipped through the void into my mind's eye. I cupped the soul's shoulders in my hands, stilling him. I leaned in close enough that when I spoke, it was hardly more than a sigh into his ear.

"Are you willing to pay the price?"

Homage to Chagall – Diana Brighouse

I have dreamed every night since the last full moon, and the moon is full again tonight. Each night the dream has been the same. I leave the church with my husband. As we walk, we start to rise up into the air, higher and higher with each step we take.

He grips my hand, and I cannot tell if it is in command or in alarm. He is lifting off the ground, shouting silently, waving his legs, pulling at my arm.

I fear that he will let go and fall. I fear that, without him anchoring me, I will rise and rise, weightless into the heavens.

At my birth I was just another white Caucasian baby, born into an ordinary English family. But it wasn't that simple. My parents were middle-class English citizens, but my mother's mother had been born in Belarus. She came to England as a child and never revisited the land of her birth. I knew little of my Belarussian heritage because it was rarely mentioned.

Things changed at puberty. On my tenth birthday my mother had given me 'the talk'. She anticipated the event by some thirty months, so when the first spots of blood finally appeared it would have been an anti-climax – if everything happened as I expected.

I had not been told that my menstrual blood would be blue – blue as ink, blue as my old primary school sweatshirt.

I told my mother that 'it' had started. I did not mention the blue blood.

I did not mention it then, nor the next time that I bled, nor when, my cycle established, I bled blue blood with every full moon. I did not know that the same thing had happened to my great grandmother.

The blue blood was just the beginning. After a few months, when my cycle had settled to a regular twenty-eight days, I started to feel my feet twitching on the fourteenth day. I had a sharp pain in my side, and my toes twitched, wriggling of their own accord. Another few months passed, and my whole foot jerked, trying to push me up onto my toes. Eventually I had to tell my mother.

She sighed, and looked at me.

'Tell me about your periods. Please don't tell me that your blood is blue.'

She looked at my face.

'They are, aren't they?'

I nodded.

'Since the beginning?'

I nodded again.

My mother ran her hands through her hair and groaned.

'We need to go and see your grandmother, see how much she can remember.'

My grandmother lives in a retirement flat, which she moved to after my grandfather died. Since she moved into the flat, my grandmother has started talking about her dead mother, and Belarus. My mother obviously thinks that my grandmother and her memories will help me understand what's happening to me. We arrange to go and visit her for tea the next day.

Our visit was obviously deemed important, because my grandmother had also made a cake, of a type that I didn't recognise. Three china teacups and saucers were already on the table, with a matching milk jug and sugar bowl.

'Come in, I'll just put the kettle on.'

She hugged us both and pushed us into the living room. Minutes later she followed us, bearing a large pot of tea.

'Mum, be careful, you shouldn't be walking around carrying all that boiling water.'

My mother's concerns were briskly waved away by my grandmother, who retorted that she wasn't senile yet. To prove her point, she poured out the tea without spilling a drop, and told us to help ourselves to food.

'What sort of cake is it?'

I looked at my grandmother expectantly, half-knowing what she was about to say.

'It's a traditional Slavic cake, my grandmother used to make it. It's honey cake. Delicious, let me cut you a slice.'

Siting with my tea and cake, I looked from my mother to my grandmother. My grandmother spoke.

'Your mother has told me what's been happening to you. It's all very difficult for you girls today. You have modern ideas, you learn about science and numbers and all the same things as the boys. You expect to go out to work when you get married – look at your mother, she's the same. Your grandfather grumbled and grumbled, told her that she should be at home looking after your father and you, but did she listen? No, she didn't. No good comes of it in the end you know.'

I wriggled in my chair. I hadn't expected to come to see granny to be told how women were expected to behave in the old days.

'No, just hear me out young lady. What's happening to you is happening. It can't be undone. I don't expect you to understand it, not now anyway. That's what I'm saying – you young girls in the west are brought up differently, there aren't the same traditions here as in the east.'

I was getting very impatient.

'But granny, what has this got to do with my twitchy feet, and... you know what?'

My mother spoke.

'Mum, is this to do with Baboushka, and the stories that she used to tell us?'

I knew that Mum had called her grandmother baboushka. Baboushka had died when I was a baby, and I had no memories of her. My own grandmother had been insistent that I call her granny, rejecting my mother's suggestion that she continue the Slavic tradition.

'It is entirely to do with baboushka, yes,' said granny,

looking tired.

'You have to understand – both of you – that even now, in the Slavic lands, there is a much greater acceptance of the blurred lines separating fact and fiction. Here in the west, everyone thinks that science has all the answers. You think that everything can be explained, and if it can't be, then it soon will be. Goodness, you young people don't even go to church anymore, even God has been thrown out of the window.'

She stopped, seemingly overcome by her own pronouncement that God had been dispatched. My mother was unwise enough to intervene.

'Mum, it's called progress. It's normal. Older people always find change hard.'

I thought my grandmother was going to explode. Her face turned a bluey-red, the colour of a Victoria plum. She gave my mother a withering look.

'I'm not talking about change. I'm talking about things that we can't explain and never will. I'm taking about the world that lies between the gaps in words and numbers, the world that *some people* have the humility to just accept.'

As she emphasised 'some people' I wasn't sure whether she was talking about me, my mother, or the whole of the western world. I still felt uncertain about how this linked to my blue blood and twitchy feet.

'Granny, please can you explain what all this has got to do with me.'

I gave her my most winning smile, and she smiled back, placated.

'If you sit still and listen, and don't interrupt,' she glared at my mother, 'I will tell you what I know. You'll have to be patient.'

I glanced across at my mother, and she nodded and settled into her chair. I looked at granny expectantly.

'This story, like all the best stories, starts with 'once upon a time'. My once upon a time begins long before baboushka was born, before her grandmother was born, and even before *her* grandmother was born. In those days Belarus didn't exist as we know it today. It was part of Lithuania, of Poland, and of the old Soviet Empire. Many people in those times just called themselves Slavs, or Eastern Slavs. Our ancestors grew up with the folklore and religious tales of the Slavs. They were handed down, grandmother to grandchild, tales told by baboushkas to their golubushkas and golubuchiks. Long before there were books, these stories were told, stories of what happened when the gods came down to earth, stories of heaven and earth and the underworld, and of travel between all three realms.'

I started to speak, having become impatient with granny's tale, but she shushed me.

'This started long ago, when the boundaries between the divine and the earthly were not as clear as they are now. Some of the stories have been forgotten and others have been banished to the pages of history, but some of them live on today. I'm going to tell you the story that will help you to understand what is happening to you, Sofia.

Long ago, in the days when the gods ruled the realm of the divine, and were worshipped by the men and women of earth, it was common for the gods to visit the earth. They took human form and moved around, living with ordinary mortals. They offered wisdom and justice wherever they went. Usually they returned to the heavenly realm, but just occasionally one of the gods fell in love with a mortal.

When this happened, the consequences were grave. If a god decided to stay on earth with a human, then they could never return to the heavens. They would be condemned to stay on earth, living a human life, and eventually dying. They were given a stark choice – relinquish your human lover, or relinquish eternal life.

Now every male god resisted the advances of mortal women, and returned to heaven. The women left behind, having experienced the love of a god, spent the rest of their lives in mourning, unable to ever love another man.

But things were different for mortal men who received the love of female gods. Some gods returned to the realm of the divine, and the men they left behind on earth soon put their divine lovers out of their minds, dismissing them as dreams, or fantasies brought on by too many drinks. They found mortal women to marry.

A few female gods decided to stay on earth, relinquishing their claim to eternal life in favour of a mortal life. They retained their human form and married their lovers. They had children and grandchildren, and when the time came, they died and were buried alongside their husbands. Years later, few people remembered that these families had been touched by gods, and that the essence of the divine ran in their bloodline. The truth became blurred, and nowadays most people believe that these were only ever stories, and that there were no real gods.

But this leaves some explaining to do. What is happening to you, Sofia? I know what will happen if we take you along to see the doctor. She will say that you are suffering from an overactive imagination. She will say that your blood is not blue, it is just a very dark red, a normal change when blood is exposed to air. She will say that your twitching feet are a manifestation of an anxiety disorder, and that you can have some medication or counselling to help you.'

'But granny,' I broke in, unable to keep quiet.

'Shush, I told you to listen. I'm telling you what the doctors will say. And if you keep going back to them and telling them that they are wrong, then they will send you to see a psychiatrist, and he will tell you that you have some delusional disorder. He will give you strong medicines, and you won't know which way is up and which way down, never mind whether your feet twitch.'

I groaned softly, but kept my mouth shut.

'Non-believers always produce answers that satisfy themselves, but they don't satisfy those of us who know the truth.

The truth, Sofia, is that you have divine blood in your veins. It has been passed down, through the generations. Those first gods who married their human husbands passed on their divine bloodline through their daughters. With the passage of time the divine influence has weakened. We believe that it is only the blood of the blue angels that remains, and only in alternate generations. I knew of just a handful of women still showing manifestations of their blue angel heritage. My mother was one of them, and like the others, she is dead. None of their grandchildren have been affected, just as your mother hasn't. We thought that it had finally died out – until you told us what had been happening to you.'

I was silent, struggling to take in the fantastic story that I had just been told. It all sounded too bizarre, too ancient. Surely nobody could believe this stuff. And what on earth were blue angels? I wasn't inclined to let my grandmother continue her strange story, but at the same time I wanted to know everything.

'Granny, what are blue angels?'

'Blue angels, my sweetheart, were those female gods who most closely resembled humans, even in their divine form. They had blue hair and wings and skin. When they took on human form their hair became brown and their skin had a normal human appearance. Their wings were absorbed under their shoulder blades. They looked no different from human women, apart from always wearing blue clothing. However, they still lost blue blood every month, and with the release of an egg in each menstrual cycle, their feet twitched and they found themselves lifted off the ground. For a short time, they became airborne, as they yearned to return to the divine realm. People who witnessed the blue angels thought that they were seeing the Virgin Mary, and new stories sprung up concerning appearances of the Holy Mother.

The descendants of the blue angels lost all traces of their

divine ancestry in their physical appearance. However, they continued to bleed blue menstrual blood, and their feet twitched at the middle of every cycle. A few women still found themselves rising into the air, just for a few seconds. They say that it is possible that a descendant of the blue angels may yet fly again, if she marries a man whose mother carries divine blood, but I have never heard of this happening.'

My grandmother stopped talking. She looked exhausted. My mother reached out her hand and took my grandmother's gnarled and veiny hand in her own.

'Mum, why have you never told me all this?'

Granny smiled, weakly.

'You never needed to know, my dear. Sofia needs to know. It affects her. Now I have told all that I know. We need not speak of it again.'

With that, she picked up her teacup and drank.

After that strange tea with granny, life carried on as before. I had an explanation, no matter how strange, for the things that happened to me each month, and I learned to hide the twitching feet from the gaze of others. As for the blue blood, well there was no-one to see it but me, so it wasn't a problem.

I never had the chance to talk to granny about it again, because a few weeks after she told me her story, she had a huge stroke and died without regaining consciousness. My mother said that all our Slavic heritage had died with her, and she looked relieved as she said it. I think that my mother had deliberately put out of her mind the Slavic things that were happening to her daughter, because we never spoke about them.

In due course I left school and went to university. There seemed an inevitability about me settling into a steady relationship in my final year with a guy called Max. As we got more serious we started to swap family stories. That was when I discovered that his father was called Ivan, and his mother Anastasia. That seemed too much of a coincidence, and sure enough, his family background was very similar to my own. His grandparents had been born in Belarus but had come to the UK as children, and his parents had done everything that they could to distance themselves from their Slavic heritage.

Despite us living together for three years, I had managed to conceal my blue blood and twitching from Max, and we never talked about our non-English heritage. One evening, over dinner in our favourite restaurant, Max produced a diamond ring and asked me to marry him. I said yes without a moment's hesitation, and admired the ring, which fitted perfectly. He told me that it had been his great grandmother's ring, and possibly her mother's before her. He thought that it might have been her only valuable possession to survive the journey from Belarus to England.

Perhaps it was an unconscious prompting from my grandmother that made me ask Max if we could have a church wedding, and his grandmother's influence that made him readily agree, because neither of us considered ourselves religious. When we visited the church, I became convinced of their influence, because the church was the church in my dream.

We made the wedding arrangements ourselves, and the morning before our wedding day complimented each other about how straightforward it had been. The newspaper was folded on the table between us. I glanced at it and realised the one thing I had overlooked.

Tomorrow there was a full moon.

Rope – Michael Thompson

Willy was old as fuck. Scratch that. *Fuck* sounds sexy. Scratch that. *Scratch that* makes you think of a cock. So does Willy in fact. Fuck.

Willy wasn't sexy; Willy was ancient. I mean, his body made noises that a body shouldn't make. When he bent over to pick up a 9gallon his back sounded like a Tudor drawbridge. His knees clicked every time he moved. Patella and patella cracking on like old pals.

I never actually found out his age and at 18 I didn't give a fuck about the specifics. He was old and bald and had the aspect of a scarecrow. I will say this for the bastard though. He was strong. I mean he didn't look it but he'd walk around the depot with a full 9 gallon like it was a tin of beans.

You see, we worked for this booze warehouse in town. The kegs would come off the trucks and we'd rope them down into the cellars. Over 30 years Willy had done every job in the company, except the ones that required any brains or paid anything more than minimum wage. The depot was where you ended up when wagon drops became too strenuous. You were put out to pasture and look after JSA fuckwits like me.

I remember my first day. Most people are nervous when they start a new job; I was pissed off. I'd only been signing on for a few months and the wankers had managed to find me something.

Anyway, I arrived at the depot and old Willy had all these cunting ropes lined up. I found out later he'd been a fisherman out of Blyth until some wanker had monopolised the sea and left it empty of anything but used condoms and needles.

'Look, youngin—' he cast a cloudy eye over me—'this is your *double braid* and this is your *three strand twisted*.'

I let it wash over me like one of those northerly squalls that had washed the best years out of him. Why did I care about fucking rope? I was gonna be out of that dump as soon as anything better came along. I was a fucking genius even if nobody realised it yet.

A few weeks in I heard the lads in the break room taking the piss out of him. He always ate his sandwiches alone on the pallets beside the cellar drop.

'Is that old bastard still going on to you about his ropes?' Melvyn said as he chomped on a cheese and pickle sandwich his fat wife had made him.

I nodded, disinterested, reading the sports section.

'Don't pay any attention.' Shaun the rat joined in. 'He used to talk the same shit to me a few years ago when I started. It doesn't make any difference. There's nothing too heavy for the weakest rope. The old cunt's cracked up.'

Inexplicably, I found myself defending old Willy. I mean, I didn't give a fuck about ropes either but I suppose in a twisted way I liked that the old fella had a hobby. 'What the fuck's it got to do with you like, rat boy?' I stood up.

Shaun the rat jumped up too but it was clear the cunt had no mettle. I would've killed me if it had been the other way round but he just hissed through his whiskers.

After lunch the day carried on as normal except come 5 o'clock I had this weird fact lodged in my noodle: 'Nylon loses 15% of its strength when wet...Polypropylene is perfect for a rescue line because it floats...'

Anyway, Willy wasn't influenced by factory politics. He only talked about the tonnage that needed dropped and what ropes were best for the job. As long as the job was done he forgave my frequent tantrums and misdemeanours. I say misdemeanours but they were more than that. Once he accidentally took a swig of my lemonade and discovered what I already knew—it was neat rum. Rum pilfered from the cunts we worked for. The old bastard's eyes watered, he swallowed it, and then said nothing.

There was another incident involving this girl Melanie that worked in the office. I'd scoped her on the floor and made my move on a Friday night at the shit tip of a bar across the street everyone drank at.

'Fancy a shag?' I whispered into her ear as she stood with a Bacardi Breezer. It wasn't a classy opener but then again she wasn't classy and neither was I.

'Who the fuck are you?'

'How dare you? Don't you know that's my drink you've got?'

'I just bought this.'

'And I lifted the bastard off the truck a few days ago.'

'What the fuck are you talking about?'

'Fine. Play hardball. Possession is 9 tenths of the law, I guess. What about the other fucking tenth though, Mel?' I yanked the bottle from her manicured clutches and took a slug.

It was madness, I realise, but offset with supreme confidence. Soon me and Mel were shagging so often that my spunk took on the consistency of skimmed milk. Anywhere and everywhere. That's why I bring Willy up. One night we were doing a dark 10-6 (a lot of international air cargo flew in by night) when I began to feel amorous.

The best spot to fuck was in long term storage. That's when Willy would really get a rope hard-on because everything would have to be dropped a few levels...Me and Mel waited until break time and started fucking on the dumpy (crashmat) below...I had Mel bent over and we were like a big horny shuddering H and I looked up as Willy was manoeuvring an 18gallon into place. The old bastard had decided to work through!

'Wait! Stop!' I shouted. (I would've rather not drawn attention to the fact that we were fucking but it was either that or risk becoming an erotic underscore).

Willy looked down and then walked off and I finished because I figured he was going to tell someone and I'd be sacked anyway...But that old bastard didn't say anything, not to me, or anyone else in the depot. You've got to respect a man like that.

The months went by and Melanie started fucking some meathead delivery driver and I threatened to stave his head in with a wrench and then quickly forgot about both of them. There was some sort of power struggle in the upper echelons of management and some set of cunts replaced another set of cunts except these cunts were even bigger cunts.

It was technology that fucked us really. I wouldn't have minded if it'd been robots like in the films because at least you've got a fighting chance against some Android wanker but it was the things that you couldn't see. The cameras came first, every inch of the depot monitored, even this shrewd bastard couldn't find a blind spot. I mean, I wasn't a model worker but I wasn't lazy either. I didn't deserve to be bellowed at through a loud speaker because I stopped to scratch my balls every now and again.

They wanted to squeeze every last drop of energy out of us and eventually they'd found a juicer powerful enough. Those cunts were trying to set up shop in our souls and then bankrupt them.

They started on with all this gear that was meant to make the job easier but didn't. We got this hydraulic lift but the bastard was always breaking down and even when it was working it was much slower. Willy refused to use it. He had his ropes. Ropes didn't break. They snapped occasionally but it didn't take 50 grand and a small army of Japanese engineers to fix them.

Willy's ropes started to rub the new floor director up the wrong way. He was a lad about my age with a new suit and a new degree and an old fashioned ruthlessness that the directors liked. Willy took his lectures from the kid like a man. He nodded slowly, without speaking, and then carried on doing things like he'd always done. I don't think he could've changed even if he'd wanted to.

Anyway, Willy was forced into retirement and it was like his entire life had never happened. That's what I remember thinking when he told me they'd let him go. All those fucking hours. All that energy expended. It didn't matter. He didn't.

I felt terrible for him but we got on with things. I'd saw this kind of rope online, the 70m Mammut Supersafe, and even though it had cost me a £100, I couldn't let him leave without something.

On our last day together we stopped for lunch and then I went back to my motor to get his gift. Everyone else was in the break room and we were sat on the pallets over beside deep storage like usual. As I walked back across the depot floor I began to think my present was ill-judged. You wouldn't buy a fucking fisherman a life jacket on his last day, would you? That was rubbing it in...Maybes he would use the rope for fishing though. When the old bastard wasn't talking about different ropes he was talking about boats (and to be fair what ropes were the best for mooring boats.) He'd get himself a little coble, maybe, and go out in it and actually fish...

I looked over towards the pallets and Willy was gone—on the beam of the hydraulic lift, a perfectly tied Jack Ketch knot, 7 loops, and a taut line leading down to the abyss. I could see the top of his head and his body suspended underneath, still twitching. I pulled out my box cutter and started slicing into the material and then the blade met the metal inner coil. There was nothing I could do. The old bastard had picked the perfect rope for the job.

I quit the depot a few weeks after I found Willy. I had a strong constitution but something about seeing that old bastard hanging there like a bag of washing, shook me up. It took an extra few nips of rum on my cornflakes in the morning to steady my hand.

Eventually I ended up in Whitby with this older sort called Louise I met when I was a cashier at William Hill. She put a roof over my head and all I had to do in turn was feed her tips from the racing form and make sure my own form never dipped when I gave her my tip.

Things were going well until I took a stroll down the harbour one afternoon. I was walking with a bag of chips and a hip flask of gin, my mind wandering, when I actually began to pay attention to that inner monologue.

'3-strand pre-stretched – you can splice normally, but use 4 or 5 tucks instead of the 3 with natural fibre.'

It was the boats. Every boat was tied up. I hadn't realised until it happened but I could tell you every type of rope and every type of knot keeping those dopey wooden elephants in place.

I packed my stuff, kissed Louise on her damp cheeks, and continued fucking off.

You know what it is? Those cunts will never get me.

Voices and Songs – Edward Sergeant

It's good to be here. Whatever happens, it's better than London. Then again, why do I have to keep telling myself this? In any case it's like London never existed. A dream. Dark mornings on the 53 bus and hazy lights streaking through breath-misted windows. The hell of the Old Kent Road. No time for coffee. Work and then back to the cramped mould and mildew infested flat below pavements. I was lost. Lost in London.

Tom Courtney as Billy Liar, his affected, clipped accent addressing the boss in the office who's not even there filters into my mind.

Of course, London's a big place. It's a very big place, Mr Shadrack. A man can lose himself in London. Lose himself. Loo-hoo-hoo-hoooose himself. Loo-hooose himself in Lon-dun...

I'm yet again spilling out a quote or song in response to a word, image or sound. It's like some sort of disease.

I'm lost here as well, I suppose. I don't know if I can really admit it. Maybe I'll be lost wherever I go. Yesterday could have given me some hope.

Yest-er-daaay, all my trub-bles seemed so faaar a-waaay...

I just want to be good at something, to know I'm not a failure. But if yesterday had gone swimmingly, would that really have been a solution? Shut up. Don't think about it. No, do think about it. You have to think about it. But oh God, I don't want to. If yesterday is anything to go by, I'm in big trouble, big trouble.

Koufax is in big fuckin' trouble, big trouble, baby. Someone get me a wiener before I die...

That's Jack Nicholson and his imaginary baseball commentary in *One Flew over the Cuckoo's Nest* in case you were wondering.

One flew east, one flew west

One flew over the cuckoo's nest

I wonder if other people have it – the spilling out of dredge by association. It's not like I can ask around, is it? Excuse me, sir, excuse me, madam – when you get off the tube at Waterloo are you always compelled to sing ABBA and The Kinks to yourself? I think not.

Sometimes I don't even need a catalyst – songs and voices appear out of nowhere, uninvited – a line from a song or a piece of dialogue from a drama, film or sitcom. I can't switch it off – sometimes it's the same thing over and over again until I'm telling myself to shut up. It's even worse when it actually comes out of my mouth and isn't just in my head. Like the time at the airport with my girlfriend.

*Truud-ee! Listen to me **very** **c**arefully. We are **not** a-**dopt**-ing a child!*

How would people around us know that the woman I'm with is not called Trudy and that this is from the *Mad Men* series we'd watched together – a line I'd repeated often but not for perhaps six months. And why should it spill out then, for Pete's sake (for Pete Campbell's sake in fact – that's the name of the character, after all) – amongst luggage and shops selling clinical bottles of perfume, gimmicky watches and alcohol in tall boxes, waiting for a flight to Amsterdam?

So much in life I can't understand – numbers make me dizzy; logic gives me vertigo; practical explanations leave me queasy – perhaps this instinctive inner-mimicry is taking up space I need for these other things.

On a day like today

We pass the time away

Writing love letters in the sand...

And here it is again. Ok, there's a logic with this song. I am walking on sand bathed in cotton-wool soft, subdued winter light, looking up at The Grand Hotel and the four undulating corner towers encrusted with white barnacle-like round windows. Behind it lurk grey skies.

You put the grey skies out of my way

You make the sun shine brighter than Doris Day...

George Michael and a white t-shirt with *Choose Life* printed on it.

Cue a Scottish accent and Ewan McGregor running down an Edinburgh street.

Choose life, choose a job, choose a career, choose a family, choose a fucking big television...

Shut up. Shut up Shut up.

Just think about the important things. Like, what am I doing and where am I going?

Do you know where you're going to?

Do you like the things that life is showing you...?

I realise I'm singing out loud and look around. Luckily no-one is nearby.

I sometimes wonder if there is anything original in me at all. Everything but everything comes from something else. My feet scatter grains of ginger-blonde sand and pop videos from the 80s come into my head – Madonna with the sea washing over her,

Cherish the thought of always havin' you

Here by my side

Glenn Medeiros in white runs along the sand with the blonde woman in pink, the waves sending splinter fingers of water towards them.

Nothing's gonna change my love for you

You oughta know by now how much I love you...

It takes me back to the cassette my brother had. I hear his voice again and the gruff undercurrent of annoyance.

"Hey! Have you seen my 80s Hits tape?"

What else was on it? Mel and Kim – '*Respectable*'; Rick Astley – '*Never Gonna Give You Up*'; '*Loco in Acapulco*' – The Four Tops. What else, what else? Kylie and Jason? That's right – Michael Jackson:

One Day in Your Life

You'll remember a Place

Someone touch-ing your face...

And Michael Jackson makes me think of Matt Hammond. I don't know why we were near Kensington Gardens at the relatively early hour we were but we noticed a small crowd standing outside a hotel. From the murmurings we found out they were waiting for Michael Jackson to appear. A black car with blacked-out windows came out and smoothly turned into Kensington High Street and a woman with mad eyes and crazy wavy hair ran out into the road after the car, shouting after it,

"I love you Michael. I'll follow you anywhere..."

Poor Michael, I think now – so sad, such a talent.

I have a talent, a wonderful thing

Everyone listens, when I start to sing...

And what happened to Matt Hammond? How did we lose touch? I close my eyes and am back in London. We sit outside the pub at the back so he can smoke. It's cold and poorly lit. He puts on a goofy expression and grabs the rectangular seat cushion, holding it upright like a surfboard and sings high-pitched,

Ev-ree-bod-eeee's goin' suuurf-iiin'

Suuurf-in' yooo essss aaaay...

How many years ago was that? Shut up, don't think about it. But what happened to Matt?

Oh, what happened to you

Whatever happened to me

And what became of the peee-pol

We used to be

Good question, mate.

Oh, *please* do shut up.

Sometimes I think it saves me – this inner me, another voice, another me almost – that takes over – it takes me away from the here and now and I can hear Simon and Garfunkel or see De Niro or whoever and whatever it is so clearly. I escape. And it's just as well, really – considering...

That interview yesterday. Well, call it an interview. I'm trying to shake it off, out of my head. I knew it was to be a group assessment. I'd told myself there would probably be ten other people but to prepare for twenty. At least thirty turn up – and all for a non-descript part-time role for sod-all hours per week and minimum wage to boot. Two girls are waiting outside when I get to the building and then more and more bodies appear – and keep appearing.

We eventually are let into the sterile smelling building and a sticker with your name is stuck to your front. Then the fun really starts. We are told to talk to our neighbour, blow up a balloon and then draw a picture of them on the aforementioned balloon with marker pen. I feel like I'm six years old again. I hated doing this shit when I was six, too. I feel old – everyone else looks younger and my neighbour is only sixteen. 'What the hell are you doing here' I say to myself. The balloon I blow up is red.

Ninety-nine red balloons

Floating in the summer sky

Panic bells, it's red alert...

The next task is to show off your 'team-working skills'. In a smaller group of five, we have the task of building a 'house' as high as possible, using a deck of cards. I hold back, knowing I'll be hopeless – a 'manager', 'architect' and 'builders' are allocated. I half-heartedly get involved with the so-called building and my attempt sends the already pathetically low effort tumbling. Notes start playing in my head, followed by the words,

The game of life is hard to play

I'm gonna lose it anyway

The losing card I'll someday lay

So this is all I have to sa-aay...

Going over it again now in my head as I come to where the beach ends, I carry on the song:

Suicide is painless

It brings on many changes...

I turn to look at the sea to my left as I begin retracing my steps and the vision of a bundle of clothes and the figure frantically rushing into the sea with music in the background – Reginald Perrin.

Ga-rate. Suuu-per

I ask myself the age-old question again – what I am to do? Before I can answer, Carly Simon does,

What else can I do?

I'm so in love with yoooo...

I look the other way and see the defunct Futurist Theatre and next to it the Coney Island entertainment arcade. I always smile when I look at it – I like the curving patterns the dancing red lights make as they travel up and down the turret.

We'll go to coe-neee

And eat balon-eee on a roll

In cen-tral park we'll stroll

And our first kiss we stole

Soul to soul

And My Fair Lay-deee

Is a ter-riffic show they say...

A dreary market place and Eliza in a drab green coat and black brimmed hat, her face all the more radiant in contrast as she dreams of better things,

All I want is a room some-way-aaar

Far a-waaay from the cold night a-yaar

Oh, look, SHUT UP, will you. SH-UTT UPP-A

Aaah, Shut-uppa your face

I walk the steps up from the beach, wishing I could shake off the songs, the images, the cultural references and wonder if mimicry is really all there is for me.

'Is that all there is...?

Is that all there is...?

If that's all there is my friends
Then let's keep dancing...'

I sigh, chuckle, shake my head, sigh again.

The other interview next week – will that be any more bearable; is it still possible that I might be offered a job from the one yesterday? I can hardly believe they'll offer me something over all those other people but I'm not definite. Will I feel the tiniest bit of pleasure or relief even if they do? Anyway, until I hear back I can fool myself there's hope. A fool...that's me. What a fool...

Day after day

Alone on a hill

The man with the foolish grin is keeping perfectly still...

I ask myself seriously, does it matter – does it matter if I can't get a job again, does it matter if I, just a tiny dot in the big wide world have no self-esteem, no so-called prospects? Does any of it matter?

'Well I guess it doesn't matt-er any-moore...'

Thanks, Buddy Holly. Very helpful.

The voices and songs – why can't they be of use?

I'm getting to my front door and know that inside there'll be more job searching, leading to more soul searching and more depression, interspersed with bouts in front of the bathroom mirror with a banana for a microphone. Pretending to be Marc Bolan will make me feel better while it lasts but worse when it ends.

Singing in front of the mirror is alright when you're twelve or maybe fifteen. I'm way too old to be doing it. Or so society tells me. Why should I care what people think – but if anyone knew I'd die of embarrassment. If you sit in an airless little box, tapping keys, talking meaningless words for no reason or purpose and then numbers in your bank account change every month it means you can look someone in the eye. Why am I embarrassed and not them?

So here I am – watching myself pretend to be Marc Bolan.

After finishing being a twentieth-century boy, I stare into the mirror again and watch my lips ask a question.

Who the hell are you talkin' to? Are you talkin' to me?

Yes, I am, De Niro. The nagging voice interrupts me – the one that always tells me what I need to do but without any real solutions. 'Go on', it says, 'get on with it – turn the laptop on and search.'

Collections and Loans Agent – no way.

Trainee Personal Trainer – as if...

Despatcher – what the hell is that?

Special Needs Home Worker, Learning Mentor, Planning Administrator...

Sigh, that's right, that's really gonna help. Close your eyes. Brilliant. And open them again and everything's hunky dory.

I go out again. Walk down to the beach again. Walking helps. Being outside helps. Helps to take my mind away. Or at least to flit.

If you see me walkin' down the street

And I start to cry each time we meet

Walk on by

I'm walkin' on sunshine...wer-hoo...

Yeah, really walking on sunshine.

Back on the sand. Look out to the grey slate sea and the sharp line of unreality that's the horizon. When you get there it just carries on or does it? There's a red blob of a buoy in amongst the water. I see Timothy Spall as Turner painting the red patch on his painting that hangs in the gallery.

Let's hear it for the ba-oyyyy

That's a good boy. And that's my mother's voice, talking to Dad. I've never heard her call him boy before. I've called an ambulance and he's horizontal on the sofa, struggling for breath. I sit there, holding his hand and wonder how long it's going to be. It seems like ages.

It's going to be here soon, Dad

And what would he think of me now? All this? I want to make you proud, Dad. I know I've let you down. I wanted to be somebody, do something for you. I still do. I know you're out there. I see myself, feel myself as a little boy, small and vulnerable and full of blank dread of what's to come and I see you, Dad, I hear you,

Remember. When you're having a bad time, just think. It won't last forever. Remember that. Nothing lasts forever.

Then Julie Andrews has to trivialise things.

Nothing comes from nothing

Nothing ever could

And I'm feeling guilt again but knowing I can't help it. It's not my decision what to think – it's my mind's. I wonder if it would ever be possible to separate myself from my mind – to leave it behind, say goodbye. Even as I think this I know I never can say goodbye.

There's a kind of flash like a camera shutter in my head and it's like she's real – a young Gloria Gaynor in a typically seventies shiny sequin spattered blood orange dress walks towards me and starts singing:

I never can say good-bye

No, no, no...I....

Never can say good-bye...

Standing Awkwardly in Rooms – Francesca Casilli

I am good at standing awkwardly in rooms. I know what corners feel like. I am on a first name basis with the floorboards as we make intimate eye contact. I like the feel of the wallpaper against my fingertips. I tell myself it's a secret code written in only a language that wallflowers can understand. I stand with my back against the brickwork to protect myself from unknown attackers and chokeholds (hey, it happens in the movies). At least now I need only worry about what is in front of me. This particular talent of mine has been finessed with time. It has become my art.

Dinner party invitations strike fear into my soul. My stomach sinks when an e-vite announces itself in my inbox. I dislike their use of clip art and the word, "soiree". I have equally grown to ultimately despise the term "networking". A handful of half-baked excuses trickle through my mind. I'm half hoping I have to work late or that I get whatever bug is going around. I stand annoyingly close to sneezing children. Mirages of overtime and illness crumble before me. I accept defeat as gracefully as I can. I make sure to arm myself with a bottle of wine as a generic token. I hope this instills that I am polite and likeable. I'm not sure I am either one.

I always ring the wrong doorbell and I never know how to get into the building. I contemplate scaling walls or waiting for a neighbour to collect their take-out Chinese. I make small talk with delivery men and slink in behind them with all the cunning of a two-ton walrus. I never know when a handshake is an appropriate greeting or whether it's a hugging occasion. I shuffle out of colleague's embraces and ching-chong-cha hand gestures until they seem to match. I even say something totally out of character like, "Ciao" (even though the most Italian thing about me is my passion for carbohydrates).

I look at the art on the walls for what seems like a little too long. I greet a few familiar faces. Some of them introduce themselves, with no idea that we have met before. Some of them I have met more than once. It makes me feel beige. I am erased from memories upon entry and exit. Wondering why I came here at all, I pace around someone else's familiar space. I pick up a family photo and look at the people standing awkwardly in it. I feel a kinship with them. I like the token ugly sweater and the golden retriever eating a hot dog out of a toddler's hands. I look for empty seats where none seem to exist. I didn't know people took up so much space. I find one open chair amongst strangers who speak passionately about the psychological benefits of breastfeeding. I label myself as anti-social. Hence, I do not engage. No one wants to talk about standing awkwardly in rooms.

The rooms make me feel small. The people inside them make me feel smaller. They put me in boxes labeled *What do you do?* and *Where are you from?* I answer their questions like my brain is made of drying paint. They ask me, "Do you like what you do?" I respond with, "Depends on the day." No one seems to like my answer very much. I wish I could give them my heart to hold so maybe then they'd understand the sum of my parts. Then they could dislike me more *fully*. I let anyone who wants to hear know that I think the food is exquisite. People raise their glasses in agreement. I don't admit that the chicken is dry and the sauce over seasoned. They don't admit it either. The potatoes need a bit of salt. I think of a girl I went to highschool with who would suck the ends of her hair when she was sad. It has taken me until adulthood to understand her.

I light a cigarette and stand by a window just to give myself something to do. This trivial act of destruction gives me momentary purpose. My purpose is to destroy myself. I notice the size of my cleavage and allow it to let me feel a little empowered. Then I allow it to let me feel a little inappropriate. I pull my top up slightly. I stand with one hand on a windowsill

Turkish Delight

that is ever so slightly too short. I look uncomfortable. Give me an oddly shaped piece of furniture and I will lean on it. I will find a too-high counter or a strangely shaped loveseat and drape myself across it. I never know what is appropriate dinnertime conversation so I talk about serial killers and their motives. I even start to make myself feel a little woozy but it's too late to swallow my words as they spill into the air. I tell people that if I had a superpower it would be to rewind time. Their polite laughter crackles like live wire. The hairs on the back of my neck stand on end. I ask them if they think they could kill someone if it came down to it.

It's hard to know when is a polite time to excuse oneself. I remind myself I have a season of reality TV pre-recorded at home. There's a tub of Bolognese sauce in the freezer. Some invisible force is keeping me here and it's stronger than frozen meat. Is it the need to feel connection with something other than my social media newsfeed? If friendship at first sight is an option then I'll take one please. This room makes me feel like the new kid on the first day of school. I'm an adult, I'm not allowed to feel this way. I tell myself I obviously wasn't hugged enough as a child. Maybe there's something to the psychological benefits of breastfeeding after all.

I don't know where this aversion to rooms began. Perhaps it is rooted in the very first rooms of my life: a nursery, a classroom, a dining room, a jumping castle, a hockey field or a public restroom. I ask myself if my parents fought around the table or if I peed myself at a kid's birthday party. There is no singular moment. There is simply a prison built out of room upon room. I want to lock myself in a nice empty one and throw away the key. Maybe every now and again someone can whisper a compliment through the keyhole to remind me I'm human. I imagine myself whispering, "What's the secret password" through a slot.

I can stand awkwardly in any room. From awkward bouquet

catching at weddings to dropping a dozen eggs on the supermarket floor. I could even make a police lineup look a little awkward. People introduce me to their babies and my response is to sit on my hands so no handover can take place. I'm that person who wears all black to a pool party. You definitely wouldn't want me at your local orgy. Even when I'm alone it can be a little awkward. I always say the wrong thing to myself and hurt my feelings.

Sometimes I catch a glimpse of someone who seems good at standing awkwardly in rooms. Their shoulders hunch over as they scroll through already-read text messages. I see myself reflected so beautifully in their body language that is permanently set somewhere been constant fear of attack and the desire to flee. I like the way he has paired a phone pair of socks with a serious pair of pants. It almost makes him seem approachable for a second. I urge myself to greet him. I urge myself to say something, anything, that will make it feel a little less like we are all just getting by. I rehearse a thousand conversations and they all end in disappointment. So I don't say anything at all. We will forever remain two strangers standing awkwardly in rooms.

Eventually I leave. The host gently protests at my departure but doesn't really care. I thank them, as we all must for the time others bestow upon us. We are constantly told that no one owes us anything. In this light everything is a kindness and not a chore. Despite this I feel constantly in debt. I vow to invite them over to my studio apartment and prepare a meal that doesn't involve the microwave. I vow to buy a bottle of wine that isn't from the bargain bin. I vow to be a more confident version of myself. I vow to never speak to anyone again.

No one wants to braid my hair or ask me how I lost my virginity. In my online language courses they teach me how to say, "He has many friends and I don't have any," in almost every tongue known to man. It's hard to know if I'll ever feel big in a room. I've always wished that in my eulogy the words, "larger than life" would be used often and without restraint. Instead I fear that the only attendee will be my Mother and one person I was nice to once in high school. Upon my death they will say I hated card games and wouldn't try anything I wasn't good at. I think it's fair to say I am not good at a lot of things, including basic algebra and not snacking between meals. But what I am most definitely, certainly, incomparably good at is standing awkwardly in rooms.

In Wolf's Clothing – Celia Law

"I'm going to be the wolf," declared Ollie over the spaghetti bolognese last night, "and I need a costume, a good one. Can you order one off the internet. Pleeease?"

"I'll make you one," I said. I'll be buggered if I'm going to pay twenty quid for some shite from China that'll catch fire if he goes too near a light switch. "Trust me," I smiled, "it'll be better than any wolf off Amazon."

So here I am, patrolling the moth infested charity shops looking for dark fur that I can turn into a wolf costume that is not going to be so good it makes any assumptions about Ollie's acting prowess but also doesn't look homemade, it's a tough line that I'm walking.

The first shop had nothing to offer except nits so against my better judgement I went into Hattie's nearly new boutique, and it was there that I saw Mrs Carmichael. Not exactly the whole Mrs Carmichael as last I heard her head was still firmly attached, but a headless mannequin sporting her coat, her blouse even her Kingfisher brooch. It was the brooch that gave her away. Last time she came up in conversation mum did tell me that she was leaving the hospital and heading to The Hollies retirement village. Mum had been more worried about who would buy the house adjoining hers than she had about Mrs Carmichael finishing her days in a PVC chair being spoon fed by a stranger.

The kingfisher's eye twinkled and as clear as if it was yesterday I can remember his eyes in the semi darkness, wide open and his index finger on his lips telling me to be quiet. I had been quiet for as long as I could, but eventually I told. It was one thing not saying anything and it was another thing entirely to bare face lie to a policeman who was asking you directly if you had seen Sarah go. I had seen her go. I had seen her go with him. She had waved to me and he had tussled my hair over the low garden wall as they left hand in hand, her carrying a pink Benetton duffle bag over one shoulder. They had both looked like adults to me, they were both tall and had a full set of second teeth. The fact that he was much older than her escaped me at the time. I suppose it would, I was only eight.

Mrs Carmichael was sad after Sarah left, I can't remember her being particularly happy before, but she was definitely worse once she had gone. She used to sit in the upstairs window and watch for hours and hours at a time. I used to wave sometimes but then I'd feel bad because if I had said at the time she could have stopped her leaving and she'd be cooking the dinner now, not staring into the distance waiting. Everyone said it wasn't my fault but the guilt stuck like a smell, it followed me and wouldn't wash off. Eventually, it just became part of me, my brand.

I used to fantasise about Sarah's new life; that she'd run away with the circus and was a famous acrobat going by a different name, The Amazing Angelica who could fly and spin and catch the swing at the very last second leaving the audience gasping for breath and the asthmatics reaching for their inhalers. Or that she was a spy, weaving through life like the shadow of a cat, able to change her appearance at whim and blend into a crowd without so much as an excuse me please. Sarah was living the dream, of that I was certain.

"We have a mirror in the changing room if you'd like to try it on," said the lady in Hattie's.
"Oh no, I'm just thinking," I said as I stroked the sleeve of the coat.

Mrs Carmichael never went on holiday and she left the living room light on at night just in case Sarah came home. She didn't. When I was much older the subject of Sarah came up over our chicken casserole dinner, Sarah wasn't a subject that had come up before, probably because they didn't want me to feel bad again. Mum casually asked if I remembered when Sarah's pink Benetton bag had been found on the tow path near the canal a few weeks after she left. She said it like it wasn't news to me. I haven't eaten chicken casserole since, even the smell turns my stomach into a ball of knots.

The blouse must have cost Mrs Carmichael quite a bit, it's not a style that I would wear, or anyone under seventy would to be honest, but the material is the softest cotton and the label reads Hobbs. Mrs Carmichael always dressed well, especially after Sarah left. Mum said it was because she was always ready for Cilla Black to knock shouting "Surprise, Surprise we've found your Sarah." Cilla never did knock obviously, and eventually even the police family liaison officer retired and the new bod was probably never told about her, there were more recent runaways to be briefed on. Cases that might actually be solved.

I'm meant to be buying dark fur for my sons wolf outfit and now all I can think about is getting a cuddle from him instead. Telling him that he's wonderful and that I love him more than sunshine and chocolate. The wolf can wait. I call into the bakers and buy us each a cream cake for pudding, then into the butchers to get some mincemeat, tonight we'll have Ollie's favourite of homemade burgers and chips. Life is too short for salad and grilled chicken.

As I crawl into bed and lay next to the sleeping form of my husband, Ollie's dad, the man I love and loves me back all I can think about is Sarah. What ever happened to her? As an adult I am processing the information afresh, with new eyes, from the new perspective of maturity, and I know that what happened to Sarah is bad. I know she isn't The Amazing Angelica, or the secret-ist of secret spies. I can smell the guilt oozing from me, the guilt hasn't matured, it still hangs in the aura of my soul, as fresh as lining on a breezy clothes line, like the day the policeman sat me down with the lady from social services who had dandruff and chewed fingernails.

"Can you remember anything else? Did they get in a car perhaps?"

"I saw two red lights at the bottom of the road. But not a car, bigger."

"A van?"

"Bigger."

"A lorry?"

"Yes it could have been a lorry," I replied.

"Did you see the number plate, any of it."

"No."

I tried time and again over the first few weeks to stretch my eyes and remember the number plate, but I got nothing. I couldn't see. I played memory games and then tried to think, fast ,fast, fast as you can what can you see? Nothing. Two red tail lights and nothing else.

My sleep is broken by the Kingfisher swooping down and ruffling my hair. The man's eyes open and staring, his index finger to his lips;

"sssshhh little girl ssshhhh".

"What can you see?"

"Two big eyes."

"All the better to see you with".

"And two big ears."

"All the better to hear you with."

"And two big fangs."

"All the better to eat you with," smiles the wolf.

"Run Sarah, run for your life," and Sarah runs into the darkness beyond my dream.

More Than Life – Pete Pitman

Track 9 - Love Is Not Enough

I'm listening to my favourite album from two years ago. It was the soundtrack to our romance. A romance that started so well, it's hard to believe it could end in such tragedy.

We met downstairs in Rock City. I was there for Heart in Hand – melodic metalcore; harmonic guitar riffs, blast beats and taut, emotional vocals. They were headlining, with three bands on before them. I took up my usual position, elbow on the bar, sipping beer, observing from a distance. The Basement was black, sticky floor; black peeling walls; and a black stage with mounds of upturned Marshall Amps looking like decaying teeth, interspersed with coils of wire writhing like a pit of snakes – it was the departure lounge to Hell.

I spotted him during the second band's set, The Eyes of a Traitor – hard thrash metal, ear piercing screamo. He hit the moshpit like a demon, no, a fallen angel - part ballet dancer, part warrior. He leapt and pirouetted about the floor scything down imaginary barbarians. His body was slim and lithe, his face pale and beautiful. My heart crashed against my ribs and my eyes watered. I felt like a member of the audience at the unveiling of the Sistine Chapel ceiling. A question that had troubled me for years was answered.

The third band, More Than Life, began setting up and he jumped on stage and chatted with them. They started up and played emotional hardcore, I was well stoked, they were cool. He had good taste in friends. This time he remained in the same place, heart-wrenchingly close to me, twitching and doing jazz hands. This kid pretending to be a clumsy robot careered into him and he crashed to the floor at my feet. I helped him back up and stared at his big, brown eyes, his face still white despite his exertions and the corona of wavy black hair that surrounded it.

I had to say something, so blurted out, "Who you here to see?"

He brushed some grit from his jeans gave me a smile that paralysed my soul and answered, "Er, thanks. I was here for Whitechapel, but they pulled out at the last minute."

I said, "Wow! They're heavy – American, anti-religious deathcore." I preferred Australian deathcore.

He walked away, I kicked the bar. I'd tried to show him I knew who they were, but he must have seen that I didn't like them.

Heart in Hand hit the stage and I was soon lost in the joy of fast guitars, synchronised breakdowns and rattling blast beats.

On the way out I visited the merchantmen to get a More Than Life t-shirt in his honour. Holding my purchase close to my chest, I stepped back and banged into a passer-by. It was him, of course. I thanked the Gods, I prefer the older religions they make more sense.

"It looks like everyone's out to get me tonight," he said, playfully punching my shoulder. "My name's Tom."

"I-I'm Joey," I answered.

"He looked me up and down and said, "Where do you live?"

"I-I live in Beeston. Why?"

"Spot on. It's on my way," said Tom, pulling out a set of car keys. "I've got an apartment in Long Eaton. I can give you a lift if ya want?"

"Yes please," I said, my knees knocking together like coconuts in a basket. "That would be sweet."

As he dropped me off he said, "There's a killer band at the Greyhound on Wednesday. Fancy going?"

"Y-yeah," I said.

"Meet me at Spoons, at eight."

"Spoons?"

"Wetherspoons, ya know," he said, pulling away. I found it hard to imagine Tom in Wetherspoons.

I vaulted the front gate and skipped up the yard.

Track 7 - Do You Remember

I used to love this record and now I hate it. The first time I heard it we were in Tom's apartment. I was on the sofa his head on my lap. I stroked his silky hair and gulped at the raw emotion of the song. The singer's tortured vocals ripped into my soul and I felt the pure ecstasy of his pain. Tom twitched beneath me as I hid my weeping eyes.

We'd been to a poetry evening in the caves below the Malt Cross. I'd never been anywhere like it. The atmosphere was stunning, even the weakest poem sounded amazing. Tom seemed to know everyone there, but he remained at the back with me. Part way through, he got up and recited two of his own poems about his elder brother who'd died a couple of years before. The audience sat in silence until he'd finished and then cheered so loudly we were covered in sand.

I asked him on the way home, "I didn't know you wrote poetry?"

"Oh yeah. I'm down here doing a creative writing degree at Trent Uni. I'm originally from Sheffield. Walked out halfway through the second year. My parents don't know or they'd stop my allowance."

"Why'd you pack it up?"

"It was too prescriptive. Ben Bancroft, we called him Ben Bankrupt, one of the tutors said, writing was like baking a cake. I wanted to throttle him."

I had no real opinion. My English teacher had sat me next to Danny. Then he got upset because Danny led me astray. I preferred maths with its set rules. You can write the same thing a thousand different ways. Writing is too subjective. "Is that the only reason?" I asked.

"Course not. We had another lecturer, the feminist fatale, made us read all these women writers. Kept telling us how the literary world was so against women.

"Well, isn't it?"

"What! Not any longer." He was starting to shout and

people on the bus were looking. "Every work of serious literature will be written by a middle-class woman soon."

I didn't ask anything else, hoping he'd calm down.

He carried on, "I was brought up with Sillitoe, Barstow and Waterhouse, courtesy of mi dad." His Yorkshire accent was showing through. "And Mcewan, Amis and Barnes from my mother. They were never mentioned. Wiped from literary history..."

We'd reached his bus stop. I found out later, he'd been kicked off the course for being a disruptive influence and because he was behind with his work.

Track 7 - Do You Remember

I remember the good times. That's how our relationship progressed. Tom would ring me up and we'd go into the city. He'd shout, "Take a bus into the electric city/Or a tram toward the phosphorous glow/To the place that nettled and inspired/D H Lawrence and Alan Sillitoe. That's the first stanza of my epic poem about this epic city. I'm calling it Childe Thomas."

We'd go to Rock City, or the Jam Cafe, or a poetry evening in a pub, or the Rescue Rooms bar. He'd dazzle and sparkle and everyone would want to talk to him. I'd sit there looking cool, but with an inferno burning inside of me. He led and I followed.

We'd go back to his apartment and I'd look at his latest unfinished painting, his collage of photos that wasn't quite complete, or his half-finished poems. I'd tell him how brilliant they were and how he should finish a project before moving on to the next one. He would tousle my hair and push me onto the sofa.

We kissed and stroked each other, but never did the sex thing. Neither of us could get past the idea of putting our prized possession in a waste hole.

Track 6 - Season's Change

I remember the bad times. One day, he took me to The Bank,

which if you're feeling generous you might describe as cheap and cheerful. He got me a pint and himself a double whisky and led me past the old men with empty lives, the office workers delaying going back to their empty homes and the rowdy lads meeting for an affordable drink before they hit the town. We settled in an alcove at the back of the room. He downed his whisky and sent me to the bar for another. When I returned he'd broken his glass and was gouging at his wrist with it.

I took the glass from him and wrapped a handkerchief about his wrist which was dribbling blood on to the carpet. He apologised and I hoped it was a one-off. It wasn't of course. I'd been so dazzled by his beauty and creativity I hadn't noticed his dark side.

The following week we went to the Room with a Brew, a micro pub with a monthly poetry reading night. He criticised every turn.

I said, "Why don't you get up and show them how to do it?" I was still smitten by him, I couldn't see past his charisma.

He got up, stood still until he'd got everyone's attention. Raised his arm, pointed at the audience and snarled, "You middle-class cunts ya can't write poetry."

They, the mostly middle-class audience, sat in silence waiting for the punch-line.

Suddenly, he jumped up and down and shouted, "You middle-class can't write poems/You've no grit to work into a pearl/There's no fire or hate in your belly/You've no bloodstained flag to unfurl//Only the leisured or the angry/Can hack into the coal seam of pain/Only extreme emotions are worthy/Of reconstructing as a refrain..."

We all squirmed in our seats as he stood still again. He smiled as he recited the last stanza, "So when you fire up your laptop/And your emotions drip on to the page/Think of this working-class loudmouth/And hammer the keys with your rage."

They cheered him back to his seat.

The applause was generous but he wasn't, he said, "Come on; let's get away from these pathetic losers."

Track 8 - Sometimes

I remember the highs and the lows. For the next couple of months, he was his usual charming self. I continued to visit his apartment like an artist's favourite model.

One warm August evening, my phone rang. I recognised Tom's number, so answered, "Wh-what time is it? It's two in the morning, what's up, Tom?"

I couldn't hear anything at first, just the occasional sound, like kids playing in the distance. I realised it was actually him sobbing; it was a cry for help.

I got dressed and cycled like a maniac around to his apartment. The door was locked, but he'd given me a key. When he'd given it to me he'd said, "You're my magic wand, my muse, my Nelly Ternan, my Jeanne Duval." Despite being compared to a couple of women I'd never heard of I floated all the way home. I found him sitting in his boxers on his bedroom windowsill, legs dangling out over the Erewash Canal 40 feet below. I spent an hour coaxing him back inside, telling him how wonderful he was. This happened three more times over the next month. By this time, I felt like a worn and overused crutch.

I remember he nearly cost me my job. He'd ring me up at work and arrange to meet me lunch-time at a local pub. He'd keep me talking until I was late back and behind with my work. I felt good; I was floating, I was his go-to guy. I felt bad; having to keep my head down at work because I'd let my team down. I was on life's see-saw. And the dizziness turned to nausea.

Track 7 - Do You Remember

I hate the song because it describes a normal love affair. One that ends badly, but at least they did things together as partners, as equals. For us, there was no walking hand-in-hand across a beach with a golden setting sun as a backdrop. No kicking autumn leaves at each other behind the lake on Wollaton Park.

Title track - What's Left of Me

Not much. He had absorbed me. He was Count Dracula and I was the gibbering wreck who ate the flies. When I met Tom I was an optimistic, naive 19-year-old boy. Now, I'm an embittered, cynical old man of 21 who knows that everyone will let you down. That love can't last, that the halcyon days of first love are soon replaced by raging storms. I wasn't Joey; I was Tom's quiet friend.

Track 2 - Weight of the World

He cried Woolf once too often. I'd had enough, so didn't come running like his lap-dog. They pulled him out of the canal the following day.

His parents came down to Nottingham and asked to see me. His dad was a self-made businessman and his mother a cellist in an orchestra. They wanted to understand why he'd done it. What could I tell them? Could I hide my guilt?

His dad, short and stocky, all vigour and charm, shook my hand. I was ready for the firm grip and just kept from grimacing.

"Yo were a good mate of our Tom's, weren't yo?" His battered face creased some more. "He mentioned yo a lot."

"Yes, but I hadn't seen so much of him recently. He was concentrating on his work," I lied. He didn't need to concentrate it came naturally, what he'd needed to do was persevere. He needed his dad's work ethic.

"The police told us 'is neighbour saw 'im on the windowsill a few times, regular like."

I shrugged. I couldn't say I'd talked him down on half-a-dozen occasions.

"They say he'd been drinking and most likely just slipped."

I nodded. I couldn't say he'd threatened to jump several times to get my attention.

His mother, tall, slim, pale and delicate, pushed away her tears and said, "Had you noticed any change in him recently?"

"No," I lied, once again. "He was too clever and sensitive for his own good. Sometimes he struggled with the stupidity of people, but he was happy. I'm sure of it." I gave a reassuring smile.

"So, you think it was just an unfortunate accident?"

"I do, yes," I told them what I thought they wanted to hear.

I couldn't tell them I pushed him. That I did it out of self-preservation. That I didn't come running like his pet poodle when he called. That I sauntered around to his apartment, listening to an old album by Killing the Dream. That it wasn't out of exasperation, it wasn't a moment of madness.

I calmly picked up his phone and deleted the three messages he'd sent me. I waited until he was leaning forward and gently pressed two fingers against the smooth skin of his back. He thudded against the concrete canal-side, lay sprawled half over the edge for a second, before slipping into the turbid tranquillity.

They thanked me for my time and for being a good friend.

His dad shook my hand again, but without the grip of steel and said, "Yo'll be at the funeral tomorrow, won't yo?"

"Of course!"

And of course, I wasn't.

Take the Gamble – John Bunting

The first time Wendy caught sight of Jack, he was standing a little apart from the other onlookers, shaking his head sadly as she threw up over the daffodils in the Municipal Remembrance Gardens. She lunged at him unsteadily, determined to punch his sanctimonious face, but was stopped by a handcuff-wielding policeman. The first time Wendy spoke to Jack was four days later, outside the Magistrates' Court where she'd been fined £80 plus costs for being drunk and disorderly. It was to be a conversation that would test them both to the limit.

The dank, February mist hung heavy as Wendy marched angrily down the street, muttering vile curses on the Judge and his family. She heard someone run up behind her, and felt a tap on the shoulder. "Excuse me," a young man's voice said hesitantly, "can I speak to you, please?"

Wendy swung round angrily. "Leave me alone, sodding press." Then she saw who it was. "Oh no, not you again." She aimed her umbrella at his groin. "Buggar off!"

Jack swerved to avoid her death-thrust. "Whoa steady, I'm not the press. I want to help you."

"That's what all you bastards say." Wendy wiggled her bottom at him insultingly. "Talk to this."

"I can think of better things to do with it," smirked Jack.

Wendy squared up, teapot fashion. "I might have bloody guessed. That'll cost you a hundred."

"Oh no, I didn't mean... oh dear. I was just trying to get your attention. My name's Jack, and I've been sent to give you spiritual guidance."

"Who by? The bleeding Jehovahs?"

"Goodness me, no; dreadful people. I'm a sort of guardian angel."

"I knew it!" snorted Wendy. "You're a nutter."

"No, I am... no, not a nutter, I mean... Look, let me buy you a cup of coffee, and I'll explain." Jack smiled. "I must say, you have got lovely ears."

"Jeez," spluttered Wendy, "arse *and* ears. You're a perv as well as a nutter." She turned to walk off, but Jack pushed round, blocking her path.

"Sorry," he groaned, "I'm not very good at this am I? One more chance... please!"

Wendy looked at Jack properly for the first time. He was in his early-twenties, tall, pale-blue eyed and fair with a kindly face. "All right, I suppose you are quite good looking. You can buy me a double vodka."

"Sorry again," shrugged Jack, "but it's against the rules. How about a Full English?"

Wendy's eyes lit up. "Now you're talking."

Ten minutes later, they were sat in 'Rumbling Tums'. Wendy hadn't eaten all day, and pitched straight into her fry-up. She knew Jack was watching her, and could imagine what he was thinking – that she was probably about twenty-five, but the booze made her look a wan and puffy forty; that her tarty clothes were too tight, her hair too bleached, and her make-up too heavy. She wondered if he had any idea why. Only when she'd cleared her plate, and was drinking her coffee, did she look up. "OK, pretty perv, what's all this about?"

Jack took a deep breath. "Let me start again. I've been sent to help you find a new path in life; a way out of your troubles. You'll be dead in five years if you carry on drinking like you are doing. You're my first assignment, by the way; I only completed my training a month ago."

There was a long pause. Then Wendy said, "Finished? Good. You are bleeding Jehovahs, aren't you? Or a Latter-Day Whatsit."

"No, as I said before, I'm the real deal."

"The real deal what?"

"Guardian Angel."

Wendy looked at Jack dismissively. "Give it up. You're trying to tell me you're from... up there. That's rubbish."

"Hard to believe, isn't it? But I can prove it." Jack leaned over, and whispered in her ear for several seconds.

Wendy sat back hard in her chair, and stared at him wide-eyed. "No! I never realised! Oh my... but that means... well, you know."

"Indeed it does. And I'm impressed."

"By what? My backside? So you keep saying."

Jack laughed. "Touché. By your grasp of the implications."

"I used to be clever," said Wendy sadly. "I got a double first at Oxford."

"Wow, you have fallen a long way since then. These must be tough times."

"You're not kidding."

"Do you want to talk about them?"

"You're the Angel, don't you know already?"

"They don't tell me everything. Do you want to?"

Wendy made a big thing of not wanting to; taking off her coat as slowly as she could, and hanging it carefully over the back of her chair. Then, to waste more time, she sighed noisily, and said, "You haven't got a vape, have you?" Jack sat silent, looking at her intently. "Of course not, you're a bloody Angel." She sighed again, resigned to talking. "All right, if I can't tell you who can I? ...There was this woman; she was a senior partner at the law firm I joined after Oxford. Before her, there had only been spotty boys and smelly students. She was beautiful, intelligent, forceful; everything I'd ever dreamt of being. I couldn't resist her advances; didn't want to. I was obsessed with her. But she used me, abused me, and then spat me out. I was destroyed. Shit, I still am." Wendy started to cry, tears dripping onto her empty plate.

Jack passed her his napkin. "You gave up the law?"

"I fell in with a bent card sharp - gambling's a habit a lot of students pick up at Oxford. I was the sexy distraction while he fixed the deck. We drank and cheated our way round the country for a couple of years. Then one day I woke up, and he'd gone."

"And what have you been doing since then?"

"There's been nothing else since then." Wendy blew her nose, and dabbed her eyes. "I spend my days playing the slot machines, and drinking bootleg vodka. I can't face the world any more, it hurts too much."

"So you booze, and swear, and dress like a tart to push people away from you?"

"Jeez, you don't hold back, do you?" sobbed Wendy. "I guess so."

Wendy asked Jack to get her another coffee. She needed time to gather herself, and she could see that he needed a break too; that sitting here, face to face with this broken woman, was hard for him. She smiled through her tears as he brought the coffee back to their table. "Thank you. I'm one hell of a first assignment, aren't I?"

"Drink it up," said Jack, "it's strong and hot." His face lit up. "Hey, like me!"

"You're sweet," laughed Wendy, "I might even get to like you one day."

"I hope so. If you can't get to like your Guardian Angel, you really are messed up."

Wendy took a sip of coffee. "I'm hoping this is the point where you have a word with 'Upstairs', and 'He' makes everything better."

"Sorry, that only happens in the movies." Jack waved his hand at the world around them. "In reality, you have to sort things out for yourself."

"Really? Do you think I haven't tried?"

"Have you spoken to anyone? Asked for their help?"

"The Court made me take counselling last year, but I could tell they didn't care." Wendy shrugged. "Sod them, I stopped going."

"What about friends?"

"They disappeared fast."

"Family, then?"

"My parents have disowned me." Wendy looked down at her cup, as if that was it, but then added quietly, almost as an afterthought, "There's my sister; I haven't spoken to her for years. She's got everything; husband, kids, a good job. She knows what I've become, though, she wouldn't be interested."

"How do you know? Get in touch with her."

Wendy shook her head fiercely. "No. Leave my sister out of this. Drink is the only thing that can help me now."

"That's rubbish. In my experience talking to someone you trust is the best way."

"In your experience!" sneered Wendy. "What experience? You're a bloody trainee."

"Yes, damn it," snapped Jack, "my experience. I was a dropout junkie. My wife and kids walked out on me. I died a week later from a heroin overdose. A deliberate heroin overdose. Don't you *ever* question my experience."

Wendy reached over. "Oh, I'm sorry, I didn't... sorry."

Jack pulled his hands away. "Yes, yes, I'm sorry too; this is about you, not me."

For the next half hour, Wendy talked about the hell she'd fallen into – the alcohol, the shop lifting, and the gambling. And sometimes, when she was desperate for money, the seedy, nameless men. Jack kept encouraging her to look at the positive side of things, to find ways she could help herself, but nothing he said could shake her belief that her life was ruined; that there was no way back. Eventually they fell silent, and sat staring uneasily at each other; neither sure what to say or do next.

Wendy drank down the cold remains of her coffee. "So, my pretty Angel, what now?"

Jack shook his head. "I don't know. Why don't you tell me more about your sister? Were you close once?"

"When we were younger," Wendy said bitterly. "She's

eighteen months the older; the sensible one. She was always there with a shoulder when I needed it. She got me out of a lot of hairy corners when we were teenagers. And what did I do in return? When I went up to Oxford, I dropped her for the bright lights." Wendy wiped her nose. "I've never forgiven myself. I doubt she's forgiven me."

Jack's eyes flashed. "So I ask you again. Why don't you get in touch with her, and find out?"

"And I've told you to leave my sister out of this!"

"But why, Wendy, why?"

"Because... damn you... don't you see?" She banged her fist on the table angrily. "I'm frightened she'll put the bloody phone down on me! I can't take that gamble."

Jack banged his fist down too, deliberately matching her anger. "Then don't phone her. Fix the deck. Go and see her unannounced. Just walk in, and sit down."

"That's crazy. She'd throw me out."

"And so she might, Wendy, but there's a chance she might not. There's a chance she might still have a shoulder for her little sister, and want to help her out of another hairy corner. Remember how she used to do that? How you loved her for it?"

Wendy started to cry again, fear growing. "You bastard."

"But I could be right!" shouted Jack. "It might be your last chance. Take the ga—"

"Fuck you!" screamed Wendy, jumping up and slapping his face. "Don't you dare do this to me!"

Jack didn't flinch. He stood up, and jabbed his finger at her. "I will dare, because I'm telling you the truth, and deep down you know it. You're just too frightened to risk it."

Wendy slapped his face again, harder. "Sod you, fucking Guardian fucking Angel. I wish I'd never met you. I was all right till I did. Now... now you've said these things... fuck you!" She grabbed her coat, and ran to the door. As she hauled it open, she heard Jack shout after her, "Take it, Wendy. Take the gamble!"

Wendy ran stumbling down the street, barging and cursing past the shoppers, until she reached the steps of the Methodist church. Stopping to catch her breath, she looked round to make sure Jack hadn't followed, and went inside. She leaned against the wall at the back, and stared at the altar cross; letting her mind drift through what had just happened. All the things she had revealed to Jack, and what he had said to try and help her. Above all, that fear he had forced her to confront. Was contacting her sister really her last chance? Dare she take that gamble? What if...

A gentle voice broke her thoughts. "How do you think he got on?"

Wendy looked up at the huge crucifix hanging over the altar. "Not bad. He found it hard, bless him, but that was to be expected. He asked the right questions, and it was obvious he cared. And he was tough when he had to be. He took a gamble himself, though, trying to get me to face up to what might be my last chance. If I don't, well..."

"I agree. I'll have a word. You were very convincing, as usual; they never guess."

"Thank you. Was he a junkie?"

"Yes, a sad case. What's your next step?"

"I'll engineer an 'accidental' meet with him tomorrow, maybe another after that, and eventually let him persuade me to go and see my 'sister'. That way he won't be surprised when I disappear. He fancied me, you know."

"Bits of you, anyway," smiled the voice. "Could he cope with a real assignment?"

"As long as it's not too complex – and he or she isn't too pretty."

"Good. Thank you, as ever. Your work testing out new Guardians is invaluable."

"When can I ascend again? These sessions are tough on me too."

"I know. Hopefully next month. When you've finished with

Jack, there's one more I'd like you to check out. Theresa; she's up in Manchester."

Wendy groaned. "Another? All right, if I must. But please not vodka this time, it makes me so sick."

The voice laughed. "I saw."

"Drugs, maybe. Coke is fun."

"Hey, steady on! I can't see the Heavenly Host agreeing to us getting married if you're a junkie. That *would* be a gamble!"

Wendy giggled, and wagged her finger at the crucifix. "Gotcha. Only kidding, I'll stick to the vodka." She turned to leave. "Let me know about Theresa."

"I will. See you soon; I can't wait to start our new life together. Love you, Wendy."

"Love you."

The Last Voyage of Ferrywoman Katherine Marshall – John Bunting

Katherine's first thought as she stirred from stasis-sleep was, "Made it! Now for a quiet retirement in the desert." Her second thought was, "What the hell is all that noise!" Her third thought was, "Oh bugger, alarm bells!" She gasped as the starship's emergency revival system pressed an oxygen mask hard to her face, then wretched violently as it pulled the bio-analysis tube from her throat. Finally, as the stasis-bed lifted her into a sitting position, she vomited through the mask and all over her trousers. Ferrywoman Katherine Marshall was awake.

She dragged off the puke filled mask, and wiped her face with her shirt. "Computer," she screamed above the bedlam, "why all the alarms? Report."

"My mother told me never to talk to strange women."

"What?! Damn it, computer, it's me. Stop being bloody stupid!"

"Only following procedure; hint hint."

Katherine groaned in frustration, and eased herself off the bed. Two deep breaths, and she started towards the door, only to find herself flat on her nose as her legs refused to cooperate. Cursing loudly, she heaved herself up onto all fours, and scrambled on. She entered the Bridge on hands and knees, hauled herself up onto her Captain's chair, and pushed her hand into the DNA Analyser. "Computer, Waking Procedure Calamity; recognise Ferrywoman Marshall, Katherine Anabella, service number five one two, authorisation code Captain Alpha Female Definitely Most Definitely Bloody Female Alpha."

"Ferrywoman Marshall is recognised."

"About time. Turn off that noise! Thankyou. And the flashing lights. Now; report why."

"Report why what, Maam?"

"What! What do you mean why what? Why was every effing alarm on the ship going off? That's why what."

"Maam, twenty-two seconds ago, I detected a large unidentifiable vessel seven million miles from us on a collision course. I altered our course to avoid it, only to note with considerable consternation that one-hundredth of a second later the vessel armed its *very* big guns, and changed its course too. So I initiated your emergency waking procedure, and sounded the collision alarm. I then checked our defensive and offensive weapons systems, only to find with equal consternation that both are inoperable. So I sounded the action stations alarm. For reasons I will explain later, but to do with the fact that sixty-three percent of my other systems are down as well, I sounded the general alarm – just so as you'd know we have a number of issues to deal with. I await your instructions."

"...Pardon?"

"**Maam, twenty-two—**"

"Stop; I get it. When will it reach us?"

"**In eight minutes.**"

"Have you tried all the emergency collision manoeuvres?"

"**Yes.**"

"There's nothing we can do to avoid it?"

"**No.**"

"And it's got very big guns?"

"**Maam, it's got very bigger, faster, everythinger than us; and it's coming our way.**"

"There must be something. You're always bragging you have an IQ of two hundred."

"**Nothing.**"

Katherine sat thinking for a while, then said quietly, "So you're telling me we might be going to die. I must say, this is all very sudden."

"Technically, I won't die, I'll break up into several million pieces. But both your observations are valid."

"Well, it was always a risk of the job I guess." Katherine sniffed at her stinking clothes. "But I certainly don't want to meet my maker looking like this." She walk/crawled over to the shower room, washed herself down, and put on her best uniform. Then she stretched and eased her muscles loose. Feeling better, she went and stood by the computer. "I'm sorry it's ending this way," she sighed. "What is it; fourteen trips together?"

"It is. We've had some laughs, haven't we? Do you remember... no... best not to start that."

"No. As a matter of interest, where are we?"

"I have no idea."

"Huh?"

"Maam, when our ship arrived at where I thought Earth was, it... um... wasn't. Nor were any of the other planets or the sun. The whole bloody solar system had disappeared. I wondered if the problem might rest with me, so I carried out a wide-ranging systems test. It turned out I was A.OK – apart from the sixty-three percent of me that doesn't work. As a result, I concluded that we had been on course – it was the Earth that hadn't been."

"When was this?"

"Seven thousand four hundred and two Earth years ago. Give or take."

"Seven... and you didn't think to wake me?"

"There didn't seem much point. If I didn't know where Earth was you sure as hell wouldn't, and you'd have blundered around the Bridge getting cross with me, and using up valuable and diminishing consumables."

"Blundered arou... Computer, if I may say so, you seem to have developed a rather eccentric way of addressing your

Captain."

"Sorry, Maam. All those extra years of background radiation have not treated my linguistic circuits well. The foul expletives are your fault."

"So you've never found Earth?"

"Nope."

"Shit."

"Indeed."

They fell silent; both, in their different ways, contemplating the apparently inevitable. Katherine thought about the life she had chosen as a Ferrywoman. On the whole she'd enjoyed it. One month loading; two hundred years in stasis-sleep, only to be woken in extreme emergency; and one month unloading. And then a year off before the return trip. It was during one of those years that she'd fallen in love with the empty hotness of the Central European Desert. "It is, isn't it," she muttered to herself.

"What is what, Maam?"

"Mmm? Oh, I was thinking how ironic it is that my last ferry trip – in fact, the last ever sub-light ferry trip by anyone if they've got that faster-than-light drive to work – proves to be the only one ever lost."

"Irony is... whoa, hang on, Maam. Hang on one little-bitty minute; the unidentifiable vessel has started to slow. On current projections, it should stop one mile off our port bow in... ten seconds. And it's switched off its guns! Yippee, we're not going to die; not yet anyway."

"On screen." The vessel was a mass of white cubes and globes, joined together by an intricate maze of thick, tube-like structures. And it was huge; maybe ten miles in every direction.

"There's an audio message coming through."

"Let's hear it."

"Identify yourself," rasped a deep voice.

"Bloody hell," gasped Katherine, "it's talking in English!"

"Never mind that; identify yourself immediately!"

"I am Ferrywoman Katherine Marshall, Captain of the starferry Grinstead. I am on a peaceful mission carrying non-military supplies from the planet Oxted, in the gamma quadrant, to my home planet Earth. I mean you no harm."

"Wait while we interrogate your ship's computer."

"Ouch, that hurts!"

It's OK, computer, let them do it. We need their help."

"You speak the truth. I am Becklespinax the Ninety-Second, Captain of the Saurship Goyocephale Three. I am opening a visual channel; I think you will find what you see will be of interest."

"OMG!"

"What is *that*?"

"A dinosaur."

"Correct."

"Hey, my first alien. What a cracker!"

"I and my kind are the descendants of the First Magyarosaurus Solar Expeditionary Squadron, which had the good fortune to be in transit when that wretched meteor struck Earth, our home planet also, and killed off everysaur. How their deep space radar missed the damn thing I'll never know. Anyway, the Squadron managed to land on an habitable planet in the beta quadrant, and the rest, as you would say, is history. You are in considerable trouble, are you not?"

"You're not kidding."

"We seem to have lost Earth."

"That's because it's disappeared."

"...Continue."

"Yes! I've always wanted you to say that."

"We've no idea where to. We've been monitoring Earth's progress for several million years, and what we do know is that a while back this area of the galaxy drifted into psychedelic

space, and lots of star systems simply vanished, including yours."

"What space?"

"These parts of the space/time continuum were damaged when some mindless idiot tested a faster-than-light drive. The effect on the continuum of the impossible actually happening was similar to that on your brain if you took Lysergic Diethylamide."

"LSD?"

"No shit. Warped space!"

"Your ship entered the psychedelic space when it approached where Earth should have been. You're trapped."

"Are you... trapped?"

No. Our scientists have developed a mobile force field that can keep out psychedelic space by generating an artificial normal space around us."

"Wow; that is genuinely cool, and very, very clever. Respect to the dinosaurs."

"It's only a temporary fix. Psychedelic space is unstable and collapsing at an increasing rate. It will shortly fall into a massive black hole. We need to leave soon or we never will. And here's the thing; we've been trying unsuccessfully to rescue you for a while now."

"I don't remember any previous attempts."

"You're stuck in a time loop; each time we meet is like the first for you. That's why I've treated this meeting as a First Contact, and interrogated your systems as you would expect me to. But this must be our last attempt."

"What do you suggest?"

"Our scientists have tried every sensible idea they can think of, without success, so as a last resort we're going to try something completely crazy. LSD crazy, hopefully. Computer, what are you carrying in your cargo hold?"

"Nine hundred and eighty-two million genetically identical, butter-basted, oven-ready, frozen chickens."

"Is that animal, vegetable or mineral?"

"Good question. They contain various disgusting vegetable and mineral additives, and far too much water in my opinion, but on the whole I would say animal."

"Can you release them into space?"

"That's up to my Captain."

"Could we detach the cargo hold, and then blow a hole in it?"

"Yes, but as the man said, you're only supposed to blow the bloody—"

"Enough! And the sudden decompression should blast the hold apart?"

"Confirmed."

"We'll do that, then. Computer, make it so."

"Compliance."

"It will be sufficient."

"And then?"

"And then watch and hope. If our plan works, it will force space/time back into normality, Earth will reappear where it was, and you will wake up safe in its orbit as if none of this had happened... which... err, it won't have."

"And I can retire to the Central Earth Desert. Sounds good to me."

"But if it doesn't work, you will wake up in the middle of a collapsing black hole, which... won't be good. We have two of your minutes left; we must act now."

Katherine took a deep breath. "What are our chances?"

"Better than zero, which is what they will be if we don't do this."

"Fair point. Thank you for putting yourselves at risk for us."

"Here jolly here. You dinosaurs rock. Maybe see you on the other side!"

Katherine pressed an emergency release button, and the cargo hold drifted away for the ferry-ship. At a safe distance, she pressed another button, and the hold blew apart. Out exploded nine hundred and eighty-two million frozen chickens. Immediately, the Saurship bathed them in an orange glow of microwaves, and the chickens thawed. Exposed to the effects of psychedelic space, they started to change colour and shape, and within a few seconds nine hundred and eighty-two million pink flying pigs were grunting and flapping around helplessly. Now a green energy beam fired from the Saurship, and the pink flying pigs were somehow twisted and faded into the very fabric of the space/time continuum, which seemed to shiver as one psychedelic distortion was confronted by another. The third-to-last thing Katherine heard was herself whispering, "Our father..." The second-to-last thing she heard was, *"Goodbye Ferrywoman Katherine Marshall, and good luck."* The last thing she heard was, **"Holy shit, I hope the force is with us. Continue. Hah!"**

Katherine's first thought as she stirred from stasis-sleep was...

Angels with Razor Wings – Laure Van Rensburg

Carly Sue had floated on her back on the calm yellow waters of Wolf River. Over her, heavy branches bowed to create a makeshift foliage of arches like the cathedrals in those fancy books at the library. The blinding June sunshine filtered between waxy leaves and broke on the surface of the water into a dozen shimmers but she hadn't seen any of that.

Fish always go for the eyes first, at least that's what Jamie overheard when she went down to the County morgue to identify Carly Sue's little body. Not much of a body really, bloated flesh the ashen colour of death minus the bits the fish and other small animals had nibbled on. Not much of Carly Sue really, of the eleven-year-old Jamie knew and loved so much with knobby knees and those goddamn pink sneakers she would never take off. They didn't find those when they fished her out. She listened to them and answered their questions as best she could, standing stiff and straight as a utility pole on the Interstate. Once they were finished with her, Jamie strode outside and around the back of the building. She leaned forehead against the wall and finally puked her breakfast but, she waited until the dead of night after everybody had gone to sleep in the house to cry and scream into her pillow.

Jamie marched down toward Sal's—hands buried deep in the pockets of her army jacket and cap firmly screwed on her head, ragged visor tilted down. A week of no goddamn news, she thought as she kicked an empty can. One of the deputies at the station had told her that Memphis had sent a Detective to be in charge of the investigation and he was presently having lunch at Sal's. She wasn't sure which deputy had told her; Barlow only had two—Dumb and Dumber, she called them. She couldn't tell them apart, same look of stupid on their faces. She stepped in and scanned the inside of the dim lit room, which smelt like an ashtray stuffed with bodies in need of a good scrub. She clocked the Detective hunched over a table drinking his lunch.

"You Jimmy Whittaker?" she demanded arms crossed scowling down at him.

"Who's asking?" The question escaped amid the beer sloshing about in his mouth.

"A fucking concerned citizen."

She dropped sideways in the chair opposite him draping one arm on its back. The man in front of her parading as a Law Enforcement Officer wore a three-day stubble and a crumpled shirt that wouldn't look out of place on a wino. He stared back at her with bloodshot eyes that hadn't seen a good night sleep in a long time.

"What you concerned about little girl?" He snorted taking a swig from his drink.

"Fuck you, I ain't no little girl I'm seventeen, you old tramp. I want to know what's happening with the Fields investigation."

"Fields?"

"Carly Sue Fields, the kid you fished out of the Wolf River a week ago. What's happening? You got... what do you call them? Leads. You got any of them leads?"

"Jesus, that investigation." He rubbed the stubble on his jaw, which made a harsh grating sound. "Tell me about that one, I ask to be put on loan out of Memphis so I could stop dealing with that kind of fucked-up shit, I mean killing little kids. I'm sent out to the sticks and that's the first case I catch. That poor girl..." He drowned the images and the rest of that sentence with whatever was left in his bottle before motioning for Sal to bring him another one.

"So?"

"Sorry, can't tell you anything. You ain't family. Her folks are back in some town in Missouri."

"You listen, I was more of a family to that girl than those hicks ever were. She lived with me for going on two years now."

"Oh, so you're Ange? They told me about you at the station

you live with the old Jensen down Walton Road and you take in the strays: runaways and all other sorts of messed-up kids."

"Yeah that's me, alright."

"Why they call you Ange instead of Jamie, anyway?"

"None of your business." She shrugged. How about Carly Sue?"

"Sorry, nothing I can tell you."

"Goddamn what good are you for then?"

She stormed out tipping the chair over and leaving it on the floor. The swings of her ponytail counting the rhythm of the seething anger rising within.

She reached the house and slumped on the porch swing making the rusty chains creak under her weight. The open window behind her brought the muffled voices of the twins arguing. Nothing of concern really, they were always arguing about something. She also caught a whiff of fried catfish and pickles, sure sign that Jensen was home.

She pushed her feet against the planks of the porch and the swing whined away. She was grateful for the little wind it created. The sun had dipped behind the buildings but it had left its stuffy heat behind. It was all around her pressing against her skin, suffocating her more than usual. Frustration and memories of Carly Sue welled up in her eyes and she wiped them away with her shirt sleeve. Goddamn, she was just a sweet kid. The coroner had been reluctant but she had insisted and he had explained all that they did to her. How they molested her body and innocence until they took everything she had, but it wasn't enough and they took her life too, smothered it out of her. Jamie had seen the dark purple shadows around the frail broken neck. A scream gathered in her throat and her dirty fingernails dug into her palms.

"Hey, Ange!" Timmy chimed jumping on her lap. She swallowed the cry and manufactured a smile for him.

"Hey, monster. What you been up to?"

"Digging earthworm in the backyard with Mel."

"Well, that explains those grimy paws putting dirt all over my shirt."

She tickled him just so she could hear the tinkles of his laugh, distracting her mind for a moment from the darkness creeping at her edges. These days her hands itched to break something, to bring pain instead of comfort, especially to the particular son of a bitch who killed Carly Sue. She'd love to snap his bones and feed them to the dogs.

"Stop it!" He squirmed about digging his little elbows into her sides. "Hey, Ange?"

"Yes?"

"When's Carly Sue coming home?"

The question caught her by surprise and her fingers went dead. She had explained it all to Timmy but how much could a five-year-old understand that there's no coming back from that kind of gone? She held him tight and buried her sorrows in his hair but no matter what she did, she couldn't get rid of the anger, that was stuck in her like a knife between the ribs.

Another week of no answers. Jamie kicked the screen door open and stepped into the heatwave. She coiled her hair before trapping them beneath her cap pulling down on the frayed visor. The relentless sun bleached the sidewalk and the fried patch of lawn that clung to the dirt in the yard. She was about to turn around to check if she could find a pair of sunglasses in one of the kitchen drawers when she noticed a patrol car down the street.

"Hey stop," she yelled as she broke into a run. "Hey, wait a minute." She caught up with it and banged on the protruding boot. "Goddamn, stop!"

Finally, the car came to halt and she discovered Dumb, or was it Dumber behind the wheel.

"Hey, Deputy."

"Hi, Jamie. What do you want?"

"I spoke to the Detective…"

"Detective Whittaker?"

"Yeah, that's the one. He said you had news about Carly Sue?"

"He did?" Furrowed hesitation spread over his face as he played with his moustache.

"Sure did, said you had a lead." She grinned.

"I'm not sure…"

"C'mon, I was on my way to the station to get the lowdown so you can sure spare me the trek and just tell me now." The words escaped her mouth still painfully stretched in a wide smile. "He'll sure be glad that you saved him the time."

"Oh, ok then." Police around here, dumber than a sack of rocks. "Yeah, we got a lead alright. Some bikers witnessed Marty Wicks talked to Carly Sue before she got into his truck and he was the last person to see to her but— "

"But what?"

"We've got no evidence. It's all circumstantial as they say at the DA office in Memphis."

Jamie's hands balled into tight fist, the rage rattling her small bones building up worse than toxic fumes in a cheap meth lab. It exploded with a kick to the driver's door.

"Hey, what you do that for?"

The deputy's unanswered question disappeared in a cloud of grit as Jamie sprinted down the road.

"Is it true, you know who killed Carly Sue?" Jamie asked as she slid a chair over before straddling it. Her dark eyes probed the crumpled face of Det. Whittaker. Just look like one of his shirts, she thought.

"What makes you think— "

"Your deputy told me, goddamn is it true? Did Marty Wicks do it?"

"Damn idiot running his mouth. Yeah, Marty Wicks' our perp. He did it alright."

"So? Aren't you gonna arrest him, or something?"

"Or something," he stated into the neck of this bottle but she knew from her old man that there're never any answers to be found at the bottom of one, only problems, misery and bad hangovers, "I can't we have nothing on him, no evidence or DNA, the river washed all that away."

"How do you know it's him then?"

"Oh, it's him alright. Witnesses saw him talking to her, son of a bitch got a record too, not the first time he's done that sort of thing..." He slurred.

"How many of those you had?" she asked nodding towards the bottle in his hand.

"Not enough," he sighed finishing it before motioning to Sal to bring another.

"Can't you get him to confess?"

"Nah, he ain't stupid. He knows if he shuts his mouth we got nothin'. He's even been bragging about how he's got us."

"That's it? What y'all good for?" She snatched the bottle Sal dropped on the table and took a long swig of it. They stared at her before the Detective asked Sal for another.

"That's it. I don't like it any more then you do, kid but— "

"I ain't a kid— "

"Really pisses me off that scumbags like Marty Wicks get away with shit like this. I promise you sometimes if I wasn't a cop..." His meaty fingers strangled that bottle of beer so hard, he might shatter it. She wondered what had happened to damage him that bad but she sensed an opening in his words and in this hand around that glass neck that she couldn't ignore. She leaned forward and dropped her voice.

"If I was to take care of it, do you have my back?"

"Wait, what?"

"If I was to take care of it, do you have my back?"

He scoffed at her hard. "Whatcha' gonna do with your little freckled face and twig arms? You couldn't even win a fight with an alley cat."

She ignored his contempt and stared him down. "Answer, do you have my back?"

His eyes probed her assessing how serious she was. She didn't waiver and showed him the determination of a stray dog ready to fight to the death for a scrap of meat.

"Yeah, if you did I got your back but tell me why do they call you Ange?"

"Told you, none of your damn business. Just ain't go about forgetting your promise, Detective."

Jamie was flying down main street, one of the deputies huffing after her. She had the advantage of not having to carry the same heavy load of fat strapped to his gut. She made a hard right almost skidding to a stop. Her lungs burnt hard in her chest but the finish line came into view—the entrance to Sal's. She would find him there, spent more time in that place than at the station. Jamie crashed through the double doors and didn't slow down until she collapsed in a chair opposite Whittaker. The low thump of her body interrupted him chewing on a bacon rasher.

"Easy, kid."

She smiled in between jagged breath before downing half his beer.

"Remember your promise?" she asked after wiping her mouth with the back of her hand.

Before he could respond, the deputy stumbled through the door, his face as flustered as that of a cheating husband caught with his pants down. The sweat, he was drenched in had pooled under his armpits and the rolls of his chest darkening his shirt a nauseating shade of brown.

"Don't. Move." He ordered a chubby finger pointed at Jamie. She replied with an arched eyebrow and two raised hands showing good faith that she wasn't going anywhere.

"What seems to be the trouble, officer?" She smirked.

"Don't play smart ass, you know what's what. You need to come with me and answer some question about what happened to Marty Wicks."

Det. Whittaker's attention and face perked up at the mention of the name.

"What happened to Wicks?"

"Well, you'll know if you ever answered your damn phone." The jab earned the deputy a dark scowl that made him cower and Jamie decided that today this one was Dumber. "Wicks was found this morning in his bed, throat cut like a pig at the slaughterhouse, soaked in bleach and..."

"And, what?" Whittaker snapped.

"And with his junk cut off and stuffed in his mouth."

"Is that so?" The words were for the deputy but his attention was focused on Jamie, eyes hooked on hers as she took another gulp of his beer.

"Yeah, this one was seen leaving The Salty Dawg with him night before last."

Jamie rested her forearms on the table and leaned closer to the Detective ignoring Dumber.

"Should I tell him or you wanna do the honours?"

"What she talking about, Whittaker?"

Silence settled around the table, heavy and uncomfortable like the heatwave outside. Jamie didn't back down in her stare off with Whittaker assessing if she had bet on the right horse. He fished a pack of cigarettes out of his pocket and slid one between his lips. They waited on him as he took his time like a shy virgin on her wedding night.

"She was with me, found her drunk by the side of the road with Marty and drove her arse back home."

"Is that true?" Dumber stammered at Jamie.

"What you asking her for? You think I'm lying?"

"Sorry Detective, of course not... I just thought— "

"Don't think that's bad for you. Head back to the station

Turkish Delight

and prepare me a file on this. I'll be along in a bit."

The deputy scrammed back out knocking into chairs, and patrons on his way out. Might need a word stronger than Dumber for this one, Jamie thought smiling at his embarrassing exit.

"So how you do it?" He pinched the question along with the filter of his cigarette and she eyed him sideways.

"I mean hypothetically."

"What that means?"

"Means if it was you how you have done it. Just exchanging theories no more."

"Well, hypothetically," she said her tongue stumbling over the unfamiliar ten-Dollar word, "I would have bumped into him at The Salty Dawg and done shots with him although I would have pretended drinking some and puked the rest and just acted drunk. I would have flirted too to get him horny. Then when he was hammered, I would have suggested getting back to his. I might have let him feel me up with his sweaty paws and slobber into my neck and around my mouth to get him unsuspected." Whittaker's body moved forward drawn to her story. She rinsed her mouth with a swallow of beer and hunched over the table. "Maybe I would have let him take me to bed and insisted to keep my cap on and in his drunken state, he would have found that fucking hot. And then, when he was on top of me busy trying to stuff his junk inside me, I would just..."

Jamie pulled on the visor as she leaned closer again. A flash of silver sliced the air. Her fingers were at his throat, the cold tickle of a blade against the skin covering his jugular. She smiled at him as she lifted the razor away from his flesh and stashed it back in the frayed opening under the visor of her cap.

"Anything else?"

She leaned back into the chair, arms crossed and a smug lopsided smile on her face. He signalled for Sal to bring out two whiskeys. The old man shuffled over and settled two glasses and the bottle on the table. He didn't fancy doing the back and forth, Jamie guessed. Whittaker poured them double measures. He raised his glass to her before tossing it down his throat. Jamie slowly drank hers, tasted like honey compared to Jensen's moonshine.

"Yeah, why they call you Ange?"

"None of— "

"C'mon kid, you own me."

She shrugged. "Guess so. Old Jensen got me that nickname when he first found me all grimy and bloody. He took one look and said — child, ya' look like an ange', an ange' with a dirty face." She mimicked the chewed-up diction that came with a mouth that lacked teeth. "Kinda stuck after that."

"Huhn, how about that? I guess angels around here don't only have dirty faces they also have razor wings. Hey, where'd he found you?"

She smiled. "None of your goddamn business."

Zig Zag – Charles Osborne

I couldn't help myself. Three steps to the right; there steps to the left; three steps to the right. I missed the open door of the bus. The driver closed the door and went off without me. Another bus; another attempt at getting on. I tried to position myself in the correct spot but the next bus pulled in further up the road. I was determined not to miss this one. I was in a rush; as I zigzagged across the pavement I bumped into a woman with a young child and knocked them over. I was surrounded by a less-than-friendly crowd. The police soon arrived and arrested me for being drunk and disorderly and for common assault. This was not the first time I had been up before the judge. Yes, I have to admit that I'd had a couple of glasses of wine, but I would argue that this was medicinal to help me with my condition. But no-one believed this, least of all the judge, who put my zigzagging down to drink rather than as some sort of medical or psychiatric condition. There was no help here. So, here I was, facing the usual outcome; another six months jail term.

Crash! Bang! Plates flying; women screaming; shouting; fighting; inmates spattered in portions of pies, peas and gravy. And at the centre of the fracas, me, Maggie Meyers, in for disturbing the peace and public order offences.

Solitary confinement is no escape. Here, I felt psychologically exposed by the shiny whiteness of the newly-painted walls and the unceasing brightness of the strip-lighting.

The prison counsellor comes to see me the next day. A young man not long out of university; not yet hardened or disillusioned by the frailties and brutalities of the prison system. How long will he last, I wonder? His name is Geoffrey Wilson.

Because of cutbacks and, to many, the unattractiveness of working in the prison service, the prison has been unable to employ a fully-trained psychiatrist. What we have is Geoffrey, or Geoff, as he likes to be known, a multi-tasker, who is responsible for psychiatric counselling, creative art, and sports therapy, all rolled into one. I don't know how he copes.

'Hello Maggie,' he beams, disarmingly. 'What is this, your third time in solitary? What are we going to do about you?'

'I don't know, I can't seem to help myself,' I reply, sheepishly.

He looks at me quizzically, as if weighing up the various possibilities he has in store for me.

'I think we'll have to make an appointment for you to have a brain scan, Maggie. It's in your best interests.'

Oh, dear. Am I going crazy, I ask myself?

I turn up in my borrowed shorts and ill-fitting top. Geoff has persuaded me, despite my protests, to come in as a late replacement in the prison women's football team. They haven't won a game all season. Our lone striker, Millie, a hardened drug dealer and abuser, leads the team up front despite carrying a long-term injury. Geoff tucks me into midfield.

I'm not too bad at one-on-one but get overwhelmed by two or three opposition players ganging up on me. Millie is getting more and more infuriated at my ineffectiveness. We lose by a record 15-1.

It's a good job I can return to solitary confinement as Millie and other hardened inmates are out to get me for my poor display. Luckily, Millie is side-lined with her injury for the next game. Geoff takes a gamble and pushes me up front. I'm so nervous, my legs feel like jelly. We are losing 1-0, when the ball comes to me from the left-wing. I put on a burst of speed; three steps to the right; three steps to the left; three steps to the right, and bang, the ball's in the net. This seems to inspire the team and we run out 2-1 winners. Our first ever win. On the one hand, I'm a bit of a heroine for scoring the first goal, while on the other, Millie and her gang are out to get me as they've bet heavily on us losing. Geoff recommends I remain in solitary for now for my own safety.

In the next game, I'm on my own up front, when a long ball

reaches me. Three steps to the right, three steps to the left. I round the defender and edge the ball over the outcoming keeper. We are 1-0 ahead. With some solid defending we maintain our lead and edge the game 1-0.

Even some of the hardened inmates are impresses that we've won two games on the trot. But it's not to last. The next team we come up against have sussed out my precise manoeuvring. We lose the game 2-0. I'm in the doghouse. My temporary fame has evaporated. Geoff says 'not to worry' as we all have our setbacks.

My brain scan came back negative. Several visits to the psychiatric wing of the local hospital, under handcuffed escort, proved fruitless. I was labelled uncooperative and disruptive. Only Geoff seemed to offer any sympathy, even though I hadn't opened up to him either.

One day he brought me a tape-recorder and suggested that 'here was a chance to unburden myself.'

The next game was a crunch game against the women's prison officers team. We had to win. Somehow Geoff kept faith in me and kept me in as a lone forward. I was nervous. I had to vary my game, if I could, for us to have any chance of winning. I had been practicing my moves with the tape-recorder.

The prison officers team were expecting my usual three steps to the right, three steps to the left, so were surprised when I varied it to two steps to the left and one to the right to score our first goal. Keeping up different variations of this routine, I managed, much to the disgust of the prison officers, to score another goal. After a bruising game, we left the field in triumph, beating them comprehensively 3-1. The Prison Governor, having divided loyalties, had mixed feelings about our win, while up on the wing, illegal booze flowed freely that night.

Upon release, my sister arrived from some remote archaeological dig in south-central America. We hadn't seen each other for years. She was waiting for me at the prison gate.

We embraced warmly, and comically paired up and zig-zagged down the road together arm-in-arm.

Up until now I hadn't opened up to anyone about what underlay my condition. But the time had come. As my sister was packing, after her brief stay, to return to her dig in central America, I gathered up the wherewithal to fill her in on the details which, up until then, were unknown to her as well as to everyone else.

I explained that I had a recurring vivid dream. I was being chased by some unknown and unseen creature. Ahead of me was a large reptilian, barring my way. I tried to confuse and outwit it by taking three steps to the right, three steps to the left, and three steps to the right. It would never quite get me. I would wake with a start with sweat dripping off my brow. I was afraid to go to sleep. This must have affected me mentally, in some way, as I found myself mirroring this behaviour in real life. The dream became a waking nightmare.

My sister noticed a ribbon-hung medal taking pride of place above the mantlepiece.

'Ah, I was awarded that for scoring the winning goal that beat Arsenal's women's football team 2-1 in a charity friendly football match.

'At least something good came out of it,' she ventured, as she suggested that I might try a clinical hypnotist to see if they could help.'

It was strange. As I got to a certain stage while in prison, where, with Geoff's help, I had been making slow progress in muting my zigzagging, my footballing skills, conversely declined. After the heights of the Arsenal match nothing was ever the same again. My prowess, all built on the art, if that is what it was, of zigzagging, was ebbing away. As it turned out, the Arsenal match was my last game.

After my sister left, I made an appointment to see a clinical hypnotist, as she had suggested. After a long course of treatment, my dreams subsided; my zigzagging zagged away. I was much relieved. I could walk a straight line again.

This called for a celebration. I stopped at the wine bar for a couple of drinks.

I was on my way home. A young man was coming towards me. I stepped to the left; he stepped to the left. Then, oh my God, I took three steps to the right.

Not to worry, I'd saved my boots and football shirt.

As conveyed by Maggie Meyers to Charles Osborne.

Busting a Rhyme or Two on a Lovely Spring Morning – Sean Crawley

I promised Nina I would bite my tongue and just nod.

Last time we visited my wife's mother things went pear shaped – excuse the cliché. The old bird claimed that a comet was circling the Earth, and I asked her if she meant the comet was orbiting *the sun*.

"No," she said with authority. "It is a new comet and it is orbiting the Earth."

"Bullshit, Elsie." I couldn't help myself. I recalled a similar exchange when she claimed that chickens don't have a brain. That time I agreed to disagree, this time I would not back down.

"How dare you speak to me like that!"

"I'll call bullshit, bullshit, when I hear it, Elsie. You don't get off the hook just because you're my mother-in-law. Facts are facts."

Elsie faked an angina attack and we had to leave.

The next day she phoned Nina to warn her about me.

"You know what they say, Dear. *A dimple on the chin, the devil within*," she said.

"Don't be silly, Mum. Now have you heard back from the doctors?" My wife can deflect like a pro.

"So where is Jason at the moment, Dear? Is he at work? What is that new job of his? It's in Darlinghurst isn't it? Does he ever work late? You know there are a lot of temptations for a man in that suburb. Don't be surprised if he strays, Nina."

"Mum! Jason's business is Jason's business. Now those results ... from the doctor?"

Elsie took about two months to calm down and recover from *my outburst* before inviting us over for a cuppa and some of her burnt scones. I mean they weren't burnt when she invited us, they would be though when we sat down on her precious Sanderson print lounge suite to listen to her latest ravings. As you can see, I'm maybe not quite ready to go back there, yet. But for my wife, I will do it.

I will bite my tongue and just nod. I will detach myself and float above as a remote observer. I will laugh in the face of insanity – to myself that is.

When we arrived, Elsie decided to have tea and scones on the deck outside. It was a lovely spring morning, the sun was shining and the wisteria was in flower. The scones were baked to perfection and the conversation, though superficial, was pleasant and devoid of false astronomy. Apart from saying hello on arrival I remained tight lipped. I nodded in acknowledgement and occasionally dared to offer a *mmm* in affirmation.

"Did you see the sunset last night?" my wife asked her mother.

"Oh yes, Dear. That is why it is such a lovely day today. You know, *red sky at night, shepherd's delight*. It's never wrong."

I choked and some scone flew out of my mouth and landed on the table next to the green depression-glass butter dish.

Everyone pretended not to notice.

Nina, asked if I was alright. I nodded, took a swig of tea, patted my chest and said, "I'm fine. Go on, Elsie." My wife smiled at me, I was doing very well indeed.

Elsie went on, and on and on. The old wives' tales and pseudo-science polluted the crisp morning air. She was obviously fishing for a bite from her son-in-law. I just nodded in agreement and ate scones. Lots of scones.

My wife must've been too relaxed, possibly because of my exemplary behaviour, when she let out, "Jason has had some issues with his oesophagus lately. He's seeing the doctor on Monday."

I nearly choked again. I could sense that things were likely going to crash and burn real fast – again excuse my cliché –

they must be contagious I tell you. Nina, my beautiful and caring wife had slipped. Her usual tactic of being a grey rock, just flew out the window – even though we were on the deck outside. This tactic was taught to Nina by her counsellor, specifically to cope with the mother. It entails being bland and not giving away too much information.

I looked at Nina, she looked at me. She said sorry with her eyes. I reassured her with a wink and a nod, and a big smile. I could handle this, I was prepared. I would *not* take any bait offered by Elsie, the old fisher-woman.

And by George, Elsie was off. The tit bit of information about my oesophagus was like the starting gun in the hundred yard dash.

"Well, if you ask me *an apple a day keeps the doctor away.*"

I nodded.

"Nina, go inside and get an apple from the fruit bowl on the kitchen bench. You know, *a stitch in time saves nine.*"

I nodded.

Nina wouldn't normally obey her mother's army like orders, but I figured that she was kicking herself for *feeding the beast*, as I called it. She went inside to find an apple.

"I once had a friend who always used to stay up late and sleep in all morning, she got oesophageal cancer and died at 58. *Early to bed and early to rise, keeps one healthy, wealthy and wise.* That's my motto, Jason. Couldn't be a more sage piece of advice if you ask me."

Despite no one asking her anything, Elsie ploughed on.

"Beatrice was her name. She was a dancer, and you know what that lot are like! *Birds of a feather flock together*, no truer a word than that."

I nodded. I was tempted to point out that her rhyming aphorism was actually six words and not one, and that I knew a dancer who bluntly refused to socialise with the troupe she was in.

Nina returned with an apple from which I quickly took a

massive bite.

"Now, what time do you go to bed and when do you get up in the morning, Jason?"

I pointed to my full mouth and held up a hand to indicate I couldn't speak.

"Mum! Leave Jason be. He has good sleeping habits, don't you worry."

"But I want to worry, Dear."

I choked on my cancer preventative apple. A small piece took flight and landed right next to the small piece of scone next to the butter dish.

Everyone pretended not to notice.

"Talk about worry," said Nina, "Auntie Mary rang me last week and told me that Frank was likely to loose his superannuation due to his business partner gambling it all away."

I love my wife. Not only can she deflect and be a grey rock, but when her long fuse runs out, she can give as good as she gets. Nina knows that her mother hasn't talked to her sister, Mary, for years. Apparently, Mary gave Elsie the flick when she grew tired of her sister's flirtatious ways with her husband, Frank.

"Oh, poor Frank." said Elsie. "Mary has no place telling this kind of private information to the world. You know, *loose lips sink ships*."

I nodded and thought, *takes one to know one*.

"I know. I will send Frank a lovely card and a lottery ticket. You know, *a friend in need is a friend indeed*." The old biddy looked straight at me. With my mouth purposely refilled with apple, I simply nodded.

"Mum! You're kidding aren't you? Don't you think that would be an insult to Mary?"

"No, I don't! That woman is as hard as nails and a mean one to boot. You know when we were young …"

Nina interjected, "Yes Mum! I've heard it many times. Mary, on her way to school used to step on the cracks in the pavement and sing, *step on a crack, break your mother's back.* That's right, isn't it?"

Go Nina!

"That is right, Christina. And your dear grandmother died a broken woman. These things should not be fooled around with, they have a truth to them."

"Bullshit, Mum. Nan died of emphysema caused by fifty years of smoking."

Touché, Nina.

"Well, that's what the doctors say," said Elsie, never a backward step from this old battleaxe. "I hope for my sake *you* didn't step on any cracks in the pavement when you were young."

Nina looked over at me with eyes wide open in frustration. I nodded. Inside, I laughed out aloud at the insanity.

"OK, Mum, we have to go now. Thanks for the tea and scones, have a lovely day. I'll take the tray inside for you." Nina needed to get away from this irrepressible matriarch – quick smart.

Elsie looked at me and said, "Well you've been very quiet today, young man. What, the cat got your tongue?"

With Nina gone, I was very tempted to let loose. The saying, *empty vessels make the most noise,* came to mind, but I held my tongue.

"Come on, speak up for yourself. Has the wifey got you on a promise?"

I took a deep breath. Elsie was champing at the bit for a reaction. A reaction that could be used later as evidence in the Family Court of Recriminations. I was a bit at sea, so I took a second deep breath.

Perhaps it was the thick fog of rhymes that was hanging around, perhaps it was just plain good fortune, but whatever it was, thankfully, a poem from my distant childhood came floating like a life raft into my reach.

"Elsie," I said. "I've been admiring all those wonderful wisdoms that you have been espousing this morning. And they rhyme so eloquently. It gives them a much greater authority don't you feel?"

My mother-in-law for all her conniving cleverness is a total sucker for flattery. "Oh yes, I have always used those sayings to guide my own journey."

I continued, calm and resolute, rubbing the devil cleft in my chin, "I will never forget a poem I learnt in fourth grade at school. It went, *A wise old owl lived in an oak, The more he saw, the less he spoke, The less he spoke, the more he heard, Now, wasn't he a wise old bird?*"

Nina returned, ready to escape. She'd missed the poem but could see her mother convulsing and choking on something. She quickly went around behind her and smacked her fair and square in the middle of the upper back.

Elsie's denture popped out of her mouth, flew through the air in slow motion, and landed on the table, right on top of the small pieces of scone and apple that I had deposited there earlier.

Aspirational – Jennifer Hayashi Danns

Am I happy? Is anyone truly happy? I am happier now than when we were in school. I am glad I have you, Toby and Uncle John. I wish Mum wasn't dead but I can shroud myself in Toby's London. The art galleries, the theatre. I love that he loves all that kind of stuff. Pretty much every Thursday we have a dinner party with his friends. Your favourite Kate was raving about my new hair.

"Wow! How did you get it so straight? It's gorgeous and the colour, it really suits you, you look so, how can I say this? So classy. Don't you think so Tobes?"

Toby thankfully agreed.

When he first saw me he was shocked, "What have you done?"

Toby found his manners and added, "It's nice but it's so different... It's really blonde. And straight"

It is really blonde but I didn't like the way he said it.

"How many women in your work have curly hair?"

"What's that got to do with anything?"

"I'm just saying, curly isn't very professional is it?"

"But you don't work in the city."

"Fuck off Toby."

"What did I say? I don't understand?"

He never bloody does but I was made up Kate liked it. I know you don't like her. You would have hated her last Thursday.

"I was on the district line the other day and I could have sworn I wasn't in London. The Americans who come here must not believe their eyes. Or their ears."

Kate has a way of telling a story which forces you to ask her questions thus making you complicit in whatever point she is

Turkish Delight

making.

"Why what happened?" Emily dutifully asked.

You haven't met Emily, she is Kate lite, she isn't quite as pretty, clever, or as confident as Kate, and Kate knows it.

"I was resting my eyes for a couple of minutes and all I could hear was 'not English',"

"Really? That's unbelievable," said Emily.

"I know! I am willing to bet of all the people in the carriage I was the only one who spoke English."

"It's not a bad thing though is it sweetheart?" said Felix

"I am not saying it is bad per se," Kate snapped, "I am just saying I find it strange when I am on a British train in Britain and no one can speak English. How do they get by day to day?"

"It must be so hard for them, especially the kids," Emily said feigning compassion.

"But what about the people they are interacting with? It's not fair. In other parts of Europe they have tried to ban the burka. Good on them. We don't have the guts to do it here. There was one of them on the train and it is just so intimidating."

"You are afraid of a woman with a bit of cloth over her face are you?" said Tom tapping the stem of his wine glass.

Kate glared at him, "No, of course not, but who knows if it is a woman underneath there it could be anyone."

Tom scoffed and said, "Was she even wearing a burka or was she wearing a niqab?"

"What difference does it make? It could have been a man or a woman. It's hard to tell by just the eyes, they don't all wear eye makeup do they?"

"I never thought of it like that. It could be anyone underneath there," Emily shivered, "How scary."

"It's unlikely to be anyone more dangerous than you. They do say ignorance is the most dangerous weapon of all."

Emily laughed at Tom but then looked confused, "Who has

ever said that?"

"What do you think Tobes?" Kate purred.

Toby mumbled something incoherent and looked at me.

"What about you Nats, if you went to, say, the doctors for example, would you be comfortable if the doctor was in a burka?"

"Are you sure you mean burka?"

"For god's sake Tom! You know what I mean,"

"Being uncomfortable is different to feeling intimidated," I said.

"Is it?" said Kate.

"Yes, I think so" I said.

"Well I for one wouldn't like it, fortunately most of the surgeries around here have British doctors." Kate said.

"They might be British and wear a niqab," said Tom

"Don't be ridiculous darling," said Emily.

"Why not? They could be a British Muslim."

"I would love to wear a burka for a day," said Felix, he was prone to these kinds of pronouncements, "I would like to experience the freedom of totally anonymity, the smooth material on my bare skin and the sensation of knowing I could see people but they couldn't see me."

He was also prone to sounding like a pervert.

"Now that is exactly the point," said Kate.

Was it? I thought.

"You could wear a burka-" She eyeballed Tom, "and we would have no idea it was you underneath there."

"Don't they have those little peep holes for their eyes. You could tell it was Felix through them," said Emily

"Maybe he could wear sunglasses too," said Tom.

"Coolio, then I would be totally incognito," said Felix.

"One time I was in the toilets at Euston and there was a woman in there who had just unveiled. I don't know why but I felt quite privileged to see her face. It felt... I don't know... quite intimate, I can't really explain it." I said.

"Wow, this really puts the whole thing into perspective doesn't it?" said Felix.

Does it? I thought.

"Thank you for sharing your precious moment."

If Tom said that to me I would know he was taking the piss, but Felix was serious. He's like a snake charmer. He hisses praise after everything I say, I often expect to look down and see my knickers around my ankles. He makes my skin crawl. Despite this Kate married him. She thought lots of other women would want to marry him and of course because Toby never got around to asking her.

No one has perfect friends do they? They can't all be like you. You probably would have punched Kate but to be honest I look forward to Thursdays with them because it means I'm not in work. My job is probably not the best but at least in the pub I feel like Charlie takes me seriously and he treats me better than Michelle. I hate her, it doesn't help that our names get mixed up because people think we look alike. I do take pleasure in making her polish mountains of cutlery way past closing. She thinks if she does these pointless tasks well she will eventually get my job but the more menial things I ask her to do the less Charlie views her as management material.

You won't believe what happened the other day. Some family came in, stuffed their faces and everything was fine until they asked for the bill. I was hiding in the office doing pretty much nothing when Michelle banged on the door. I could see her on the security camera so at first I didn't answer. She was waving pieces of paper. I let her in, she had ten £100 vouchers from another brewery. The lucky cow, someone must have given them to her as a tip.

"My table gave me these!"

Yes, I know. Stupid bitch.

"Lucky you. Close the door on your way out."

She stood there dumbfounded then over enunciated, "No. They are trying to pay with these."

Oh bloody hell please god no.

I snatched them out of her hand and ran downstairs to a purple faced man throbbing by the till.

"I am terribly sorry Sir," I think I may have bowed to convey humility, "But we," I glanced at Michelle, as far as I was concerned we were in this together. Charlie was upstairs, technically at home on his day off, "Cannot accept these vouchers."

"Who the hell are you?" He boomed.

My hand trembled as I tried to return his vouchers, "If you look here Sir, you can see this is not our company logo."

"What?" The man pointed a stubby finger at Michelle, "Why didn't she say something before we started ordering?"

"Sir there is no way she could have known you intended to pay with these vouchers."

"Get the manager."

"I am the manager."

"Are you?"

"Yes I am."

"I want to see another one."

"I am sorry Sir I am the only manager available today."

"But you are obviously going to take her side."

That's not true Sir, I hate her as much as you do, but that's beside the point.

"That is not true Sir, I am sorry that this has happened but I will have to ask yourself and the rest of your party to pay this bill."

"Preposterous! There is no way I am paying £1000 for that."

"Sorry Sir, I am afraid that is the total of your bill."

"But we only had that much because of the vouchers."

"I am sorry Sir. I would encourage you to discuss this with the rest of your party. I will wait here."

When he left I realised Michelle was beside me, practically hugging my waist.

"Get off Michelle! Go back to work."

"No, I want to stay with you."

I have to admit it was quite comforting having her there, "Ok, but back off a bit."

The family, lead by the wife, marched over. She threw the bill at me and screeched, "We are not paying it."

This really wasn't going well. All six of them were jabbering and pointing at me. It was the last thing I wanted to do but I whispered to Michelle to go upstairs and knock on Charlie's door.

Michelle came back breathless, she whispered gleefully in my ear, "He answered in his boxers!" God, I hate her. "He said if they walk out without paying, call the police."

"Police?" bellowed the man, "What's this about? What's going on?"

I swallowed bile, thanks for nothing Charlie. "I am sorry Sir but I must insist you pay this bill or I will have no other option but to call the police."

"This is unbelievable! I can't... I have never..." He grabbed the vouchers off the bar, stuffed them into his inner jacket pocket and threw a platinum credit card at me.

"Enter your pin please Sir."

For two excruciating minutes I stared at the card machine and almost cheered when the paper burst from the bottom of the hand held device.

He snatched his card and receipt from my hand. He leaned in close, snarling at me and Michelle and sneered,

"This is what happens when you pay peanuts, you get fucking monkeys."

It is times like these when I most miss my Mum. We were so unalike I was often able to hear other people's unguarded opinions of her. She had bright blonde hair, deep green eyes and red lips which could spit the foulest, most cruel and funny words imaginable.

"That woman is dangerous," They said.

They were right, she was. But she was my mother and I love her and I miss her so much it hurts. Like with Father Tom, she would have ripped this pompous bastard a new arsehole.

My mum used to attend church, well, religiously, every Sunday morning she would be at St Mary's in the back pew. Praying for a morning without a hangover. Donating our gas money to the collection plate. She loved the Church but not Father Tom. Mum would often mimic his nervous tic in a way which didn't seem synonymous with Christianity.

I loved Christmas. Every year I prayed to be Mary and every year I was cast as one of the three wise men. One year my mum asked, "What are you doing in the Nativity this year?"

I told her.

"Weren't you a wise man last year? Don't you want to be Mary?"

Which to be honest, even at that age, I knew to be an idiotic question. Of course, every girl wanted to be Mary. The following Sunday my mother sat in the front pew, and when the service was over she sweetly asked Father Tom, "Could I have a word?"

He looked horrified, but he obliged. Off they went through the door which the altar boys usually slide in and out. I was left alone in the church and I offered up a prayer to God that Father Tom could keep a secret. Clearly God was not listening and Father Tom was incapable, because in the evening over our Sunday roast my Mum asked me, "Have you ever done a wee in church?"

The answer is yes, and it still makes me feel angry to think Father Tom had obviously passed judgement over me when he clearly couldn't hold his own water. During a rehearsal I was desperate for the toilet but I didn't want to mess up the practice. At the back of the church with the other wise men I started to wee. I weed all the way up the aisle towards the altar, stepped into the scene and in my opinion, like a true professional, delivered my line,

"He truly is the son of God."

I ignored her question and ate my tea with my head down. I was scared she was going to start kicking off so as soon as possible I went upstairs out of her way.

Later I heard Uncle John arrive. I could hear his cans clinking in the hallway. I crept down the stairs and listened at the kitchen door. Mum was laughing so hard she could barely speak.

"I told that Father Tic, why the hell are you telling tales on a little girl? So what if she pissed herself? What has that got to do with her not being Mary?"

"What did he say then?"

I knew Mum was doing her cruel impression of Father Tic, sorry Tom, because Uncle John was banging his hand on the table and laughing so hard I had to shove my fist in my mouth to not join him.

"I said, listen Father we both know what's going on here. I don't care if she took a dump in the holy water"

There was a sound like an elephant spraying water from its trunk.

"Oh, bloody hell John!"

"Sorry Pat, I couldn't help it."

"Here you are, quick, wipe it up."

"I'm sorry love, I wasn't expecting you to say that, go on."

"I said to him, I don't care if she took a dump in the holy water, my girl best be Mary this year."

"You've got some front, you Pat, I can't believe you!"

"Well wouldn't you have done the same? I've never liked that man, he needed ripping a new arsehole anyway, so I gave him a massive one."

At which they both collapsed into childish giggles.

That Christmas I was Mary. I was happy.

The Nervous Bread Van – Michael Demus Hanson

"David, is there anybody you know in this part of the world who can help you?" I was facing the Salvation Army Brigadier who sat opposite me.

"You see I wrote to the prison on your behalf to try to find out something about you. I made several enquiries about your parole terms and came up with some relatively interesting answers. In the time, you were inside I have been able, because of my particular relationship with the Governor, to determine that your wife divorced you and remarried and is now I believe living in Canada with your children, is that correct?"

"Yes, sir it is."

"And would I be right in thinking that you left the halfway house in Battersea of your vocation, and in effect contravened the parole terms of your early release?"

I rubbed the sleep from my eyes.

"Yes, sir that is true. I think it is because I could not work in the egg factory anymore...sir."

"The egg factory?"

"Yes, sir it was where they wanted me to work, and I could not pack eggs anymore, so I ran away."

He screwed up his eyes. "But is that not a means of income and at least a job of honest work?"

"Sir with all respect it was a way into insanity. I could not face the repetition...the constant conveyor belt was churning out the eggs that had to get packed in their varying sizes and everyone that smashed to the floor they deducted a penny from your wages." He looked at me and shook his head.

"Sir, I tried for six weeks to meet the terms. I tried to be enthusiastic about my humble work, but all I saw was the misery and petty mindedness of it all. The foreman was a bastard. He knew of my past that I was an ex-con, and he played in his bored little sadistic empire with my nerves, and I could not tolerate the goings-on any longer. So, I ran. I got my few belongings and thought I would take the risk. After prison sir, I could not tolerate this offering of so-called freedom. It was breaking my willpower and my mind."

He looked at me thoughtfully. In that instant, I did not know what he would do. The phone was by his elbow; he could easily pick it up and ring the authorities and have me returned to prison.

"You see David my responsibilities are really to God and His work, and although I try not err on the side of the Law, there comes a time when we have to make decisions... I am grateful for the work you have done in the kitchens, and individual members of my army think the world of you and ..." he lingered as if deep in thought, "I have been no... I have decided that there is a way forward for you if I chose to ignore the so-called mistakes you have made... Yesterday I received correspondence from our missing person's bureau. You probably know we trace those that have left or ran away, for whatever reason, in the belief that they may wish to remain either known to their loved ones or to at least let their loved ones know they are well and alive. In some cases, they return to the life, they have left behind, or they chose to carry on with their anonymity. However, a certain Neil Ingram has been asking for your whereabouts or if indeed we are aware of them..."

It was a voice calling to me from a long-lost past. Neil... I had almost forgotten about him as indeed I had forgotten about most things. Events tended to hit me in swarms. It is never just one thing at a time. Inside my head I watched a black scorpion trying to fend off a small army of red ants, its tail whipping over time and time again, and stinging nothing. In desperation, it sought to run but was unable to, weighed down by the multitude.

I could not say anything. I began rocking on my chair.

Could I face going back to prison? Why does everything always have to be in a state of flux? The Salvation Army was the only place that allowed me time to find out who I was. It was a gentle place. I was feeling a sickness in my stomach at the thought of losing the little I had. Could I face the journey north? Was the Brigadier giving me some ultimatum that if I continued living here, he would be unable to sustain his policy with God, of truthfulness and honesty?

"Sir..." I faltered. "I have very little sir. I have finished up here a man with nothing...no home to go to, very few friends. I could not return to prison of that I'm certain. Neil is a boyhood friend, the last person I know who is aware of my history, which of course comforts me to some extent. Without guys like him, I have no past...he helps make my past. And if he goes away and I never set eyes on him again then my past also goes away because there will be no reliving of that past. And part of me wants him to go away and never come back. To never make enquiries about me or to even consider that I might be alive. Because to some extent, I get so saddened with the life I have led and where it has taken me. But then if I made contact at least I would have a friend and a possible new start..."

The Brigadier sat up in his chair. He said nothing for a while, and we sat in silence listening to the heavy traffic going by on Victoria Road. Through the window, at altitude, a silver coloured jet plane was leaving a white stream of vapour across the clear blue sky. He folded his hands on his desk.

"You see David you know surely my predicament? You have employment here, and to some degree, I am your employer...and I am interested in your welfare; I want you to do well for yourself...but I am bound by the Law to a certain amount not to condone known felons." I felt the rage coming into my body. All I wanted was to be left alone. I concentrated on his face,

"Sir, it seems for these past few years that my entire life is always at the mercy of others. It is always what they want…always their situation over mine. Their concerns, their fucking lives! When in all of this have I ever asked for anything? I leave people alone I respect them but Christ! It's hard getting by without having to be one thing or another. Sir, what do you want from me? That I should go? For what reason because I have stood up for myself and decided to leave a lousy job? I'm no different in my values than any other person with sense."

I wanted to summon more anger. To shout from my very soul at the snivelling, petty-mindedness of it all, but there seemed so little point, this so-called wise old man did not appear to comprehend what he was doing. I told him to hang onto the details, and that I would go away and think about what I would do. I stood up, and he shook my hand. It was indeed a solemn occasion for me…*the crazy self-righteous, sanctimonious fucker!*

I came out of the building and walked down through Parliament Square going towards the embankment by Westminster Bridge. It was a bright autumn day in early October and not a cloud in sight. The dead leaves from nearby trees swirled among the barren flowerbeds. I went down into the underground and jumped on a Circle Line train not knowing where it was going, and not caring.

Anonymous, islanded people surrounded me behind newspapers, behind makeup, fat, fleshy masks and flat eyes. I watched the blank faces – no one looked at me. I looked at the ads, unreal women and pink-cheeked men smiled cheesy grins to sell shaving cream, nightgowns, chewing gum, sex; *'Flash half a tit and I'll buy your toothpaste. Show me the outline of your buttocks, and I'll see your show.'*

Sex drier than sand, and more secret than death. The train stopped. More people got on and everybody trying not to look at

Turkish Delight

each other; how many secret places are there in the carriage? I smelled dirty.

A young white couple stood opposite. The girl had her back to me she was hanging on to her boyfriend's arm. He was the rugby type, tall, blond, and ruddy. Despite the month, they were dressed in summer clothes. When the wind blew from the carriage doors, she squealed, holding her printed dress at the hem so that it would not lift up. He said something, which made her laugh, and she turned and looked at me, and the smile died. I looked back at the ads. Then I hated them. I wanted to do something to make them hurt, something that would crack the naïve, stupid, pink-cheeked masks. They got off at the next stop without looking back.

I wanted a drink. I got off at Temple and went to a rundown shop that sold cheap booze at Surrey Street. My people, my people, stood all around. I bought four cans of Super-strength lager, the strongest you could get, and sat down on a bench nearby. Old men, young men, mostly in ill-fitting clothes tipped the drink down their unwashed necks. I unclicked a can and bolted it down. *God save the Queen! God save us all!*

I kept on drinking, listening to the voices of my people; some raised in anger others slurring and shouting, few were laughing. I kept on drinking by myself, saying to myself after each drink, *'now I'll go.'* But I was afraid. In this small garden, we were all one.

The afternoon passed on and, by early evening, there were few of us left. I didn't want to sleep in the hostel. I didn't want to go to sleep. I kept on drinking, buying more cans, becoming drunker by the hour, and listening to Peter playing his violin by the kerbside as he begged for money. I thought of the Brigadier and Neil. It was possible. If for instance, I got him to come to London he could take me from the hostel to a new life.

I could in an instant leave all this behind. I longed for an opening, some sign, because I did not seem to have a place anywhere, and I desperately wanted to belong. I thought I don't walk the streets anymore; I crawl. I've never been like this before. Now when I go to strange places, I wonder what will happen. Sometimes I'm afraid, and I don't know what of. Other people, the young children in the parks, the old men walking their dogs, mothers pushing prams, talk and laugh in the streets. Somewhere in my mind, I could once do that.

Peter in mock imitation was going around the garden shouting "Last orders at the bar!" and we piled down to the off-licence, and with the last bit of my money I bought six cans of witch's piss for the coming night, and we set off for the bridge at Waterloo..."*We few, we happy few, we band of brothers;*"

***

My dad called me the *fly in the ointment*. It was always strange when I was a kid to be called this...a fly. I spoiled the ointment. He rubbed the balm of life onto his body, and somehow, I had discoloured it and made it ineffective by simply being. One day I read about Wittgenstein. Somebody said to him *'What's your aim in philosophy?* He replied, *"To show the fly the way out of the fly-bottle."*

***

It was Sunday when I awoke under the bridge. Peter had gone off somewhere with his fiddle, no doubt begging. The rain was falling. I felt hung-over and cold. The streets were empty and stiff with boredom. I needed change desperately but did not at that moment know how to go about this. I was also broke, and if the day was to pass in marginal comfort, I needed a few coppers.

Turkish Delight

On the one hand, I need to live, and on the other, I need a change. There was nothing spontaneous in my life. It was like I was stuck in a groove, and the groove only ended in a sour death on some cold riverbank, under some shit awful sky, with nothing but black buildings, and the bare trees of autumn... I wanted to get out of the bottle in more ways than one.

The cold, miserable morning by Waterloo Bridge was culminating into some intervention. Maybe the combination of my unremarkable existence and the haunting repetition of the dream I seemed to be living in, was taking effect. I found a can of lager and stood there drinking it, as a red route-master passed by with its decks full of waving Japanese tourists. It was a regular service. It came through the gap in the wall at one side and disappeared down the road out of the other side. I was never sure whether it was a real service or not. I kept thinking... *I must be having a nervous bread van.*

With it being Sunday there were not many people around, and pickings were hard. I shuffled over the bridge towards the Strand, in the vain hope of some success. It was a cold day, and I had a stiff neck. My shoulders ached. The day had started for me, and already I was trying to inject a semblance of goodwill into myself. Something that will pick me up and make me feel that life is worth living again.

All I see is dullness and poverty; there is no rose-tipped dawn, just a grey smudge. But in some little way, I was trying to stand up for myself. Shaking my can on street corners, with my head low, hoping my hand did not appear to be weak and fragile, but strong and determined like the charity tin holders-*shaking for Jesus man shaking for Jesus! "Will ya come to the Mission will ya come – bring your cup and saucer and a bun..."*

***

I was looking at the sundial in the park. It had been marked out on the lawn in Roman numerals, and the figures were made of purple wood sorrel. There was a large, cast iron centrepiece sticking up in the middle, which the sun caught, and cast the shadow to tell the time. A plaque nearby read, *"Our days on Earth are but a shadow, and there is none about!"* I smiled. I sat on a bench and looked at the clouds passing in front of the sun.

I kept thinking if I arranged with the Brigadier would I be ready if Neil came for me? Would I be able to leave on the day stipulated? I was free of *smack* now. I realised there would be alcohol up north so I wouldn't be giving up too much up at this stage. The task seemed daunting. But equally, I could not stay here. The city was killing me, albeit slowly. I also knew that if I went with him, there would be lots of talking to do. It had been over ten years since last, I saw him. I was a different person then. I was stronger and living up there in the world. I walked taller and was beholding to no man; those were the days of foolish pride, jauntiness and self-regard.

Now I shook tin cans, and rummaged through waste bins, and could find little refuge anywhere. Days were spent picking the bones from a fat, silent society that walked around me. My life was a hand in Fenchurch Street station, waving from the carriage of a passing train, a small pulsating embryo on the pavement. Sperm swimming up the fallopian tube, seeking creation. The never-ending cycle being played out in a predatory world. I was no longer a logical optimist.

I loved Twilight. Along the river, the reflected street lamps would dance in the water. Mountainous office blocks would display a checkerboard of yellow lights. Sentinels got posted on the walls of the city. The sun would sink lower in the sky, preparing itself for its exit, and I would sense the waiting night.

It was in darkness that my fears came, the cold, clammy darkness from out of the caves and hollows, which masked the face of an agonising death. I would seek comfort with the small animals in the woods by the river, the squirrels, and the voles. Little timid field mice would scurry out of their holes and nibble the fallen seed. I would smell the earth under the starlit sky, and watch the flickering constellations, and sense the vastness of the universe in my murmuring wilderness.

I would awaken, wrapped in the grey mist from the river, and listen to the fish jumping.

The city was killing me, even though it did smile occasionally. Somewhere Neil was seeking me, offering a strong hand, preparing to take me away to goodness knows what, and the conflict was with myself, and whether I wanted to go.

Five Pound Notes and Fluffy Bunnies – Mary Charnley

'That was an awesome dinner, darling. You must give me the recipe for that marvellous Tagine,' Soraya drawls, spilt wine seeping like blood onto her silk blouse, just above her heart. Emily plays with her knife. If only... Emily thought, if only... perhaps she could take that ghastly Toby down as well.

It's the Saturday after Christmas and the party season is starting to take its toll. Emily looks at her guests, at the empty plates littering the table, the sputtering candle and wishes that they would just go. She's tired, and to be honest, rather bored. Conversation has come to a halt. Joe is worse than useless, sitting there, slurring and hiccupping, his head nodding over his wine, just on the verge of consciousness. There's no chance of any help from him after they've all gone home.

'We'll leave the clearing up till the morning, shall we darling? Get off to bed?' But she knows that she simply won't be able to.

The dining room is crowded and hot, and the smell of garlic and expensive perfume is making her feel sick. Family duties, she thinks, it's that Christmas thing. Thank goodness they don't have to see them for the rest of the year, particularly when the duty involves the objectionable Toby.

The streets are quiet now, just the scream of a distant siren. Rain lashes against the windows.

She makes a show of looking at her watch. It's 1am. Dear God, are they never going to go? There is only so much one can take of Toby's drunken flirting. Soraya picks up a grape, pops it into her mouth as though she's taking part in a Roman orgy. She'll start on the after-dinner mints next. No wonder she's putting on weight; not that anyone would dare to mention it of course. Toby has eaten very little. He's become a vegan recently. Soraya says it's because of his new job at the research lab. He can't allow anything taken from animals to pass his lips. It's all very well, but it does make planning a dinner party very tedious. Personally, she doesn't see why she should bother. It's like dealing with children really, you just tell them to eat what they're given. What's wrong with a plateful of organic vegetables after all? He picks at the cheese, crumbs of Stilton clinging to the designer stubble.

Cheese. Isn't that an animal product? Aha; a pick and mix vegan, she thinks to herself. She keeps her mouth shut. It doesn't do to argue with Toby, it's the season of goodwill after all. Rumour has it that he was seen eating a bacon butty the other day.

'Coconut latte for you Toby?' Toby grunts, nods his head, and reaching into the pocket of his tan leather jacket, he pulls out a small white envelope. He pushes the overlong dark hair out of his eyes in a gesture more reminiscent of the romantic poets than a research scientist. He chooses his image well, even down to the heavy framed glasses pushed up on his head. He takes a five pound note out of his wallet and rolls it carefully and then clears a space on the dining table and unwraps the small white package.

'You're not doing that here, are you? For goodness sake Toby, show a little respect.' He glares at her, gets up and heads towards the bathroom. Soraya looks at him with something like contempt, knowing that he's going to become argumentative, more arrogant than usual, but it's too late now, she'll have to wait for him to come down before she can call a taxi.

Soraya feels Emily looking at her, wondering why she doesn't do something about him. Get him to see someone. She sighs and wonders how long it will take him to come down so that she can call a taxi. They don't know what it's like for her; the come down, the aggression, the terrible moods when he can't get a hit, the despair that always lies beneath the surface. If he can't see the problem, he's not going to listen to her.

He returns to the table, takes a sip of wine. Coke and alcohol? He picks up his fork and waves it in the air, the five-pound note, still neatly rolled, lies beside him. Emily notices his eyeballs dilating by the second. He's about to make a pronouncement.

'It's an absolute disgrace...'

He waits for a response. Nobody speaks, unwilling to encourage the inevitable verbal diarrhoea.

'I said, it's an absolute disgrace, in fact it makes me feel physically sick...' Emily gets up to clear the table, hurrying to stack dirty plates and glasses before he gets into full flow. She glares at Soraya, daring her to take him home.

Toby's face is flushed.

'These new five pound notes.' He waves the offending note in the air, having ingested most of the contents, and looks around the table.'Did you know they contain animal fats? I mean the thought of it, it's outrageous.'

'What is?' Emily picks up a bottle and pours a little more red wine into her glass.

'You know, some poor defenceless animal having to die, just so these notes can go through someone's washing machine. I mean what will they think of next?' Soraya joins in:

'Shoes made of leather, your wallet, that new bag you insisted on me buying you for Christmas?'

Toby ignores her.

'Who asked them, eh? Who asked them if they minded being turned into banknotes? If they minded being slaughtered, boiled down, and then their remains going to some landfill or other...?'

Soraya's lips are working. She's trying to say something, to interrupt the flow.

'What about the coke? It's all right with you is it, knowing that some poor child in South America is being pulled from their bed, threatened with God knows what and being sent out into the fields...?'

'Oh, for goodness sake, darling, don't come the bleeding heart with me. They have a choice; poor little defenceless animals don't.' He wipes a tear from his eye. 'Anyway, what do you know about it, sitting at home all day, only getting up off your fat arse to do the school run in that gas guzzling sarcophagus you call a car?'

'I seem to remember you chose it…'

'Toby darling,' Soraya touches his arm. 'Crying isn't going to help. Such a waste of money seeing all that expensive powder being washed down your left nostril.'

'Well, I'm going to complain, where's your sense of duty eh? Don't you even care?' He waves his arms. One of Emily's precious Waterford glasses crashes to the floor. 'It has to stop.'

'What? Exploitation of children in South America. Drug cartels, the shooting, and the violence?'

'Just shut up can't you Soraya. Is anyone listening to me?'

'Well if you don't like it, why not give it to that bloke we passed on the way here.'

'Which bloke?'

'You know the homeless one in the doorway of Waitrose. With the sleeping bag and the dog. He's not going to worry if his fiver contains animal fats.'

'That's not the point, and anyway; homeless? I bet he's collected a few bob for the next bottle of vodka and then he'll be home to his nice warm flat taking the bloody dog with him. Alcohol addiction, that's their problem.'

Joe is snoring loudly, his glass lying on its side.

Toby takes a sip of his coconut milk latte

'That's a bit rich coming from you Toby. You can hardly go a day without snorting something up your nose. What's the difference except that you can afford it?'

'What's the difference? The difference is…' He gets up, paces the room, waving his glass in the air. He's shouting at them now, his hands agitated, his voice high.

'The difference is that I know how to control myself. And I earn the money to pay for it. I don't hang around the doorways of perfectly respectable shops waiting for handouts from passers-by. Anyway, I like it.'

'You could always give it up you know…'Emily dares to

interrupt. Toby shouts her down.

'What the coke? I need it to... You don't know what it's like, the pressures of the job, the...'

'No. Being a vegan. It must be so inconvenient for Soraya having to cook for you, day after day.'

'That's all very well for you to talk and anyway it's none of your bloody business. You don't have to go into work every day and watch people injecting those poor little bunny rabbits with cannabis to see how they react.' He gets up, the sweat starting to pour off his forehead and starts pacing the room an unhealthy gleam in his bloodshot eyes.

'Can't someone open a bloody window: It's stifling in here.'

Emily can't help but smile.

'I would have thought they rather enjoyed it, the bunnies I mean. After all possession isn't illegal for rabbits. They can have as much as they want and then when they get the munchies there's always someone there to feed them. A stoned rabbit! There's a thought. Better not let my cat near them.'

Soraya joins in hoping to lighten the mood.

'And those poor dogs and their cigarettes.'

'At least they get them for free. What are they now? Five pounds a pack? It's outrageous.'

Toby isn't listening. He continues to pace round and round and round until Emily starts to feel dizzy. Soraya looks at him in disgust. She thinks that she hates him now; the aggression, the feeling that he's invincible. She remembers where it all started, the night club mixing with the rich and successful, Toby thinking it would do the same for him, not realising that he had neither the talent nor the commitment to be a success. She sighs. He's off again.

'I'm going to write to the Treasury, demand that they stop.'

'Stop what?' Emily asks. She's not really been paying attention.

'Making those notes, demand that they burn them all before more innocent animals have to die.' Emily wonders if he's joking.

'What about all those toxins they'll be releasing into the atmosphere. I suppose you don't care about that? Anyway, you could always try a plastic straw? I believe it gives a better hit.'

Joe wakes up and fights to get a word in.

'Plastic straws? How do you dispose of a plastic straw? Is it recyclable?'

Emily goes out to the kitchen. Perhaps if she collects their coats, they might get the hint.

'Talking about recycling, did you know that thirty percent of householders are still failing to recycle their waste? It's a scandal on a national scale.' Joe is about to climb on to his hobby horse, a glass of the finest brandy in one hand and a set of ideologies in the other.

He takes a cream cracker and spreads it with cheese.

'Yes, and in some boroughs, they're employing spies to check out if people have recycled and if they haven't, they're refusing to collect their rubbish.' Toby stops pacing, sits down on the floor and glares at Joe. *Brotherly love.* Emily thinks. *Is there such a thing?*

'What? Oh, for Christ's sake, how much are they paying them? I reckon they could spend that money better on employing a few more nurses, keep the NHS running.'

Emily returns with the coats. No one takes any notice and she lays them down on the chair next to Soraya and sits down. Joe is wide awake now, spoiling for a fight. When did he start to drink too much? Meetings in the pub after work, long business lunches? The bottle of red wine every evening in front of the television?

'Camilla spent five hours in A and E yesterday with a badly cut finger. Constant pain, and nobody even came near her. In the end, she went into Boots and had to use her own money to buy some plasters. It's not right, and it's going to get worse. I mean what do we pay our national insurance for?'

Toby takes out the white packet again, looks at it longingly.

Soraya is fiddling with her bag, getting ready to go. Perhaps she'll just leave him behind. A thin trickle of blood runs from his nose. He dabs at it with his napkin.

'I'm all for private health care myself. If you can afford it, you should pay for it. And leave the creaking NHS to the elderly and the low lifes. People are too used to handouts these days, getting something for nothing. That's why we've got this broken welfare state. Too many scroungers and illegal immigrants. It's an absolute scandal.'

Emily sighs. Maybe she'll just go off to bed and ignore the lot of them.

'Of course, Christmas; it's that time of year, you know. And New Year; people coming in drunk, getting into fights abusing the staff. They should just throw them out refuse to treat them.'

'That's all very well but you can't throw them out if they're bleeding from a head would or a stab in the chest.'

'Serve them bloody right; they should think about that before they get drunk.' Soraya tries to change the subject hoping to get on to safer ground.

'Talking about Christmas... she says, 'I hear that Oxfam was selling off its goat's half price this year. People don't want them anymore, so destructive to the environment.'

'At least they're not being butchered to make five- pound notes...' Toby is off again but Soraya interrupts

'Fiona gave her children a cow last Christmas.' Emily stares at her.

'What a real one?'

'No of course not; a cow for one of those poor families in the Sudan.'

'Good job they're not vegan then.' Emily looks at Toby, a slight smile touching her lips.

'She's thinking about some piglets for next year but she says she can't bear the thought of the poor little things being slaughtered. You know they're supposed to be as intelligent as dogs?'

Toby is taking his clothes off now, peeling off his sweater and his shirt.

'At least you don't need to wrap them. All that expensive paper and ribbons and things. Bloody Christmas' He's shouting again, hands waving wildly, his pupils like a hunter's moon.

Joe takes a sip of his brandy, fully awake now.

'How many trees had to be cut down to provide all that Christmas wrapping? And then everyone just having great big bonfires to get rid of it all…. polluting the environment. They'll never get them back, you know, replace them and after all it takes …' He hiccups, and continues; 'years and years for them to reach full size. We used newspaper this year didn't we Emily?'

Emily has had enough

'For goodness sake, Joe, shut up. What do you do to protect the environment with your fuck off bloody sports car?'

Toby gets out his little envelope again and reluctantly invites Joe to have a snort. A thin trickle of blood runs from his nose and he dabs at it with his starched napkin.

Joe waves him away.

'Not my kind of thing I'm afraid. I prefer good old cigarettes.' Toby looks at him with disbelief.

'You're not still smoking surely? Nobody smokes these days. Well I hope you're going to go outside, not contaminate us with your filthy fumes. Did you know that 20% of all lung cancer is linked to passive smoking? It's a filthy habit.'

He glares at Joe, sniffing at the air.

'And the smell, how can you bear it? At least there's no such thing as passive coke.' It's disgusting, I don't know how Emily puts up with it. puts up with it.' Joe gets out his Rizlas and his tobacco pouch, rolls a cigarette and starts to get up from the table

Soraya has had enough, she gets out her phone and calls a taxi. It won't be the first time the driver has had a druggie in his cab. She grabs the coats and pushes Toby out the door.

Emily sits at the table, her head in her hands. That's it then, over for another year.

She surveys the wreckage; the dirty plates, the empty wine bottles. Candlelight catches the shard of broken glass on the floor. Broken lives, she thinks, Joe and his alcohol, Toby and his coke, And us, me, and Soraya, what about our lives? Why should we put up with it? Don't our lives matter anymore?

A new year? A new life perhaps? Sighing, she collects the dirty plates.

How to Commit a Perfect Murder – John Notley

The plan suddenly made sense. There was no other way. He had thought it out over and over again the past few weeks. He was certain that he had covered it from every angle. Nothing could possibly go wrong His two problems, money, or rather the lack of it, and his bitch of a wife would be solved at a stroke. It was now time to put that plan into action.

Richard opened the side door of the garage and walked across to the cupboard which housed his treasured bag of Yonex golf clubs. He put his hand in and selected a wedge which he weighed in his hand, considered it fit for his purpose, then quietly entered the house. For Richard Worthington, failing businessman, there was no turning back now.

****

"Well, Inspector, aren't you going to listen to my messages?"

"Of course, Sir, right now" replied Detective Inspector Johnson as he turned to the telephone and pushed the re-play button. "This should enable me to eliminate you from our enquiries." He sat back in the armchair, listening intently, his arms folded across his chest. His host, the recently bereaved Richard Worthington sat opposite him, an anxious expression on his face.

"Hello Darling, it's Rich. Are you OK? Just having a couple of drinks with some friends in "The Two Brewers" I'll be home soon, but don't wait up if you're tired. Let's see, it's eight-fifteen now, I should be home by about half past nine. Cheers for now. Love you."

Detective Inspector Johnson switched off the

answerphone. "That seems clear enough".

A smile of relief broke over Richard's face. "Thank God I left that message, Inspector, otherwise it could have looked bad for me."

"What time did your wife usually take her bath and get ready to retire?"

"At eight o'clock, immediately after Coronation Street finished."

"Therefore we can assume" continued the Inspector "that she had just finished her bath and probably heard a noise downstairs which caused her to go down and investigate And that was when she was killed. That would put the time of her death at about 8.30 – 8.40. So tell me again, Mr Worthington, how did you find your wife's body?".

"I left the Two Brewers at 9.30, having had a couple more lagers than I should have. Alan dropped me off , he's my neighbour and he's not really a drinker. When we reached my house I asked him to pop in just to say "hello" to Maureen. He was as shaken as I was when we found her lying on the floor of the lounge. It was he who called the police. I couldn't, I was too stunned to speak."

"I don't think I have to ask you anything further at this point" said the Inspector "I will need you to come down to the station tomorrow to make a formal statement and, of course an autopsy will have to take place. As there is no evident sign of a break-in it seems that your wife must have opened the door to the killer, maybe it was someone known to her. If you can think of any reason why your wife should have been killed then please inform me immediately. Perhaps you would also list any stolen items for me. And of course I shall have to take the tape" he said, removing it from the machine. I must not intrude on your grief any longer. Thank you for your help."

Turkish Delight

Richard closed the door behind the policeman, mopped his brow with his handkerchief and went to the small bar in the corner of the lounge, pouring himself a generous shot of whisky. "Thank goodness that's over" he thought as he re-filled the glass once more.

The plan had come to his mind three months before on the day his wife Maureen had mentioned the vase He remembered it now. The small cheap looking vase which Maureen's grandfather had given to her on their wedding day twenty-five years ago. Her grandfather was quite ill at the time and he said that he wanted her to have it to remember him by. He had explained to her that he had acquired the object, which looked like a large, ornate Easter egg, from a Russian soldier for a very small sum of money when he was serving in Berlin at the end of World War 2. His last words to her were "Look after it Luv, it could be worth a lot of money in years to come."

Maureen hadn't been too impressed with it either as she wasn't one to litter her house with useless ornaments for the sake of it. After unpacking the rest of their wedding presents she had wrapped the object in newspaper and together with other items of pottery had relegated them all to the loft where they had remained ever since.

A few weeks before, in one of their rare moments of civility towards each other, Maureen had pointed out to him an article she had been reading in the Sunday newspaper. It seems that some American guy, a scrap metal dealer, had bought a similar object in a flea market with the intention of selling it on for its gold content. Unable to find someone to offer him the right price he sat on it for a few years. He then read an article which referred to the Easter eggs made for the Russian Imperial family by the master goldsmith Peter Carl Faberge. This excited him so much that in 2014 he contacted a well known London auction house whose expert confirmed that it was one of seven missing eggs and worth in the region of £20 million. Talk about winning the lottery!

Richard finished reading and threw the paper back to his wife. "So what?"

"Well it sounds a little like the piece of pottery grandad gave to me for our wedding."

"So you think your grandad was lucky enough to get hold of a piece of junk like that which turns out to be worth millions. You must be joking."

"You never can tell" said Maureen "I'll go up in the loft at the weekend and see if it's still there. It might only be worth a few hundred pounds but that wouldn't be so bad."

Richard was so intrigued that he decided to do some research himself on the subject. He learned that the House of Faberge in St. Petersburg were commissioned to produce gold, jewelled eggs each year from 1885-1916. These were given at Easter by Tsar Alexander III and then his son, Tsar Nicholas II to their respective wives. Fifty of these eggs were produced until the overthrow of Tsar Nicholas by the Bolsheviks in 1917. Although 43 of them were in museums or private collections the whereabouts of the remaining seven were unknown.

"What if? The idea came to him, despite what he had told Maureen, that it could just be possible that he was sitting on his own (or rather his wife's) personal gold mine. This would be the end of all his troubles. Then a terrible thought crossed his mind. Suppose Maureen, in one of her fits of spring cleaning, had thrown out all the junk which had accumulated in the loft over the years. She certainly wouldn't have bothered to tell him.

He waited until she had left for work at the bank the

following morning, telling her that he had a dental appointment later. It was only such mundane matters as this that they managed to talk about these days. More often than not they sat in their respective armchairs either reading or watching telly for hours without a word passing between them.

As soon as the door closed behind her, he rushed up the stairs, pulled down the aluminium loft ladder and slid back the cover. It was years since he had ventured up there and when he switched on the single light bulb he couldn't believe the number of boxes, suitcases and carrier bags which were scattered over the floor. It took him about 40 minutes searching through various items until he came across a carrier bag containing half a dozen pieces of pottery which clinked against each other as he lifted it up. As he uncovered the third one from its wrapping of yellowed newspaper he knew he was holding grandfather's present.

The enamelled egg he removed from its wrapping was about five inches high and studded with a number of what he assumed to be jewels of various colours. It stood on a small delicate stand and reminded him more of a rugby ball. The piece was dulled by the layer of dust and grime which

covered it. He wouldn't have offered more than a fiver for it at a boot fair. But then he had never shown any interest in antiques or objets d'art. However, if this was the real thing, he was holding something worth millions in his hand.

The first thing to do was photograph it in preparation for a valuation. Then replace it where he had found it. If she discovered it was genuine and its potential worth she would be off like a shot, taking it with her. Over the past few years they had bickered continuously, sometimes almost coming to blows, and Maureen had threatened to leave him more than once. Things had come to a head in the previous months.

His once flourishing import/export business which he had taken over from his father had been steadily losing money for the past three years. He had laid off two employees and been forced to re-mortgage his substantial detached house in Purley, Surrey. His marriage was falling apart and they had no children to keep them together. Maureen had been gaining weight steadily and any feelings they may have had for each other had long since evaporated. They were very private people and tried to keep their differences to themselves but Richard felt that at the age of 49 life was passing him by.

Richard had not helped matters by starting an affair with a much younger woman who he had met on the train while travelling to work. Maureen had her suspicions but so far had not uncovered any concrete evidence. If he were to leave her now and she knew the value of the Golden Egg, she would, without doubt, take him to the cleaners for as much as she could. It was then that Richard had the idea of committing the perfect murder and laid his plans accordingly.

Instead of replacing the egg he put the carrier bag where he had found it then closed the loft, taking with him the egg and newspaper wrapping. Entering his study he placed the egg on the desk, having given it a quick polish, and took a photo of it which he would soon send to an auction house for appraisal. That done he locked it in his wall safe, he being the only keyholder, and left the house for his fictitious dental appointment.

When they both returned from work and were eating their evening meal Richard said casually: "Oh by the way, I went up in the loft and found that old vase we were talking about. I've put it in my safe. We wouldn't want it to be stolen, would we?", his voice full of sarcasm.

As soon as he arrived at the office next morning he

Turkish Delight

contacted Christie's the London auctioneers and asked if they were interested in looking at what could possibly be a Faberge Easter egg. They were of course delighted and asked him to send them a photograph. A couple of days later their ceramics specialist gave him the news he had been hoping to receive. Their expert was of the opinion that this could be the missing Alexander III Commemorative egg produced for the Imperial family for Easter 1909. They would of course need to examine the egg, if he would kindly bring it to their offices, to verify its authenticity.

The murder had been quite simple really. Wait for Maureen to settle down in her armchair to watch "Coronation Street", come up behind her with one of his irons from the golf bag he kept in the garage, strike her hard on the back of the head, and Bob's your Uncle. Wipe the head of the club and replace it in the garage with the others. Take the few pieces of jewellery she possessed from the dressing table and put them in his safe. They would be dumped later. It had taken less than ten minutes. He opened the front door and peered out. Seeing no one about he walked briskly along The Avenue until it joined the main road and, in less than fifteen minutes had reached "The Two Brewers, his local. He hadn't even felt a tinge of regret.

The morning after the burglary Richard reported to the local Police Station as instructed and was

ushered into Inspector Johnson's office. After he had taken his seat opposite the Inspector and his clerk, who was already preparing to take notes, the Inspector opened proceedings.

"This is clearly going to be a difficult case. On the face of it a burglary which went wrong. Have

you brought a list of any missing items of value?". Richard passed a short list of half a dozen items which he had prepared for him.

"Basically three or four pieces of your wife's jewellery and a couple of ceramic vases, one in the shape of an Easter egg. You have not given any estimation of their value. Why is that?"

"Well, I've no idea really. The jewellery was bought some years ago and is probably worth in total about £2,000. The egg shaped vase was given to my wife by her grandfather and is worth, I would guess, no more than £1,000 at the most".

"Were they insured?"

"No. I didn't think it warranted the premium they were asking in view of their low value."

The Inspector clasped his hands together, leaned forward and looked Richard straight in the eyes.

"Precisely, hardly a large enough sum for a petty thief to risk a murder charge, don't you agree?"

Richard shrugged his shoulders "He may have thought there were more valuable things in the house"

The Inspector continued: "Was your wife in the habit of opening the front door to unknown visitors at night?"

"Well, she was a very trusting person. And it's not often we had surprise visits from anyone, except perhaps a Jehovah's Witness now and again. Although, now I think of it, a couple of nights before, some strange guy knocked at our door asking about a friend of his who he thought had lived there before."

The Inspector sighed: "We'll look into that. "Would you please make a sketch of the missing egg vase, as close as you can get it. Our best chance is that the burglar will try to sell it through a fence as this is a fairly unusual type of ornament and is therefore more easily traced."

"I can do better than that" said Richard and obligingly handed him a copy of the photo he had taken.

The Inspector looked at his watch "Interview concluded at 11.15 am." He thanked Richard and said he would contact him again if there was anything to report.

When Richard had left the office D.I. Johnson turned to

his colleague and said: "A very puzzling case. No sign of a break-in, no weapon, no fingerprints, no suspects, just a few items of little value taken – you could almost call it the perfect murder. We'll see about that!"

After allowing a suitable period of mourning to pass Richard moved his new lady friend into the house and looked forward to starting another chapter in his life. The police had not come up with any evidence which would enable the Crown Prosecution Service to present a case. Meanwhile he held on to the Easter egg knowing that it would be unwise to dispose of it too soon after his wife's murder. Christie's had been pleased to confirm to him that the egg was indeed genuine and, subject to his consent, would like to include it in their New York autumn sale. Of course, he had agreed, now everything was falling into place.

October 2016 and D.I. Johnson was relaxing alone in his study with only a couple of months to go before his retirement after thirty years of service. He was proud of his record in clearing up most of the tricky investigations put before him, although one or two unsolved cases still bugged him. Turning to the arts page of the Sunday Times one particular headline caught his attention. "Record price paid for yet another discovered Faberge Easter Egg. The egg which has been missing since 1917 was sold to an anonymous buyer for the record price of £22 million in Christie's New York autumn sale."

Inspector Johnson looked at the accompanying photograph closely and a satisfied smile crossed his face. "Now where have I seen that before? There had to be a motive". A quick call to Christie's elicited the name of a Mr. R Worthington of London as the seller. "Got the bastard at last".

1½ Minutes. (Approx.) – Lee Wadmore

He had spent the morning reading. Short stories as it happens, at a literature class held in a church hall not far from his home. Nice little group. Friendly. Intelligent. No-one he'd make friends with as such, but they were interesting people and they all had something to say about the stories they shared every week. He suspected that they all had their own stories to tell: the old lady whose husband was ill at home with Alzheimer's, the Indian gentleman who'd shared a shocking fact- that he had been molested by a Catholic priest when he was just seven- and Mags, who had spent a lifetime living in all kinds of exotic places and Holland.

For lunch he had met up with some ex-work colleagues. A little routine of theirs: same place, same time, same subjects of conversation. Poached eggs on toast. Strong coffee afterwards. And then he'd walked to his car, parked around a corner to avoid paying the parking fee right outside the cafe, and made for home.

Home... his haven. He'd moved there with his partner twelve years ago. A beautiful little lane, tucked onto a long, long country road, leafy among the woods all around, and green or yellowish-orange depending on the season. Twelve houses. Twelve houses away from the noise and busyness of the town which was no more than a mile away. It had been, and still was, an affordable bliss.

Pulling off the main road, he spotted an estate car parked right across their drive. The side gate, which led through to the expansive back garden and to the fields beyond, was wide open. The window cleaners were there. But the way they'd parked this time prevented him from getting his own car onto the drive, and he was forced to leave it parked awkwardly on the lane. He hoped no other car needed to come up or down for a minute or two at least, as he was blocking it.

--

Can you remember the make of the car? **the young police officer asks.** *And you're sure it was grey, not silver? What about the reg?* **He's kind, too nice to do this job really.**

--

He jumped out, slammed the car door shut, and click-locked it with a schhhttt. A force of habit. He felt the air crisper now; some of the trees were already starting to lose their leaves. A carpet lay underfoot in some places; here he could still walk on the black tarmac. He'd have to get the window-cleaners to move the car, adopting a blokey manner with them, something he didn't find easy. He quickly rehearsed the line in his head, *You'll need to move the car so I can get mine on the drive...*

He entered through the open gate, walked two paces up the path, and before he could turn the corner onto the patio, he found himself face to face with them. *They're not the usual window-cleaners. Oh fuck!* The counting began. **One...**

Fear gripped him immediately. The looks on their faces told him he wasn't safe. He wasn't safe here, in his home, their haven. He needed to get out! Young. White. Clean-shaven. Rough. Hoodies. Dark hair. He had to run, out the way he came, so he turned. And in the second he was turning, he saw/heard the one on the right say/shout, "Grab 'im!" And he was grabbed, from behind. **Four...**

--

Just take your time, **he continues.** *I'm writing down everything you say. I know,* **I think.** *You're pressing hard on my pine table top. I'll have it there forever now.*

--

And he tried to run, like a fox chased by dogs, tearing at him, at his jacket, overwhelming him, as he found he was trapped, trapped in his own home, his garden, an Eden his partner had lovingly created for them both. **Nine...** He made it to the gate, he had almost made his escape but *almost* wasn't good enough, was it? He struggled, calling out to them, to anyone who might suddenly turn the corner of the lane (*Please may the postman be late today... Where was the dog-walker who passed every day? Will a neighbour's car suddenly swing round the bend?*) and he was trying to shout, *No!*

"Grab 'is neck!" Another instruction. From one to the other. **Thirteen...** Then an arm appeared from behind, throttling him, pressing hard on his Adam's apple, choking him, and his head was pulled, bending him backwards until he was thrust against the back of their car. **Twenty-one...**

--

I'm going to show you an image of a car now, **he says. *Was it this car that was parked on your drive?* He looks disappointed when I shake my head.**

--

He tried to call, but it was hopeless, and he felt himself give up the struggle as commands were given. "Don't move! DON'T MOVE!" It would have been hard for him to do anything now; he needed help but the leaves on the trees just rustled, and the birds hopped and dived. **Twenty-nine...**

He was amazed at how empty his mind became in those seconds, and all he could think of was survival. What would it actually feel like to have a knife slice into your rib-cage? Would you feel pain? *Real* pain or would you simply feel your life ebb away, peacefully giving in to death? More shouting. From them, not him. How could he? But he couldn't hear the words; the malice was muffled.

--

Did you recognize an accent all? **the other one asks. He's a bit older, eager to gather as much information as possible. But I don't. I'm not good with things like that.**

Turkish Delight

--

Thirty-eight... and he was shoved to the ground, behind their car, hidden now, secreted from the postman, the dog-walker, the neighbours who weren't going to appear anyhow. He was face down, pinned on the tarmac drive by them. Grit pierced his left hand which bloodied quickly; his right still clutched onto his keys which once used to shut out the world from his home, his car, his- "Grab 'is watch!"

Forty-nine... Rough fingers jabbed his wrist, sliding between watch-face and flesh, pulling at it, yanking at it wildly, and his head- still in a tight grasp and still pulled back, away from the ground- was suddenly flooded with thoughts of his wrist which might be broken in the attack. Oh, this watch had been a gift, a birthday gift, not yet a year old... He felt like he was drowning, the sea overpowering him, moving him around, a force on top of him, scum washing over him, and he tried to speak.

Fifty-eight... "I'll take it off! You can have it!" It wasn't his normal voice; this was some strange croaking sound unfamiliar to him, but it seemed to appease them. For a second- **One minute, nine...** -they seemed to relax their grip around his throat, although their weight upon his back was unrelenting, and a fragment of hope entered his mind. A buoy was bobbing on the horizon.

"Get 'is keys!" Another command before they were snatched greedily out of his right hand which had fumbled at his wrist-watch for them. **One minute, eighteen...** He felt a push against his back, but his neck, sore from the throttling, was let go of, and as he lay there, a pathetic heap, he heard a car pull away at speed. His as well as theirs?

--

***Here are the tracks, look, across the front lawn.* That's the Detective Constable who's arrived wearing a**

raincoat. I thought they only wore them in films...

--

It was all beginning to make sense now- they had reversed theirs on at an angle for a quick getaway. For a moment or two he lay there, drifting in a sea of confusion, but- **One minute, twenty-four**- instinct told him he could get up, get up, get up as quickly as he could and shout, "Help! Help!" as he ran down the lane towards neighbours' cars. He was going to heave himself at someone's door. He prayed he wasn't being pursued...

One minute, thirty-seven... He almost deafened himself with the banging, using his bloodied hands to hammer the front door. It was only when he went to speak to a neighbour looking as confused as he was that he realized he couldn't. He was panting, from running, from choking, from distress, but he made himself understood. Help was on the way...

--

We have the call logged at 14.04. **The young one checks the record sheet, looking at the older one, pleased he's doing all right.** *And how long would you say the whole incident lasted?* **he asks.** *Just roughly.* **And I tell him that it's no more than two minutes. Less. Probably about a minute and a half. I see what he writes:** *1 ½ minutes. (Approx.)*

--

Walking back towards his home, the lane so quiet once again, browned leaves gently falling, the sound of birds high in the oaks, he dared to make his way through the side gate, turning the corner onto the patio to see the back door groaning after an attack. Mangled draught-excluders wired themselves outwards, huge broken splinters had showered the mat and the kitchen table, and the floor glistened under an archipelago of shattered glass.

--

You haven't touched anything, have you? **the forensics girl asks. She looks at me with those eyes that tell me she's sorry that she's got to do this. She photographs my home. I hear the noise of the camera.**

--

Tip-toeing over it, he peered into rooms downstairs. The television is no longer on its stand. Upstairs the wardrobe doors had been left neatly opened, a large crowbar sat menacingly in the middle of their bed, and a small bed-side cabinet had been rifled through, its drawer revealing the gaps where their possessions had once belonged.

But the strangest thing, the most baffling of all was the missing pillow-case from the bed.

--

They always do it, **confesses the Detective Constable.** *They use your pillowcase to stash your belongings in...* **And I wonder why they don't bother to bring their own, save themselves the time.**

--

And as he looked out of the window, waiting for the police to arrive, he heard the magpies chattering, probably discussing what they'd seen and heard in those 1½ minutes. (Approx.)

Stalking the Muse – Steve Wade

The month was December, the evening almost closed. My mam gave me the envelope when I got in from school. The first envelope I ever received addressed to me. I tore it open. The Texaco Children's Art Competition, I was a runner-up. When I finally shouted myself to hoarseness, I took off for a walk in the fields at the top of the road with Ben, my Red-Setter. God, I loved that dog.

The sugar-frosted grass, lit up by the bony moonlight, was a black and white photo. Since that day, twenty-four years ago, I can't remember ever witnessing a sight more incredible than the whitened fields, and the dark bands of bushes and trees surrounding the fields. Above us a sky dappled with a trillion stars. In my memory a barn owl flies ghostly by, its plumage as white as the frost covered field. But I can't be definite about the owl.

Heedless of the folds in the earth or the grass that grew in clumps - perilous obstacles that threatened to twist my ankle or worse - I began to run. Nothing could touch or harm me now, not even the skinheads who sometimes used the fields for drinking parties. I was invincible.

From stumbles, tumbles and falls I rolled to my feet and went on running, flying really, Ben loping by my side, gripping playfully my flapping jacket.

Over the years, I've entered countless art competitions without so much as a note announcing that they regretted that I hadn't, this time, been chosen as a winner. Got so as all I craved was the note in a letter with those two words of encouragement and promise: *this time*. A phrase bursting and bloated with good wishes and hang in there, buddy sentiment.

I still like to do a bit of sketching and doodling, but entering art competitions is as dead and futile as trying to retrieve my boyhood. These days I concentrate on creating imaginary worlds by filling up blank pages with black squiggles recognised as vowel and consonant sounds that together build phonemes and syllables that shape into words, which, strung together, produce sentences that graduate into paragraphs, which, piled atop other paragraphs, strive to take the reader on a journey to a place where feelings of enlightenment are evoked, ambitions triggered, jealousies aroused and overcome; where they can construct images of people they have never met and things they have yet to see but have somehow known always and seen often in forgotten dreams; dreams crowded with heady scents, intricate shapes and dazzling colours, where fingertips explore forbidden flesh, where ideas, disturbed or philosophic are whispered, sung, bellowed or screamed from hallowed halls or drowning seas, seas whose thrashing waters engender a craving, an appetite that plays upon, stimulates, tickles, and burns a thousand tongues.

My stories then, were my calling, the search for what McGahern called "the truth in the simplest detail", the fictive dream that would return to me the feeling that has eluded me for two decades. The dream, till this day, remained a dream. Despite amassing quite a collection of short stories, a few plays, two completed novels, a dozen or so poems, a batch of essays, and a first draft of a screenplay, I'd been placed in less literary competitions than my hero Van Gogh sold paintings - during his lifetime, that is.

So there I am this afternoon, once more, sitting before a computer screen, waiting for the elusive something, the sweet, subtle pheromone-laden scent secreted by the muse: the what if, the shock of recognition I would recognise as the entrance to a tale as hauntingly disturbing as the story of Ralph and Piggy on that island, as passionate as any of Jack London's tales that pit man against nature or beast, and as stylistically wrought as anything that came from the craftsmanship of McGahern or William Trevor, when the preset alarm on my phone alerts the muse to my predatory presence. 3.00pm - time to get ready for work.

Along with my creative drive, I take pride in my day-job. Being self-employed has a lot to do with it. It's a job that requires physical fitness, dedication to detail, intuitiveness, deep awareness of human nature, and the ability to harness and transform my understanding of the way people are, what they do and why they do it into profit. After all, everyone has to survive.

So out the door to meet the afternoon. An afternoon that would bring with it everything and more I'd been trying and failing to hunt down since I was a kid.

Sylvia Grogan, single, my latest client – although she doesn't know it - this hot July afternoon, runs a small but successful art gallery in the city centre. Sylvia made her way on foot to the Dart station this morning. I followed her (we've never met), and waited till she was safely aboard, watched her take her seat, her eyes through the window fixed on the platform, not noticing me watching her. She wouldn't know me had she looked my way. God I love my job.

At 4.15pm I arrive at the Grogan's place. Perfect. The cleaner, a Polish girl named Aleksandra, who lets herself into the house with her own key, generally finishes up her shift at 4.18pm. The front gate is left permanently open - well, not after today it won't be.

With my mobile pressed to my ear, listening to a recorded woman's voice bleating out the time, I say, "Yes, okay sir. Nobody's disputing the figures. It's not that – " I pause, make sounds that I'm agreeing with the disembodied voice who isn't on the end of the line, occasionally interrupting to make a point about imaginary facts and figures about which I couldn't begin to give a damn.

I bang on like this in the porch entrance, and continue talking when I see, through the opaque glass, a silhouetted figure coming down the stairs. The door opens a few inches. A chain.

"Yes," the girl says.

"Listen," I say into the phone. "We'll run over everything again at the meeting ... this day week. Okay, okay. Catch you then. Ciao."

"Ms Banaszewski?" I say to the girl in the basic Polish I've picked up from the beginner's manual and CD over the past few weeks. "I'm from the Embassy."

"Just a second," she says, and closes the door, slides the chain free and reopens it, which saves me needless energy output.

Uninvited, I step over the threshold and into the house. The girl reverses automatically. She's twenty-three, compact and small. She smells of hard work and garlic; a smell that makes me shiver.

Inside the hallway, the front door now shut behind us, by me, Aleksandra Banaszewski says something to me in Polish, her eyes the eyes of a startled deer seconds before the deer flees from the unexpected confrontation with a waiting hunter.

With no idea what her words mean, I smile and make a 'come again' sound, a sound that might reassure her.

"You are not Polish?" she says inside the hallway.

I explain to her that the Polish Embassy employs me, but, no, I'm Irish. The effect of her deep tones and accent put a slight tremble I hope she hasn't detected into my voice.

"What is problem?" she says. "I am is working in this country. I am is paying taxes – "

I interrupt her and tell her how we're quite satisfied in that area, and that I'm here for another matter entirely. An invisible claw rakes down my spine.

"My brother," she says. "Something happens to Mateusz. Please to tell me."

I shake my head, fascinated at the tears slipping from her eyes and sliding down her face faster than she can wipe them away with the heels of her hands.

"It's nothing," I say, indicating that we move down the hall to somewhere we can sit and talk. "Really, it's just a formality." On the ass of her red tracksuit bottoms, in white lettering, is the word 'RICH'. Rich indeed, I think.

I scan the large living room quickly as we enter: high-ceilinged, modern furniture – vintage design, polished wooden floor, but there, on the wall is the reason I'm here. But I'll need to examine things more closely. I sit down in a black leather armchair that squeaks. The girl sits opposite me on the edge of the matching sofa, her knees, together and her hands, white-knuckled, joined on her lap as though in prayer.

"Okay," I say. "What I need from you Ms Banaszewski is a signature." I click open my briefcase and pull out a first draft of one of my stories.

"What is it?" she says. She stretches her neck higher, as though that would make a difference.

"Hmmm," I say. "This isn't right. I don't think this is you." I turn the pages over. "No, definitely, this isn't you, is it?" I hold the papers up, but don't show her the printed side - we all know where that kind of slip-up can lead.

As predicted, the girl gets to her feet – they generally do - and works her way round the magazine-strewn coffee table to me. This is the part I do not enjoy. The part that is most predictably unpredictable.

The snap of the handcuffs I remove from the briefcase and slap around her wrist causes her to scream and fall backwards. I go with her to the floor, clamp my hand over her mouth and make shushing sounds.

"I won't hurt you, Aleksandra," I say. She struggles and tries to bite me. "Hey," I shout. "Don't be a silly girl. You're not the reason I'm here, okay?" I reiterate this a bit until the tenseness leaves her body. Her heartbeat I feel pounding against my chest - or could be it's my own. I get to my feet and ease her to hers. I then manoeuvre her to the couch.

She pleads with me when I leave her sitting on the couch, one hand handcuffed to the stem of a tall floor lamp as I fumble inside my jacket pocket.

"This is for your own safety," I tell her while I gag her with the silk scarf and handcuff her hands together. Around her ankles I place a wheel tie. Carefully, I then lay her down on the sofa, resisting the overwhelming urge to peel the scarf from

Turkish Delight

her mouth and crush my mouth to hers. I have business to get on with.

Who-hah! Among the original paintings on the walls are a Louis Le Brocquy and a William Orpen. I check the time: 4.31pm. Sylvia Grogan won't be here for hours. I fish around inside my briefcase and find what I'm after. The girl's muffled screams, however, as her eyes lock to the wooden-handled Shepherd's knife in my hand, draw me to her the way, for a parent, a child's incessant crying is irresistible.

"It's for the paintings," I tell her. "Shhhhh," I say, brushing strands of sweat-soaked hair from her brow. "It'll be all over soon."

She shakes her head, a gurgling scream coming from her throat.

"Look," I say, sort of sidling over to the Le Brocquy painting. Despite the slight tremble in my hand, I cut the painting free of its frame with extra precision. I do the same with the Orpen. I then clack the knife shut and bury it in my trousers pocket.

"That's it," I say. "Finito. Gotowy. Over. All done. Okay?"

The girl kind of nods, but looks a million away from okay.

"Right so," I say. "Now I'm sorry for this, but you're going to have to stay as you are till Mrs Grogan gets back. Shouldn't be too long. A couple of hours and you'll be good to go."

The girl's eyes won't leave me alone. I ask her if I could get her anything before I leave, a glass of water, something to eat maybe ... does she want the TV on?

Her dropped eyes kind of slide down her own body. She creases slightly at the waist, squints, and then flicks her eyes towards the open door. I know exactly what she wants.

"The toilet?" I say. "You need to use the bathroom?"

She nods furiously, and those tears that are streaming are positively raging when out again comes my knife. This time I give no explanation, just cut through the tie around her ankles and make this expression at her. I indicate she walk ahead of me to the stairs.

"Don't be long," I say as she enters the ensuite bathroom in one of the bedrooms upstairs. She pushes the door closed behind her.

Within seconds I realise what she's up to.

"Open this door, Aleksandra. What do you think I'm some kind of idiot?"

No answer. Just the sound of her angry snivelling and snuffling, playing over the obvious sounds that are made when a locked window is being forced to open.

The first kick I slam at the door with the sole of my foot opens it. I grab the girl from the sink where she's climbed and drag her back.

"Help," she screams towards the open window.

I pull the window shut, ignore the girl's teeth biting into my hand and drag her to the double-bed. "Now look what you've done," I say to her. The blood runs down my hand and drips onto the pale duvet cover.

"Bastard," she screams and spits into my face.

I wipe away the pungent spittle from my nose and eye and run my bleeding hand across her face, putting colour in her cheek that matches her tracksuit.

And then, without invitation or warning, *she* arrives.

The muse arrives to arouse us when we least expect her. And when she comes we must recognise and embrace her. Without arousal, there can be no continuance, without the muse, no creativity.

"Brace yourself," I say.

She does so and more. Her legs clamp together and her hands battle against my fumbling efforts to tear away her clothes. I win.

Revulsion, shock and fear are what I see in the girl's face as I, a willing passenger on the same journey, rocket towards a different destination to the girl. I am back among the frost-covered fields of childhood. My dog Ben is running by my side. The ground, over which we sprint, encased in frozen water crystals, crunches beneath our feet. Apart from the white owl that spirits by on silent wings, we are the only beings in the universe. My body, too, lifts off the ground - or is it my mind slipping from my body? I glide; I soar upwards towards the star-speckled sky.

Lucky Number Seven – N.B. Cara

They say if you tell it seven times to seven different people you'll get over it. Seven opinions on the same scenario, surely then someone would tell you what you wanted to hear? Does anyone really listen to the advice they're given anyway? I don't. I never have. I've never been able to quit whilst I was ahead. I remember being young, perhaps six or seven, away on holiday with my parents in one of those badly carpeted, dusty smelling holiday park arcades with a plastic tub in my hand. "That's all you are having, when it's gone it's gone so don't ask for any more," my mother would say as she shared out a heap of two pence pieces between the four of us children. Although I heard the words she had said and of course I knew she really meant it, it didn't stop me or hardly even slow me down. One, two, three of my two pence pieces balancing irritatingly on top of each other right on the edge of the shelf, winning me nothing in return. I'd bang the glass, that would make all the difference. Four coins, five coins and still, I had won nothing. Soon enough I'd put in all that I had, all of it gone only to spend the rest of the evening disappointed and upset with myself. How foolish. Fast forward almost twenty years and I still haven't quite got the hang of not investing everything all at once. Admittedly I haven't matured into having a full-blown gambling addiction, and the reality isn't that coin machines are ruling my life but regardless of the context I have never managed to stop myself from ignoring the solid advice given and keeping a little bit to one side for later.

So here I am. Twenty-five. Twenty-five and surrounded by happier people. Happy relationships, new babies and career-driven people landing their dream jobs, waking up and throwing on their immaculate high-waisted skirt and blouse ensemble, hair effortless yet flawless with blemish-free skin to match. It's 2017 and apparently most of the females my age have become wedding planners. Heaven forbid I express how I would like to have any single one of those things. "You aren't even thirty yet!" Neither are you. I've come to realise, after

Turkish Delight

hearing it in a film, that sometimes people's lives just don't turn out the way they had hoped. "Every family has a faller, maybe it's me. Maybe I'm our faller." There it is, the penny drops. I had watched this film several times but for some reason, that day I really heard it. I have never heard words ring so true in my mind. It suddenly became apparent to me that everything I do, with a whole heart of good intention never quite deserves the massive fall to follow or those pangs of disappointment that reoccur when your minding your own business slumped at your desk at work with a cold cup of tea to your left. The phone is ringing.

"You haven't received your delivery yet? Let me just find out where it is for you. One moment, please hold," I say as I roll my eyes and catch my colleague grinning. She knows I've left my patience at home today. "It's 10.24 am, I hardly think your delivery is AWOL quite yet," I mumble to myself as I punch in the numbers to dial through to the designated lorry driver. He sounds how I feel. Unenthusiastic and unable to even attempt to act as though he has any intention of speeding things along. "I'll get there when I get there," he states aggressively and he abruptly ends the conversation. With not much to relay to the customer in way of a positive outcome I contemplate hanging up the phone to divert the call to someone else. Someone who will at least pretend to be sympathetic to the fact that they know the customer is in desperate need of a delivery and they know that the customer says that every week and still the customer is calling disappointed. "Well I suppose there's nothing I can do about it is there! So it will HAVE to be okay," and she too slams the phone down. I think this is what they mean by shooting the messenger, it must be, how in this day and age can it be about cowboys in the west with strands of barley hanging from their mouths and hats tilted down to avoid the sun. Someone has to keep the saying alive, I suppose.

Lunchtime arrives. I believe this is the time in which you're supposed to enjoy the nutritious, colourful meal you prepared for yourself before you left the house this morning. I rummage through my little black bag and collect all the coins, odd chewing gums and loose hairs from the grottiness that is the bottom of my handbag. Thirty-eight pence. I look at the coins in the palm of my hand and can't help but think how much my six-year-old self would have appreciated all those two pence pieces. Second to that, the thought crossed my mind of how, if I could be there as me now, I'd tell her not to cry because her pile of two pence pieces had gone and that years later she will feel exactly the same, though this time with two and a half weeks until payday it seems that shrapnel is all she has left. Never mind, at least we don't pay for tea bags at work. A cup of tea and four biscuits from my desk drawer and I'm away, leaving the office for thirty whole minutes - minus the two minutes I have to allow myself to get back to my desk to satisfy the clock watcher. I check my phone, of course I haven't heard from him. Not even a text. I sit there in my thirty minutes of screenless serenity frustrated by the fact that the screen in front of me is empty. Torn between choosing to appear too keen and needy and sending a quick message or just accepting the fact that wherever he is and whatever he is doing he would rather do that than check in with me. I dunk my biscuits and confirm to myself that if he wanted to speak to me he would have, if he cared what kind of day I was having I wouldn't need to prompt him to ask. It was during this moment of realisation that I felt my fingers sting and looked up just in time to see the soggy half of my biscuit drowning in my tea. I open up a blank text, and spend the next twenty minutes moaning about his behaviour to a friend. She, like me, has very little patience. "Oh please. Why do you still bother with him? Do you even realise you've been complaining about him for as long as you have known him? I don't want to hear it all the time I've already told you how I feel about it and about him. When will you realise you can do so much better?" I sigh, I know she's right, but I reassure myself that she's only under that impression because I've forgotten to fill her in on anything but the bad bits, which coincidently are quite bad. I close Annabel's chat without even responding, whatever I say now I'll only appear even more pathetic. After all she's only the fourth person with the same opinion.

Heart of Gold – Wanda Dakin

"She tells me you're a good friend," Tiffany is saying.

"Really?" I reply, peering through the clammy atmosphere, still in a semi-daydream.

"I was talking about Letitia Green, you do *know* her."

"Yes, but....."

The woman, whom I regard as my best friend, is now tapping at her watch, and walking towards the coffee shop door. I am left alone wondering how Tiffany and Letitia are acquainted, and how my own name even came up. And I start to think of Letitia, the friend I apparently have, but not yet acknowledged as such.

That Letitia regards me as a good friend comes as a surprise, considering I think of her as simply one of my customers. She has been coming to my house for beauty treatment for several years, declining my mobile service.

"It gets me out of the house. I'm always stuck at the computer – freelance writing," she informed me initially. I know nothing much else about her, except she is married with two sons (no names ever supplied). It is like the old-fashioned version of pass the parcel game, where you keep tearing off layers but never seem to get any further. And of course it is all part of my job to promote a pleasant, mindless chatter, to go over familiar ground and put on the brakes before anything is said to make my clients feel uneasy.

Letitia is usually my last customer of the day, which, in itself, would make me on edge. *Stay, stay and have a cup of tea, coffee, anything but please don't go,* I long to say, as my mind paddles along frantically through icy water. I don't say anything; she is after all just one of my customers; it wouldn't be appropriate. The lift of a hand, a cursory "thanks," and the sudden shock of isolation. Now all I can do is wait and pray.

"You always exaggerate," Tiffany suggests one day, "all relationships have their wobbles." Maybe it *is* my fault, I think, if I act differently, then things might improve.

Instead they get worse. Here I am in the middle of shaping Letitia's eyebrows,

"What's up?" she says, "you don't seem your usual cheery self." I rip the wax strip off a little too quickly causing my customer to wince, but rather than apologising, I just blurt out "Is that what you think cheery ... my life ... that's a joke?"

"It's your husband, isn't it?" I take a step backwards, the wax strip shaking in my hand. How does she know? I keep my arms strategically covered; my hair loose over my neck and shoulders. Did my friend, Tiffany, tell her anything? I doubt that. The moment stretches out; embarrassment crawls over both of us before she speaks,

"Sorry it's none of my business," she jumps to her feet, one eyebrow left untamed. "Look, if you need to leave, I've a spare room, my elder son has just moved out ...... minimal rent." Why does the minimal rent distance me again? Perhaps the detail seems out of place, mixed in with the unlikely swoop of generosity. But as she walks towards the door, any business-like aloofness is replaced by a warm, "Well, think about it."

I do think about it. A few days later, I am dragging my suitcase out of my car on the other side of town. I take in the stubborn array of weeds pushing through the gravel pathway that leads to the front door. And inside, continues a theme – peeling, outdated wallpaper; an aroma which I associate with nursing homes, and before me, the reason perhaps: a man in a wheelchair. Letitia greets me with introductions.

"Mike, my husband, he has MS." The tone is abrupt, almost dismissive as if he has a superficial injury attempting something irresponsible. "And this is my younger son, James. He's studying family law, which may be useful to you, if you – well - need it," she nods at the young man, who has inherited her fair complexion. I observe the wine-stained trickle of embarrassment ignite the skin on his neck.

"I'll bear that in mind," I reply, feeling I have to say something, "But I'm not quite at that stage yet." I laugh to disguise the brusqueness in my tone; mother and son smile, the same closed-in smile.

A few days later, Letitia and I are on our own in the kitchen. She lifts her perfectly groomed right eyebrow, opening her pale, heavy face.

"I know what you have been through," she says.

"Mike," my mouth shapes the word, but I only manage a bemused whisper.

"But you never …," I start.

"Left," she finishes for me. He got sick. I couldn't go then. And before, he was so clever hiding it from the boys; I thought when they are older, I would escape. But the escape never came."

"You deserve so much better."

"Well, I can't leave now" she snaps and the fan of wrinkles by the side of her eyes deepen as she tenses her face. I recall that pain only too well; the slow grinding down of your own personality; that monumental effort to leave when you have lost faith in yourself.

I meet up with my best friend, Tiffany, at the coffee shop. Her angular features; her dark, deeply set eyes are cold like muddy pools. She shows a fleeting interest in my living arrangements, "I knew you would end up buddies. You're two peas in a pod."

"But what about us?" I query. She stares down at her coffee mug. Suddenly, out of nowhere, we seem to have nothing to say to one other.

Meanwhile, my relationship with Letitia is also changing, though I never quite think of it as friendship; maybe the age gap of fifteen years makes it subtly different from the kind of friendship I am used to. A welcome mug of tea on my return from work progresses into a glass of wine; soon we are eating our evening meal together.

Tiffany is right. Letitia and I do have more in common than I could ever imagine.

"My parents passed away when I was still a teenager. I don't know what I would have done if I hadn't met Mike," she confides.

"Stop, listen to yourself!" I am surprised at my harsh tone. How easy it was to be judgmental from this side of the fence! Then I probe further,

"Didn't you have any brothers and sisters?"

"No siblings, no aunts, uncles nor family friends. So when Mike came along…"

"You could be describing my own life." We look at each other, and laugh, a painful laugh.

"There's a difference between us," she reminds me.

"There's still time for you," I say, stretching forward and touching her on the arm. "How about I look after Mike this Sunday; give you and James a break?" I struggle to say the words "look after"; he is the last person I want to do anything for, despite his illness.

"Are you sure?" she cocks her head on one side. For a moment I feel a rustle of indignation inside me - does she doubt my ability to cope? But I have misjudged her, not for the first time.

"I mean it's very kind of you – to give up your day off. He doesn't deserve it, *any* kindness," her eyes warm with gratitude.

"I'm doing it for you, not him," I remind her.

When Sunday arrives, Letitia is still concerned, "Do you really feel .. you can.. after all you've been through?"

"I'll be fine," I reassure her. But the situation is harder, much harder than I could have imagined. Somehow I need to probe beneath his frail affability. That cannot be difficult - I glance across at him, slumped in his wheelchair. I am the one in control, surely?

By evening, I can hold back no longer, my words stumble out,

"Why did you treat Letitia so badly?" I want his answers; those answers I craved all my married life; why, what gives anyone the right?

Turkish Delight

For a moment it looks as if he is going to clutch the table, to help him reposition himself in the chair, or maybe these words have been too much, he is feeling ill. For seconds, I forget; for seconds only, I transform myself into the attentive carer. But then I realise his intention: one clammy hand somehow finds the strength to hold my wrist like a vice, while the other stretches out towards the vase of flowers; the china breaks against the table edge; cuts against my hand.

I am still clearing up when Letitia walks in; her face loses colour.

"My mother's vase," are her first words.

"I'm sorry," I mumble.

"These things happen," she replies as she helps me tidy up. Do I detect a look of triumph in his eyes? But Letitia is one step ahead of him, "I know he did it," she whispers to me, as we crouch over the shattered pieces of ornate porcelain. To my despair she adds,

"But it's best to play along, otherwise he will be difficult later."

****

It is never my intention to stay with Letitia for months; I plan to get somewhere of my own. But business is very slow – some of my clients, contacts made initially through my husband, have unsurprisingly gone elsewhere; also a new salon has opened in town.

"You're back early again," says Letitia, in her exaggerated tone of showing more concern than really necessary. Her voice swivels, immediately upbeat once more.

"Go and see them at the salon," she encourages. "what have you to lose?"

Was it later that next day, or the following week when I am offered the job when I realise? The deepening of friendship; a scattering of the pleasantries which we so often hide behind? I remember standing in the kitchen as we often do, clearing away the dishes. Her face is opened into the partial sunlight, staggered behind blinds. I have no recollection of what we are discussing, but it happens then – the realisation -the parcel is finally unwrapped, revealing the ultimate prize.

"Pure gold," Tiff would have said in her sweeping way "I told you so."

My once best- friend, Tiffany, my ex-husband's sister.

****

Months trickle by. My marital home sold, I can certainly afford my own place now. I think repeatedly I should leave but never do. Meanwhile, Mike moves into a care home. Almost immediately, I see the difference in Letitia, beyond the usual, indefatigable care of her appearance. As if she has been lifted up; given a crisper outline; her features give the illusion of been subtly rearranged, more attractively. She goes out in the evenings; James and I are often home alone.

And here I am now perched on the edge of the bath, head in hands, waiting. Waiting, and watching the testing stick at my side. Holding my breath, I glance down; my heart skips a beat. How could this happen; in my late thirties? And yet there is a prickle of excitement; the leap into the unknown. He takes it well, very well; we make plans. I must tell Letitia. I don't think she even suspects there is anything going on between me and her son, not alone my other news. Will she be happy for us, or shocked, feeling we have sneaked behind her back? I am fearful of anything jeopardising our friendship, so I do the worst thing, I keep urging him not to tell her.

One evening when I come into the living room; Letitia is in a buoyant mood.

"I got the job," she tells me excitedly, as she opens a bottle of wine. I have been so wrapped up in my own world, I completely forgot about her interview.

"You're more than a friend, you're like family now," she gushes handing me a glass. For one blissful moment I assume by these words, she already knows; but as I glance; across the room at

James, he gives a slight shake of the head. I turn to face her; let the words spill out.

How well I know her from the outside, on skin level, probably better than anyone. Her eyebrows sprinkled with grey before I tint them; her arms dusted with gingery, light hairs before I wax them; her carefully manicured fingernails are red daggers from the crater-like surface of a blotched hand. But now all that matters is what is going on inside her mind. Her words, when they do reach me, appear across a chasm.

"Tiffany was right about you," she says with sudden spite in her voice.

"Tiffany, how do you even know Tiffany?"

"We've been friends for ages. We met at Zumba. We were both as hopeless as each other," she laughs at herself, but this does not suggest I am in any way forgiven.

"I didn't know that."

"You don't know everything - about either of us."

The news of this Tiffany-Letitia friendship knocks me sideways, washes over me, igniting all the nerves in my body. I feel the type of betrayal from an inexplicable exclusion; the unknown words passing between two people I thought I knew so well. It is followed by a sharp jolt of possibility – could it be more than friendship – I've been aware of Tiffany's sexuality for years; maybe, maybe Letitia...... how well do you know anybody? I am so absorbed with this information, I almost forget the origin of her ill feeling. But then she says,

"I think you should leave," with a tone of finality in her voice. Quietly I go upstairs and pack up. I wait for James to stop me, but he does nothing. He lets me leave.

I find a hotel nearby. I sit on the bed, thinking of the friends I have lost. With Tiffany, when I think about it, there was always something superficial; an uncertainty; with Letitia how long and hard we had fought for a quality of friendship to be blown away in a moment. And this whole friendship between Letitia and Tiffany, was it just flung at me in revenge? Isn't that precisely what I have been doing, when I was sneaking around with James; making the choice, for some reason, to withhold information; a breach of friendship? I was afraid, of course, she would disapprove of the age-gap, that I was not good enough for her son. Would she come round? I cannot rely on it. It seems strange, however, that I have agonised over my loss of friendship more than over my relationship with James. I feel it now though, sharp like bee stings, one after the other.

With one hand resting protectively over the slight dome of my stomach, I stand by the window. Below me, in the street, I am aware of the pattern of life going on outside me. Then I see him. It is really him, not my hopeful imagination. His tall, slim, rather awkward features seem slumped; the lack of positivity in his gait, what does that mean? Maybe nothing. He is here, after all.

How I saver these moments of hope!

I turn away from the window, and make my way downstairs.

The Kite – Hannah Van-de-Peer

The eighth of July was a particularly picturesque one. Heated rays of golden sunshine coated the green canvas of the Windborne hills. Weeping willows served as a mystical entry to a peppermint footpath that'd seen many a welly boot in its time. The wind was soft; yet potentially volatile. It could caress you, pleasantly, but if it caught you in the wrong spot on the back of your neck; or slapped you across the face, it was icy enough to do raw damage. Happy, young oak trees sat peacefully all the way up the hill; and the sky was powder-blue with the optimism of summer.

Softly grazing along the watercolour sky was a kite; a lively, homemade little thing bearing a family crest of fuchsia, marmalade and grape. The string led all the way down to the bottom of the magical footpath; that was so full of promise. At the end of the string, was a little girl. Her melodious laughter filled the air with whimsy; a heart-melting tune guaranteed to crack even the stoniest of faces. Red Wellington boots running (and, occasionally stumbling) up the grassy footpath, and a red-and-white chequered dress billowing in the cold wind; this could have been the perfect stock image for the front of a Kentish postcard.

The sky darkened slightly; and the wind became more aggressive. Passive, however, the little girl carried on up the hill with her beloved kite in tow. There wasn't far to go now, and she was looking forward to seeing her own creation in the sky with God's. She was infatuated at the thought of gliding her graceful little kite along the infinite sky; making friends with the lark, sneering at the sun...

It was in the midst of this fantasy that the wind took a violent turn; the little girl was suddenly *blasted* in the face with a powerful gust of freezing wind, knocking her over onto her backside, leaving her, therefore, in a bit of a daze. Getting up, and inspecting herself for cuts and bruises, it dawned on her... she'd let go of the kite! How disappointed are Mummy and Daddy going to be when they've discovered their efforts had gone to waste? She knew she just had to get it back. She started running; picking up the pace, bypassing the adolescent oak, clawing back the weeping willow, stomping in the mint green footpath, desperately trying to grab it to safety...

But it was gone.

* * *

The room was narrow, white, and artificial. There were no windows, anywhere. Only doors. Black doors. They had these oversized latches in the middle of them to keep people out; rather than keeping them in. My God, you wouldn't want to be kept in here...

The dead silence that had infected the room for hours was suddenly broken. The metallic clanking of the latch was enough to wake the deceased; followed by footsteps. Gentle footsteps. *'Clack...clack...clack...'*

They stood there together. Two women; one in her mid-to-late thirties, dressed professionally in a pinstriped skirt-suit and a patent pair of Louboutins (bought for her by her husband on their first anniversary). The second woman, however, was not so prim and proper. She was dressed in an oversized cardigan, cream in colour; almost matching the artificial white walls that surrounded her. She looked as if she was in her mid-forties, and her ebony, shoulder-length hair was wildly unkempt and unwashed. She had a man with her; same age, but much younger in appearance. He was of a muscular build, with sand-coloured hair and a conventionally attractive, blue-eyes-and-button-nose-face. It was grey in colour, though. Microscopic beads of sweat were carefully placed on his forehead; strategic, almost as artificial as the room itself.

Turkish Delight

The pinstripe woman was the first to break the deafening silence. She uttered seven words. Seven; cutting, venomous, yet softly-spoken words.

"Mr and Mrs Thompson, are you ready?"

Mrs Thompson uttered a dazed collection of vowels, as Mr Thompson wearily nodded his head. His eyes seemed to be unfocused; black, as if the colour and spark that was once there had been drained out of them. The pinstripe woman walked, slowly, to a charcoal-coloured slab in the middle of the unfeeling room, and sluggishly peeled back the long, sickly bed sheet. Mr and Mrs Thompson instantly eroded like the white cliffs of Dover; clutching each-other and howling as they stared ahead of them. And what stared back? A limp, lifeless little girl, wearing a red-and-white chequered dress, and matching red Wellington boots.

Back at home, Mr and Mrs Thompson sat; hunched over, as if in agony, on their brown leather sofa. Mr Thompson had his frozen hands wrapped around a mug of hot tea. Ironically, the printed words on the mug read, '*Keep Calm and Carry On*'. Mrs Thompson was staring, up at the ceiling, her red eyes still brimming with salty tears. A man stood in front of them. A solemn man, wearing a PCSO's uniform; talking to them. But they couldn't listen to a word.

"...lastly, I just wanted to say how profusely sorry I am that this has happened to you, Mr and Mrs Thompson, and I can assure you that whoever committed this..." he stuttered. "This... disgusting atrocity..." he gulped the words down, as if he were swallowing a ladle full of cod-liver oil, "...will be brought to justice". He turned to Mr Thompson, and indicated at the frail-statured; green-faced old lady sat next to him. She was still staring at the ceiling. "Is she going to be okay?" he inquired.

"She'll be fine.' Replied Mr Thompson, quietly.

"Are you sure? It's just that we can always arrang-"

"She'll be fine."

The morbid figure in the police-officer's uniform took one last look at an oblivious Mrs Thompson, before he nodded; and respectfully turned to walk out.

"Goodbye, then. Obviously you'll be the first to hear any news."

Silence. Eventually broken by the *'creeeaak'* of the front door, and consequent, gentle, closing. The married couple stared at each-other, aimlessly. Mr Thompson breathed in, and started talking.

"They were very nice up there, weren't they?"

Silence. "I mean, they didn't rush us or anything. That was nice." More silence. Mrs Thompson's eyes were fixated, and squinting a little, on the ceiling...

She was imagining a different era; a sepia-tinted memory of picnicking in the Windborne hills. Jam sandwiches, pork pies, a Victoria sponge... just her, her husband, and...

"Karen, you really need to stop this. Talk to me. Please?" Karen suddenly snapped out of it; as if she'd just been slapped around the face with his vile, inappropriate words.

"Fuck. You. Jonathan." She proclaimed; teary but firm.

"What?" Jonathan was taken aback.

Karen rose up from her haunch, taking hold of a vase; one that she had made herself, on a family holiday. With, of course, a little help from...

"Fuck you!" She screamed, hurling the homemade commodity at the papered walls. Jonathan saw a flash of blue, orange, green... then heard a stifling *'CRASH!'* as one of their only physical memories of their baby was demolished before their eyes. Karen looked at him with dull, empty eyes and whimpered. She lifted her bony, withered hands with her chewed fingernails to her sunken face; and collapsed on the floor. *An image almost guaranteed to crack even the stoniest of faces.* Yet Jonathan stood there; unsympathetic, under Medusa's curse.

Turkish Delight

* * *

"*...And it seems to me, you lived your life like a candle in the wind...*" Elton John's rich, recorded vocals echoed out of the church; as everyone stood up in unison. Six young men, dressed in mahogany velvet tuxedoes slowly made their way in; carrying above their heads a fuchsia, child-sized coffin. Sounds of sobbing streamed in from every aisle in the crammed church; friends, relatives, teachers, club-leaders... but the loudest, most cutting sobs were produced by Mrs Thompson. Dressed in a midnight midi-dress, with a red-rose pattern; and clutching a silk, slightly damp handkerchief, she cried;

"I love you sweetheart!" as the coffin was rested at the top of the ancient, gaudy church.

"She knew, Karen." A lady next to Mrs Thompson comforted her. She looked a lot like her actually, but more fresh-faced and well-rested. Her skin was peachy soft, as opposed to Karen's maudlin, leathery shell. She put her arm around her, "She always knew, darling."

Jonathan stood, staring. Alternating his eyes between the coffin and his brown loafers. His stony face was that familiar grey-colour again, and he didn't say a word all service.

* * *

"Right, have you packed everything away?" inquired a heavily pregnant Karen. It had been a year. Efforts to find out what happened had proved fruitless. Mr and Mrs Thompson were trying their best to ignore it; to trowel fresh cement over the irreparable cracks in their collective heart. They were having counselling; bereavement as individuals, and marriage as a couple. They were coping, not thriving.

"Still got a couple to do, love." Jonathan extended an arm and rested it on his wife's shoulder. She shrugged it off.

"Good, okay, well, hurry up then." She dithered, and briskly walked off.

All Jonathan had ever wanted was the love of his wife. The

thing is, he became unfaithful so soon after their first baby was born. Their golden girl. Karen found out; and she never quite forgave him. The fact that she even became pregnant a second time was something of a mystery. How would he be able to look his second-born in the eye, knowing that he was just the product of a drunken night consisting of emotionless, flat, validation sex...?

"That's the last of the boxes, I think."

"What did we do with all her old school things?"

"They're in the box marked *Loft*".

The unhappy couple got into the van, and looked at each-other. For a moment, there was a resemblance of feeling between the two. But, it was scarce, and gone within a micro-second. The baby would be born in a couple of month's time, and then... well, they didn't know. The van whirred and spluttered as a lethargic Mr Thompson started it up. It slowly reduced itself to a mild hum; as they drove off. Speeding away from the inevitable; a getaway from their inescapable problems; a remnant of salvation was felt, until... the familiar numbness.

* * *

The wind took a violent turn; the little girl was suddenly blasted in the face with a powerful gust of freezing wind, knocking her over onto her backside, leaving her, therefore, in a bit of a daze. Getting up, and inspecting herself for cuts and bruises, it dawned on her... she'd let go of the kite! How disappointed are Mummy and Daddy going to be when they've discovered their efforts had gone to waste? She knew she just had to get it back. She started running; picking up the pace, bypassing the adolescent oak, clawing back the weeping willow, stomping in the mint green footpath, desperately trying to grab it to safety...

But it was gone.

"Anabelle!"

That dreaded sound; gruff, purposeful. Like he was going to... not again...

"Anabelle!"

If she kept quiet, maybe he'd give up and go away. She couldn't bear the thought of facing him; the man who haunted her nightmares. But this was more than a nightmare to her. After all, nightmares end. He persevered; up the hill. The wind grew icier, the sky greyed over. Anabelle closed her eyes...

"Anabelle, for God's sake, what're you hiding from?" The horrid man called. His sand-coloured hair was blowing in the wind. His face was... grey.

"Nothing, Daddy." Anabelle said, in her smallest voice.

"Well! Come on then, let's see your kite!" Daddy exclaimed. Daddy didn't smell too fresh. In fact, Daddy smelt like the place you go when you want to order drinks at the pub. He always went funny when he smelt like this. He didn't act very much like a daddy when he smelt like this... he sharply nudged his daughter; "Come on! Where is it?!" He suddenly stopped acting jolly and silly. He had a serious look on his face. "You haven't... *lost* it, have you, 'Belle?"

Anabelle looked at her father; the man who would shape her view of the male sex for years to come, the one man she was supposed to trust. She looked at him, meekly, through her eyelids. In a wobbly, quiet voice, she whispered;

"Yes."

Her father looked straight at her. Rage flickered across his face like a faulty light bulb struggling to provide a red-hot glow.

"You... *stupid* little brat!" he snarled, "You ruin everything." He went to turn away. Anabelle thought she'd got off lightly, and breathed a sigh of relief. However, he advanced towards her, and spoke again,

"You've ruined my marriage." He shoved her. "You've ruined my health." He shoved her again, harder this time. He paused for a minute. "You ruined my *fucking kite*-" he stopped mid-sentence... and inhaled the soured, Kentish air. He shoved her again, one, final time. Before he did, he howled at her; four words. Four, harrowing words;

 "You've ruined my *life*!"

On the final push, young, sweet Anabelle fell to the floor; and hit her soft, fragile head on the whimsical, peppermint footpath.

The Cold Records – Dan Patton

The nightmares, which had begun to plague Adam, played on a common theme; they featured the same nameless man, immersed in an ice-water bath, screaming in agony as his extremities froze white.

That such horrors could have been perpetrated by scientists like himself was unthinkable. On the other hand, Adam's research into new approaches to preventing and treating hypothermia had recently hit a brick wall. So far all he had to show for nine month's work was a hypothesis based on mice; a credible milestone, but – and it was a significant 'but' – animals and humans differed widely in their physiological response to cold. If Adam could only prove his theories with reference to human data, he was convinced his current funding would be extended for another year. In fact, the university's Research Funding Committee had hinted that his sponsor, Avithermotech, a dry-suit manufacturer for the aviation industry, might increase their commitment, thus allowing Adam to hire a team.

Frustratingly for Adam and due to a clumsy oversight on his part, he'd discovered, since agreeing to the sponsor's brief, that the coldest temperature he was allowed to expose a human subject to – namely 36 degrees – was not low enough to replicate conditions faced by flight-crews downed in sub-zero seas. Unfortunately it was precisely such conditions – and the body's physiological response to them – that his sponsor enthusiastically believed held the key to a patentable new dry-suit technology.

It wasn't simply a matter of finding a willing human subject to freeze; the test would have to be approved by the university. If Adam went ahead without approval, not only would he be sacked, no reputable research journal would publish his paper.

He'd seen the hypothermia project as a stepping-stone towards promotion and maybe some lucrative consultancy work, but without publication his research findings would remain unaccredited and commercially worthless.

He could see no alternative, but to incorporate the hypothermia study dated from wartime Germany, but there was a problem. How big a problem he wasn't yet sure, but it was potentially so serious that he kept putting off finding out, just in case the 'no' he dreaded hearing turned out to be definitive, rather than the start of a lively negotiation.

The problem was this. The only data Adam had found on the effects of freezing human subjects to a potentially lethal temperature was in the records of one Dr Sigmund Rascher, the Nazi camp-doctor at Dachau. Morally tainted as the data was, mining its forbidden knowledge surely meant that some good could come from the victims' deaths. Was that morally justifiable? The scientist in him said yes; all knowledge was progress and as such, inevitable. There was also the utilitarian argument that said: Capitalise on the knowledge now, even if obtained by evil means, rather than wait for ethical research to catch up – at the cost of further lives.

It wasn't just Adam's call though. If he strayed too close to the edge of what the medical research community considered ethically tolerable, he'd be ostracised. He'd seen it happen to colleagues; once their reputations were even slightly tarnished, the medical research journals circled their wagons, funding dried up and careers ground to a halt. If, God forbid, the press got wind of rogue science at work, especially if they could turn you into some sort of Frankenstein figure, you could add 'public hate figure' to your list of negative accolades.

He needed to ask Gabe's advice. Normally he wouldn't dream of involving a rival researcher, due to the intense competition for funding and the consequent risk of his work being co-opted before it could be rightfully ascribed to him. Gabe, however, was not only a good friend; he sat on the university's Research Ethics Committee. He was therefore unlikely to view Adam's research with a covetous eye. The problem was Adam had an inkling, more than an inkling in fact, that Gabe might be opposed in principle, given his Jewish heritage. Adam's fervent hope was that Gabe's passion for scientific enquiry would overcome any moral dilemma about using data from a Nazi prison camp.

The research lab allocated to Adam for his project was cramped, due to the extra equipment he'd needed to install. There was a large chest freezer, an industrial icemaker; on loan from a catering supplies company and a plumbed-in bath, which could be used for rewarming or freezing. There was also an ECG monitor and portable blood analyser borrowed from the university's hospital.

Rory, Adam's lab technician was at his computer deep in concentration. He wore an ill-fitting lab coat and large, ear-covering headphones. Rory didn't notice Adam at first; Adam had to wave across his line of vision in the manner of a mime artist pretending to wash a window. Eventually Rory looked up, startled, then relieved. He removed his headphones and acknowledged Adam's presence.

"Hey Adam, wassup?" he enquired casually.

Adam regarded Rory with mild contempt, inwardly despairing at the unkempt beard, poppy-seed bracelet and Guns N' Roses t-shirt, visible inside his unfastened white coat. When the university had promised Adam some assistance on his project, he had imagined a small team of qualified researchers. What he got was Rory. Oh well. At least Rory turned up most of the time, did exactly what he was asked, and appeared to have no interest whatsoever in the philosophical questions which Adam's research tended to provoke in even mildly curious minds.

"Hi, Rory," said Adam evenly. "How's Millie coming along? Have you had a chance to plot her resuscitation data yet?"

"Sure," replied Rory. "Dropped it in your folder a moment ago".

Adam gave Rory a thumbs-up, sat down at his own screen and clicked on the project file called: *Rapid Active Rewarming: The New Frontier in Hypothermia Treatment.* He reviewed the lab-report on Millie the brown rat. He'd frozen Millie gradually over a period of several hours in order to prevent her going into shock, then attempted to revive her in a bowl of hot water. Reading through the report he felt once again the shiver of excitement he'd experienced when Millie had regained consciousness. She'd lived for a further two days before dying from heart failure. To an outsider this might seem like a small achievement, but in scientific terms it was significant.

He was due to meet Gabe for coffee in the canteen at 11:30am, but first he wanted to prepare his arguments by reading more widely both about Doctor Rascher's research and contemporary views on rewarming hypothermia victims. As far as he could discern, Rascher had discovered rapid rewarming as a technique to resuscitate his frozen subjects. In complete contradiction to accepted methods of slow passive rewarming, which used the patient's own body heat, Rascher found exposing his subjects to external heat – typically immersing them in a hot bath – to be the most successful means of reviving them.

Adam spent the next hour searching the university's digital library for references to currently practiced rewarming techniques. Interestingly treatments for extreme cases of hypothermia, such as a pilot would experience within an hour of ditching into cold seas, appeared to lack a rigorous scientific foundation. The problem was this. No researcher, since Rascher, had been permitted to expose human subjects to

Turkish Delight

temperatures below 36 degrees; nor had anyone built upon the records found at Dachau, made public during the Nuremburg war-crime trials.

Quite apart from the ethical dilemma of using data from, often fatal, experiments inflicted on unwilling prisoners, little of the Dachau research had been formally published. Consequently modern day doctors were unable to accurately calibrate their treatment of hypothermia to a patient's clinical path to revival. Hospitals, even military facilities, baulked at rapid external rewarming due to the high risk of fatality, normally from shock induced by unimaginable pain. The most common approach was to induce warm fluids into body cavities through the peritoneum, rectum or bladder. However, survival rates were low, even where the patient had been wearing a dry-suit. There was a consensus of opinion that passive rewarming was often 'too little, too late'.

Adam clicked back to an analysis of Doctor Rascher's methods. In order to assist the Luftwaffe, Rascher had duplicated thermal conditions faced by its pilots ditching into the North Sea. Over the course of the programme he had subjected some 300 prisoners to sub-36-degree temperatures, recording their shock from exposure, before rewarming them in a hot bath. A third of his subjects died as a direct result. But, thought Adam, that meant two thirds survived – and presumably more would have done so, had Rascher perfected his technique.

Gabe was waiting for Adam at the entrance to the University's canteen.

"Hey man," he greeted Adam with a playful thump on his arm. "How's it going? Wow, you're so cold!" he added, quickly retracting his hand and laughing at his own joke.

They bought two lattes and sat at a quiet table.

After Adam had brought Gabe up to speed, there was an

uncomfortable pause. Gabe massaged his own temples and screwed up his face in concentration. Then he folded his hands together and spoke in a measured tone.

"Adam, I've gotta tell you, I'm not familiar with Rascher's work on hypothermia, but *all* the studies carried out at Dachau and the other death camps are not science, they're premeditated murder masquerading as research! There's at least two reasons why the research you're talking about wasn't submitted for publication at the time:

"Number one. It isn't scientifically robust. I mean God only knows what state those poor bastards were in by the time Rascher got his hands on them, or what other abuses they were being subjected to at the same time.

"Number 2. These are criminal acts; war crimes in fact".

Adam shifted uncomfortably in his seat. Gabe's reaction was even more negative than he feared.

"Listen Gabe," he began hesitantly. "Don't misunderstand me. I'm not morally comfortable with this, but isn't there an argument that says it's criminal *not* to use the data, precisely because lives were lost. For example, I constantly hear the argument that it's our moral duty as citizens to vote because people died fighting for our right – maybe it's not the best example, but am I not even slightly right?"

Gabe was shaking his head emphatically.

"Adam, I'm sorry, but you simply cannot confront the ethical dilemma of using Rascher's data without sensitizing yourself to the images of the frozen, the injected, the tortured, the killed…millions of innocent men, women and children".

Adam sensed he'd already lost the argument, but played his trump card anyway.

"I hear you Gabe, but surely as a scientist you acknowledge that data is knowledge and all knowledge represents progress in the service of humanity."

Adam gave a hollow laugh.

"Nice try Adam," he replied. "But isn't the word 'data' a smokescreen obscuring the reality of human suffering. How about we substitute the word 'data' for a bar of soap from Dachau; a vile bar of soap made from the remains of murder victims".

Adam sighed. This was not good. If Adam's views represented those of the ethics committee – and he had little reason to believe otherwise – his research project was doomed.

Later, back at the lab, Adam clicked a link, which Gabe had just emailed to him. It was an eye-witness account from Dachau. It read: 'Doctor Rascher immersed his subjects in vats of ice water, or left them out to freeze in the winter cold. As the prisoners excreted mucus, fainted and slipped into unconsciousness, he meticulously recorded the changes in their body temperature, heart rate, muscle response, and urine. The shrieks of pain from the hypothermia victims were so intense and frequent that Doctor Rascher once requested his lab be transferred to a much larger facility at Auschwitz, where his concentration wouldn't constantly be broken by his victims' screams.

That night Adam was unable to sleep. His thoughts kept returning to the Gordian knot of his stricken project. His rational self knew there was probably no solution, but every time he felt the welcome-sign of sleep approaching, his subconscious bade him to have one last attempt at unpicking the moral dilemma in a way that might convince Gabe – and ultimately the university – to let him build a working hypothesis using Rasher's findings.

When sleep finally drew Adam into its undertow, he dreamt again of the frozen man, screaming in agony. He recoiled from the image and staggered into the bathroom. He showered, luxuriating in the warm lather of the soap as it washed away the sweat of this night terrors. As he rinsed the bar of soap,

Adam noticed that it was leaking red dye into the plug-hole. He examined the bar more closely and found to his horror that it was made of flesh and blood; sinews, veins, fingernails, eyelashes; crumbling apart in his fingers until he was standing ankle-deep in blood and human entrails. He woke up with a jolt and the stark realisation that he simply couldn't use any of Doctor Rascher's research.

For the next few days, Adam's sleep was thankfully uninterrupted by nightmares. However, his waking hours were a living torment. Despite his determination to salvage at least some of his research, each new day brought more setbacks. The Research Ethics Committee had reviewed his project and concluded that the university could not and would not sanction the deliberate exposure of human subjects to hypothermia, even if Adam found volunteers willing to sign a waiver, which had been Adam's hopeful suggestion.

As a result the university's research board had seen fit to inform Avithermotech that the project was in jeopardy, behind Adam's back. The sponsor was now threatening to sue both the university and Adam personally for breach of contract and financial damages. At a meeting with one of the university's lawyers, Adam was told that the board suspected Avithermotech had known for some time, possibly always known, that the project was undeliverable and had an ulterior motive, namely publicity for their existing products and/or financial compensation. If they assumed that the university would be inclined to pay up rather than enter into a costly and reputation-damaging fight, they had judged the situation rather well. Adam's prospects looked increasingly bleak, but there was one more avenue he hadn't explored.

It was Rory's idea. In less desperate circumstances, Adam would have dismissed it out of hand, but his lab technician's ignorance about accepted scientific methods had allowed him to spot the obvious solution to saving the project. 'Out of the mouths of babes and fools,' Adam reflected once he'd come to accept the naïve brilliance of Rory's suggestion.

***

The water was bloody cold, almost unbearably so. Adam gritted his teeth and leant back in the ice-bath, careful not to dislodge any of the electrodes monitoring his vital signs. Rory moved his computer screen so that Adam could see his body temperature as it dropped. Then he sat at the other screen and started to monitor the data from the machines, ready to record it at key intervals. On his desk was a hypodermic syringe of adrenaline, which Adam had taught him to inject if absolutely necessary along with the phone number of the hospital's A&E, just in case Adam went into cardiac arrest. As previously instructed, Rory put on his headphones and listened to a heavy rock compilation he'd made. Adam had warned him that he might cry out in pain or beg Rory get him out of the bath. On no account, Adam had insisted, was Rory to allow that to happen until the experiment was complete.

10 minutes had elapsed. Adam was shivering uncontrollably and there was an acute discomfort in his eardrums. He saw that his temperature had fallen to 36 degrees, but using a mindfulness technique he was able to partially separate his conscious mind from his physiological response. This left him feeling numb rather than freezing cold and he was able to briefly reflect with triumph on the experiment he was undertaking. He couldn't wait to tell Gabe that he'd solved the ethical dilemma that had prevented any progress in hypothermia treatments for so long. Obviously he couldn't just use himself as a test subject, but surely his colleagues would relent once they were forced to accept both the validity of his data and the fact that his method of obtaining it was safe, or at least not fatal.

After 15 minutes, Adam's temperature had fallen to 35 degrees. He felt like an astronaut about to set foot on a new planet, despite the pain which was becoming hard to bear, most likely because his thoughts had drifted away from the mindfulness routine. He focused again on his breathing, but found it impossible to ignore the burning sensation in his limbs. He could barely see the monitor anymore due to a thin film of ice coating his eyeballs, but was fairly certain he saw it flick to 34 degrees. He needed to endure this temperature for at least 10 minutes, but he was beginning to doubt whether he actually could; he was literally freezing solid. He tried to lift his head out of the water, then his arm, but they were both dead weights. The pain was excruciating. He tried to cry out, dislodging frozen flakes of saliva from his mouth and throat.

Suddenly Adam was floating above the bath looking down at its ice-bound occupant; unrecognisable; nameless; face twisted in a rictus of pain. Why didn't the lab technician notice him? Was he complicit in the victim's suffering? Why was he glued to his screen, apparently typing, while the man in the bath, immersed in icewater up to his neck screamed in agony as his extremities froze white.

Then Adam and the man from his nightmares fused back into one, just before a wave of blackness descended and the sharp stars pin-pricking his eyelids winked out one by one.

Sonata for Sausage Roll and Exploding Foam – Richard Salsbury

I

Vols-au-vent. Veal carpaccio. Caviar in crystal dishes. Bloody *caviar*. And, of course, it all tasted wonderful. It was the conspicuousness that annoyed Don. 'Just a little something to eat' was how Sebastian had phrased it, implying that if he put his mind to it he could conjure something far more opulent. Or at least pay someone to do it for him.

Even the sound system offended: it tinkled with chamber music, cultured to the point of intimidation.

Don hung around the safety of the buffet. The house was vast – the sort of place you could walk round for hours and miss the Louis Quinze wing entirely. Linda had already abandoned him, off in search of news about the rest of her family. She might already be lost forever.

He glanced at his watch and sighed. A decent conversation wouldn't go amiss – something that didn't revolve around collateralised debt obligations or credit default swaps.

'No sausage rolls?' he said, maybe a little louder than necessary. Those who turned away he could safely ignore. A man at the end of the table with steel-rimmed glasses and an unruly beard wandered over.

'I know what you mean,' he said. 'This is a bit rich for my blood. Still, I intend to eat as much as possible. Redistribution of the wealth and all that.'

'I'm Don.' They shook hands.

'Phil. Sebastian's cousin.'

'I'm Linda's husband. Surprised we haven't met before.'

'I don't usually turn up to these things, but sometimes it's good not to have to cook.'

'Thought you'd grab some crumbs from the rich man's table?'

'Something like that,' Phil said. 'So, what do you do for a living, Don?'

'Ah ... well ... yes.'

'It can't be that bad. Everyone makes their contribution to society.'

'I'm a game designer.'

'Computer games?'

'No: board games.'

'Oh, really? Can you make a living out of that?'

'I do now. I've been designing games since the 80s, but I've only gone full time in the last couple of years. Although maybe I should have stuck with teaching English.'

'You regret making the change, then?'

'It was a compromise. I took a full-time position with a company called Game Factory, who focus on family games, and after I'd been there 6 months the CEO shifted towards a "more plastic, less strategy" kind of ethos. Anything to get us on the shelves at Toys R Us. From there, it's all been downhill. The minimum age for our games seems to drop every year. I'm waiting for us to release something for babies to play while they're still in the womb.'

'It would have to be small ...'

'I used to design games about the Battle of Waterloo or the building of the American railroad. Meaty, interesting stuff. But this last thing I did ... it's just awful.' Don didn't want to talk about it.

'In what way?'

On second thoughts – he *did* want to talk about it. 'It's basically a plastic telephone box – a base with four hinged sides and a removable lid which keeps the whole thing together. Players take turns to stuff these squidgy foam people in through the holes in the sides.'

'How many people can you fit in a telephone box?'

'Exactly. Eventually the box can't take the pressure and it

explodes, scattering foam people all over the place. And voilà: you have your loser. The rules are so short they're printed on the back of the box.'

Phil was nodding slowly.

'I'm sorry,' said Don. 'I'm venting and I've only just met you.'

'Not at all. It's good to vent every once in a while.'

'So, uh ... what do you do, Phil?'

'I'm a psychotherapist.'

Oh, for goodness' sake.

Phil laughed. 'No need to pull that face – I'm off duty.'

It was almost like Phil was giving him permission to continue. Well, why not? Don could always blame the champagne.

'What annoys me is that what I do – what I'm good at – is no longer valued. Whereas Sebastian invents some "financial instrument" that no-one understands and the entire banking sector wants to ...' he was going to say 'suck his cock', but managed to stop himself in time. 'He's got everything, hasn't he? He's richer than me, smarter than me, better looking. And he's a decade younger.'

'Do you resent him?' Phil said with a quirk of the lips.

'Of course I resent him!' Don said. 'I thought you were supposed to be off duty.'

'Yes, quite right. If it's any consolation, I resent him too.'

Don clinked glasses. 'Cheers. Have a vol-au-vent.'

Later in the evening, when Phil had excused himself to search for his wife, Sebastian appeared at the buffet to reload his plate.

'Like the music?' he asked. Without waiting for an answer he added, 'Bach's sonatas for violin and harpsichord. Wonderful. You're familiar with the sonata form, I assume?'

'Uh ... not really.'

'There are three movements, you see. The first introduces

the theme, the second takes off in another direction, and the third returns to the first theme but transformed by the second. Listen and you'll hear it.'

Don goldfished for a few seconds.

Sebastian changed tack. 'The caviar's fresh in from the Caspian. Do try it.'

'I have,' Don said.

'Still making those little games of yours?'

'Oh, yes ... yes.'

A few years ago he would have defended himself against that word 'little', made a case for what he did. Significant that nowadays he didn't. And yet Sebastian himself was also a game player. Isn't that what investment banking was all about – gambling? At least Don didn't gamble with other peoples' money.

Sebastian moved closer and lowered his voice. 'Listen, while Linda's not around I wanted to ask you something. Are you, uh, okay for money?'

It was typical of Sebastian – offer and humiliation in one neat package.

'Yes,' Don said. 'Yes, we're fine, actually, thank you.'

II

The post arrived at midday, just the two letters. Don retreated to his armchair in the lounge to read them. One was addressed in a calligraphic font he had learned to recognise.

'Oh, God,' he said on opening it.

Linda's voice came through from the kitchen, where she was chopping carrots. 'What is it?'

'An invitation to another of your brother's soirées. I suppose you'll want to go.'

'Of course. Wouldn't you, if it was your brother?'

Don cast his eyes over Sebastian's flowery prose with distaste. It was only once Linda appeared in the doorway, knife in hand, that he realised an answer had been required of him.

'Yes, all right – we'll go,' he said, 'just put the knife down.'

It was the sort of thing that made her laugh, but not this time. She tilted her head. 'You don't need to compete with him, you know.'

'I ... it's not that I ...'

'I didn't marry you for your investment portfolio. I'm quite happy with what we have.'

'Really?' It was the kind of reassurance he needed.

'You think I'd rather be married to Sebastian?'

'The thought had crossed my mind.'

'That would be incest, darling. Anyway, you were having a good chat with Phil at the last one.'

'Yes, it'll be good to talk to Phil. Assuming he's there, of course.'

'*That's* what I married you for,' she said, drifting back into the kitchen, 'your optimism.'

He ripped open the second letter. It contained a photograph and a note, handwritten in blue biro. The photo was of a game of Telephone Box, post explosion, foam men scattered over a white table. Sitting behind it was a dark-haired boy, eyes squeezed shut, mouth wide. His arms were blurred – he appeared to be batting the table with his palms.

He read the note.

Dear Mr Redwood,

This might seem a bit wierd, me writing to you out of the blue like this. I asked the people at Game Factory for your address. I hope you don't mind.

My son is autistic. He's called Ben. His dad left the scene a long time ago, so I brought him up alone. It hasn't been easy. I'm not asking for sympathy or nothing like that, but it definitely has not been easy.

Anyway, I'm writing about your game, Telephone Box. I

bought it for Ben a couple of months ago. The first time we played it he was literaly crying with laughter when the box burst. He set me off too. Usually he gets upset if he loses something. But he didn't care. He loves losing now.

I've included a photo of Ben so you can see how much he enjoys it.

We play Telephone Box every day. He always plays with the orange men because orange is his favourite colour.

Yours gratefully,

Kayleigh Martin

III

Foie gras, quails eggs, gravadlax. And sausage rolls. Don had slipped them onto the table at the start of the evening while Linda, wavering between amusement and disapproval, had provided cover.

Phil sidled up to him, one of Don's pastries in hand. 'Are these anything to do with you?'

'Guilty as charged.'

'They're excellent. Make them yourself?'

'Delia's recipe, my handiwork.'

Phil's wife arrived to steer him pointedly away from the buffet. He winked at Don and swiped another sausage roll on the way past.

This time Don made more of an effort to circulate. He even rustled up the confidence to rib the other bankers about the unreality of their jobs. They weren't offended – in fact, they agreed with him. Perhaps they were human beings after all.

Sebastian swung into his orbit, champagne flute in hand. 'Like the music?'

'Bach's sonatas for violin and harpsichord, isn't it?'

Sebastian blinked twice. 'Oh. You know it?'

'To be honest, I prefer AC/DC for a party.'

Sebastian looked like he'd just swallowed a cherry stone.

'Not a rock and roll kind of guy, then?' Don said.

'Not *exactly*, no.'

Of course not – that would be like ordering Prosecco for the party instead of Krug. Imagine what your colleagues would say behind your back.

Don really should do something about this cynicism of his.

'Work going well?' Sebastian asked.

'Not bad. I've resurrected a game I shelved years ago about silk trading in Renaissance Italy.'

Sebastian glanced over his shoulder, then back again. 'Really?'

'There must be, oh, at least a dozen people in Britain crying out for such a thing. I'm going to self-publish it as a limited edition.'

'Don't get me wrong, but is that really …' Sebastian looked pained, apologetic '… worth the effort?'

'Oh, yes. Of course it is. It'll make a dozen people ecstatic.' He said it with a conviction that even he found surprising.

Sebastian cocked his head and his expression relaxed. 'Well, yes, when you put it like that, I suppose … That's the advantage of doing a job where you actually produce something physical. Whereas my job is just numbers, numbers, numbers.' He barked a short laugh.

'But those numbers could make such a difference to someone. You remember last time we met I, uh … refused your offer of money?'

'Yes?'

'How about donating to a charity instead?'

'Yes. Yes, of course. I'd be delighted.' Sebastian reached into his pocket. Don thought he might be about to whip out a chequebook, right there and then, but no – it was his phone. 'Did you have one in mind?'

'The National Autistic Society.'

Sebastian tapped in a reminder to himself. 'A thousand sound all right?'

Good God. Just like that. 'Sounds wonderful.'

'I'll do a bank transfer tomorrow. Linda always said you were full of good ideas.' Sebastian tilted his champagne glass in a little salute, then disappeared back into the crowd.

Linda was right – these parties weren't so bad. Don sauntered back to the buffet for a celebratory sausage roll. He was too late. The plate contained only crumbs.

Starving – Yvonne Popplewell

Peggy Strange never reacted particularly well to being broken up with. She didn't like it, at all. It made her feel vulnerable and alone in a way that often sent her over the edge of bad behaviour. She'd be the first to admit she made mistakes in the past, but to the best of her knowledge she had never joined a cult of undead man murdering vampires before. The fact that she did this time was *entirely* Sam Diaz's fault.

In Peggy's defence the whole man killing vampire thing seemed kind of cool after two bottles of prosecco and twelve episodes of *Gossip Girl*. Give her a break, she'd been broken up with, she was definitely not in the right state of mind to make significant life decisions, or any decision at all really. She was sad and angry and she wanted Sam Diaz to pay for her pain. So when a group of the hottest girls she had ever seen told her they could give her the revenge she'd been dreaming of Peggy jumped at the chance.

Also it turns out man murdering vampires are actually super fun. They pulled Peggy out of her pity party and rebuilt her wounded ego in less than two hours. She wanted to be friends with them, she wanted to be part of their clique. They were her kind of people, apart from the murdering.

It goes like this, Peggy was at home starring into the abyss of an empty ice cream container getting angry at Netflix for asking yet again whether or not she's still watching. Of course she's still watching, she had nothing else to do, she'd been abandoned and left alone to wallow in the company of terrible TV for the rest of existence. She wasn't planning on showering ever again and had practically moved into her pyjamas. She was sad and she was going to stay that way.

That's when they burst into the room. A flurry of colour and beauty. So much energy Peggy was exhausted watching them. She had no idea who they were but they made her feel comfortable, they even binged with her for a bit til she felt comfortable enough to shower. By the time she was clean they had put the mess of her life back together in a way that made them feel indispensable.

They took her dancing, they made her feel sexy, they listened to her complain about Sam Diaz as much as she wanted. Then at the end of the night they told her they could fix all of her problems. They would rebuild her world from the ground up and all she had to give up was her soul. A reasonable request. Peggy wasn't even sure she had a soul to begin with.

If it sounded too good to be true that's because it was, although they never technically lied. Not really. They just didn't explain things in words Peggy could understand. Revenge to her meant putting dog poo in his favourite sneakers. For her new friends, revenge meant murder. Like real murder. Bloody murder. The kind of murder that only really crops up in horror movies, not the kind of thing regular folks are expected to deal with on a daily basis.

Peggy, as much as she didn't want to admit it, could probably have worked around the whole murder thing. Her new friends were really cool and if they wanted to murder some of the men that did them wrong she wasn't going to judge. The problem was murder was kind of compulsory. It was a non negotiable requirement for entry into the club and there was a catch because if Peggy didn't fill her murder quota by killing Sam Diaz, she would die herself. She really should have read the fine print on that soul exchange.

Here's the deal, in exchange for her soul Peggy got eternal life, beauty, and super strength. A total bargain, she thought. They told her it would hurt more than a little, but girls are used to suffering for their survival. Peggy could handle the pain. It was no worse than bad cramps, and she loved the way her skin cleared almost immediately. They didn't warn her about the hunger.

The pain dissipated, the worry ebbed and flowed, but she was always hungry.

At night, in the company of new friends the fresh wounds of

heartbreak still open, it all seemed perfectly reasonable. Sam deserved to die, he hurt Peggy and Peggy didn't deserve to be hurt. A whole room of women backed her up on that. Sam was the worst, he had it coming, she was doing the world a favour by getting rid of him really. It made sense, it was the only thing to do.

Unfortunately there's a certain level of clarity that comes with being dead, or undead, whatever Peggy was after her transformation. She saw, quite clearly, what she had not been able to see only a day before. Sam Diaz was definitely a dick, but he didn't deserve to die.

Peggy Strange has made mistakes before, but putting herself in the position where she had to either kill or be killed took her questionable life choices to a whole new level. It was terrifying. At the same time, it was possibly the most interesting thing that'd ever happened to her and if she survived the ordeal it would make for one hell of a story for potential grandkids. Except she wouldn't have any grandkids. Not anymore.

The clarity and understanding that allowed her to see what was right and wrong became more apparent as she heard stories from the women around her. They had real reasons to hate the men that hurt them, and if they hadn't already killed them Peggy might have done it herself. They were victims of rape, violence, and other unimaginable horrors Peggy would rather forget. The more they talked, the more it became clear, Sam Diaz did not belong with these men.

There's part of her that wants to punish him anyway. Punish him on behalf of all the women around her that have were beaten beyond repair. He's complacent, Peggy can see that, she understands the rules of gang and where they come from. All men are responsible for the actions of each other because they condone it, or they turn the other cheek, they let it happen. But if Sam is guilty then so is Peggy because she had conflated her wounded ego to the terror these women faced, she didn't deserve to be one of them.

Peggy knew what she was supposed to do, she could see the options in front of her. She saw what was right and what was wrong. But Peggy had never been a hero, she didn't care about much beyond her own pleasure and happiness. She cared about others of course, she wasn't a sociopath, she just cared about herself more. That instinct of self preservation had served her well and if she went with it she could be near invincible.

It sucked, Peggy thought, that the moment she was given the world on a platter was also the moment her conscience found a voice. If only her death had highlighted her selfishness, then she could have been happy for eternity murdering men with her new friends. Instead she was going to die a hero and it was all Sam Diaz's fault. She hated him and she hated that she couldn't use her hate to justify his death.

Peggy was really pissed off by the time night rolled around and she had to head out on her hunt. She was angry at the world, she was angry at the girls, but most of all she was angry at Sam Diaz because if he hadn't been such an asshole she wouldn't have been heartbroken enough to join an undead cult and they wouldn't be in this mess.

The girls around her watch Peggy wearily, they'd been by her side as she transitioned but at this point they seem unsure. Like they aren't convinced Peggy will follow through. They have a right to be worried.

When Peggy saw Sam she acted on instinct, one she wasn't aware she had until that moment. She asked to say goodbye. Tried to act angry, pretend she just wanted to kick him where it hurt a little before they got around to the actual killing. She didn't think they believed the bravado but apparently a final conversation was not an unusual request. They let approach her prey without a second thought.

Before anyone could change her mind Peggy grabbed Sam pulling him towards his bedroom at the back of the apartment. He seemed to be in some kind of vampire trance, Peggy wasn't aware they could do that and she was more than a little disappointed she would likely never get the chance to test the skill. She loved the idea of being able to manipulate people like that, she might be doing the heroic thing for once but Peggy Strange certainly wasn't a saint.

There was no time to see what she could get away with while Sam was under her control, unfortunately. Although she was pleased she got to slap him out of the trance. That was fun. Sam wasn't too happy about it but as she was about to save his life Peggy wasn't particularly concerned with his feelings. She told him to shut up, which was also very satisfying, and they climbed out the window and into the night.

Sam did not shut up, but he follow Peggy and Peggy didn't punch him as much as she really really wanted to. And she really really wanted to.

Once out the window Peggy really got the chance to test her new skill set because running at human speed was just not going to cut it. They needed to get as far away as possible as quickly as possible. Peggy ignored Sam's obnoxious complaints, throwing him over her shoulder and running in any direction the wind would take her. It didn't matter where they were going as long as it was not where they were.

She ran and she ran somehow able to tune out the man screaming on her shoulder. Peggy felt great. Running faster than any human could, it felt amazing, she was amazing. She was also starving.

The hunger hit her like a brick, it was unbearable. Like she hadn't eaten in weeks, months, possibly even years. Like she had walked through the desert without water and was suddenly confronted with a lake. She wasn't just hungry she was starving and there was a Happy Meal hanging off her shoulder. As if she needed a reason to hate him more than she already did. Sam Diaz really was the worst.

Peggy threw Sam on the ground, a little less gently that she probably should but she was in a lot of pain. She managed to grab him before he tried to run, despite the fact that she was doubled over as she felt her own stomach begin to eat itself. She wasn't entirely sure that was what was happening, but it sure as heck felt like it.

"Would you stop," said Peggy in despair as the man she was gripping continued to yell about nonsense. He probably had a point somewhere in his ramblings but Peggy didn't have the time or the inclination to listen so all she heard was gibberish. "I'm trying to save your life."

Sam stopped, not because he was listening to Peggy so much as he seemed to have run out of things to shout. Peggy didn't care. She was sad, and hurt, and she just wanted to go back to her *Gossip Girl* marathon but instead she had to die a painful death in company of a complete asshole who wasn't even asshole enough for her to kill without guilt. Peggy let herself cry, not holding a single tear back. If there was ever a situation that warranted tears, it was this one.

"Those women were going to kill me?" asked Sam after the silence lasted too long.

"Nah" replied Peggy. "They were going to make me kill you."

"But you wouldn't right?"

"I seriously thought about it," answered Peggy after a moment. She didn't really want to talk to him but didn't have anything better to do for the rest of her life. "Apparently I'm nicer than I thought I was."

"Why would you kill me?" asked Sam.

Peggy let out a breath of laugh. He honestly had no idea, what an asshole. "Because if I don't kill you I die."

That got to Sam. Got him thinking, Peggy didn't have to look at him to know that. She could see him calculating the options. Thinking through the possibilities. Trying to figure out how to get away from her before she snapped and killed him in her desperation to stay alive. He was tense, terrified and she did not want to ease his panic. He deserved to panic, this was all his fault after all. But Peggy didn't want to have to chase him, she was seriously tired and so so so hungry.

"Relax I'm not going to do it."

Turkish Delight

"Oh," said Sam.

"Yeah," said Peggy.

It was awkward, no getting around it. Now that the panic and drama of the kidnap and escape had dissipated they were left alone with the reality that the last time they saw each other Sam had been trying to act as though he hadn't been stuffing Peggy around for months before ditching her without warning because he met someone he actually liked. There was a lot left unsaid in the silence.

That's when Peggy realised she was about to die, like she knew before that but she hadn't really processed the reality. Instead of getting mad or sad, all she could think was that she no longer cared about social etiquette. She was absolutely not going to spend her last few moments on earth being polite.

"You're an asshole," said Peggy pointing angrily at Sam.

"Sorry," he replied awkwardly, he looked like maybe he might run again but daylight was rapidly approaching so Peggy wasn't worried about keeping him safe anymore.

"You're always sorry, and you're still an asshole."

Peggy screamed, a wave of pain took hold of her body. She was so hungry and Sam looked appetising in a way that probably would have disturbed her if she had been able to think about anything other than the pain.

"Are you okay?" asked Sam and Peggy would definitely have broken her resolve not to hit him if she had the strength but she didn't so she settled for giving him the nastiest look she could conjure.

"Am I okay?" she repeated, like she could not believe he had said anything let alone that. "I'm dying you human shaped paper cut of course I'm not okay."

Sam looked like he might stop talking but then any good instincts he had were overtaken by his asshole brain, "Can I do something?"

"Yeah," said Peggy rolling her eyes at the pleased look on Sam's face, he was excited to be of use. He always liked being useful.

"You can shut up," continued Peggy revelling in his falling expression. She probably shouldn't be enjoying his pain quite so much but as she was about to die she figured she could indulge herself a little. "Asshole."

Sam seemed to get the picture finally, he didn't speak again but he didn't leave either. He just stood awkwardly beside Peggy as she cried in pain. Peggy would never admit it because she had some pride left, but she was glad he stayed. He was the last person she wanted to be with at the end of her life but he was better than nothing. Besides it was only a couple of days ago that she would have been happy to spend her last few moments with Sam Diaz.

She tried to remember what that was like, what it felt like when she still cared about him, when she still liked him. It left a bitter taste in her mouth, although that might have been the blood she had started coughing up, much to the disgust of Sam who sort of tried to pat Peggy's back until she stared him into stopping. She didn't want to remember the good times, she didn't want to lie to herself. Sam Diaz was an asshole and she wanted to relish that reality with her dying breath.

As the first hint of sunlight hit the horizon Peggy noticed where she was. The beach was a rather poetic place to die she thought. She wondered for a moment, between gasps of pain whether Sam would be blamed for her death. That was a pleasant thought to have as her eyes started leaking what she hoped was blood but was more likely brain matter.

Sam did look genuinely traumatised as he watched Peggy waste away and it was almost worth dying just to see his face turn green. He looked like he was going to pass out but Peggy didn't get to see it. Her body, her mind gave out before he collapsed but her final thought was a happy one. Peggy Strange knew that although she had saved him, she had also without a doubt ruined Sam Diaz's life and she was absolutely sure he deserved it.

Consequences – Sen Jayaprakasam

11th April, 15:55

Squinting past eyelashes, speckled with rain and sweat, I struggle to wipe my smartphone dry. The gale cuts coarse across my jacket, deafening me as it flaps against my ears. In one final effort, the wind forces the hood clean from my head. I gasp. Icy water catches my neck and trickles down my spine.

I glance over my left shoulder: the image of Tower Bridge's walkway jars with each frantic step. But I can't afford to slow. Apart from a spattering of tourists huddling under Union Jack umbrellas, all I see are empty streets.

Yet, somehow, I know he can't be far behind.

Suddenly, my shoe catches on a cracked paving stone. The other, trying to compensate, overshoots and slips long across the waterlogged pavement.

I twist and scramble, desperate to hold my balance. My arm shoots out towards the railing. But all too late. I fall. My knee twists. The weight of my other leg crashes onto my ankle. My teeth jolt hard onto the side of my tongue.

The pain blinds me.

I release a silent scream as a metallic tang stings the back of my throat. My ankle sears hot and wet as it swells. Blood stains my torn trousers just as quick as it's washed away.

I catch my breath; the pain begins to numb. I lift my head, but once again I see nobody following behind. I look ahead and see a few more people, huddling in groups by the side of the bridge. Some glance in my direction. Most don't seem to notice. I try to lift my leg but the pain reawakens, freezing me in place.

I can't move it. My only chance is my phone – but it must have slipped free in the fall!

My eyes dart in all directions, wild in their search. Finally, they snag on its shining blue cover, dangling precariously over the drain.

I roll onto my front, teeth gritted through the pain. I crawl methodically over wet dirt and discarded cigarette butts until, eventually, I reach it. In one swift movement, I scoop the device free from the edge.

My heart sinks.

The screen's cracked and water has leaked inside. I press the power button. It responds, although almost half the screen stays grey. Still, I may have enough time to use it before the rain corrupts its circuits.

Sheltering it under me, I fumble with the touch screen.

That's when I see him. Diving past tourists as he hurtles towards me. I run my fingers along faster until, finally, I reach the saved number. I press "call".

Pick up, I demand, holding the phone to my ear. *Please, just pick up.*

The phone doesn't even ring; it goes straight to voicemail. I glance up to see Richard, hovering over my crippled body. Despair cuts deep into my eyes.

***

11th April, 15:00

The earthy aroma of freshly ground coffee beans lingers in the air while machinery hisses and hums behind. I take my time, sliding another teaspoon of chocolate dusted froth onto my tongue. It melts away into nothingness. I smile.

My attention swiftly draws to the tall figure entering the café door. Catching my eye, he offers a bleach-toothed grin as he casually strolls over in his tailored Armani suit. The clothes, I'm well aware, are for my benefit. It's Richard's not too subtle method of reminding me of his success.

'Sorry I'm late, Tom,' he says, taking a chair. 'Took a bit of time to get out.'

Punctuality has never been Richard's forte, but this time

Turkish Delight

I'm actually grateful. It's given me a chance to mentally prepare before he arrived. Now, if I can just hold my nerve for a few more minutes, this whole affair will finally be over.

'It's Jenny,' he adds. 'She's been a bit distant lately, what with my work kicking off. Took a while to convince her that she should come join us today.'

My breath falters.

'Jenny's coming... *here*?'

Richard nods. 'I hope that's OK. I can't imagine she'll be long. I figured you two have barely spoken since the wedding; maybe it'd be a good chance to catch up?'

I attempt a weak smile before averting my gaze. Jenny turning up certainly complicates things. But perhaps, if I'm quick, I can be done and gone long before she arrives.

'So,' Richard continues, 'what's new?'

'Oh, not much,' I say with a curl to my lips. 'Work's been a bit slow lately. It feels like everyone's looking for a therapist come Christmas, but after the new year, most just drop off the radar. But then...'

My words abruptly halt to the sound of Richard imitating a snore. He always did know how to get under my skin.

'Come on Tom, you know what I'm *really* asking. Nick's been spreading rumours you took some blonde home from the bar the other night,' he smirks. 'So – what's the goss?'

'*Nick* has an overactive imagination,' I reply, feeling my face flush. 'She was just a colleague who'd had too much to drink so I drove her home. Nothing happened.'

Richard's eyes light up. 'Hah – I knew it! If there's one thing you can always count on it's good old Tom striking out with another girl.'

He draws his eyes to the window before checking his phone.

'Jesus, you'd think that psychology degree would have taught you *something*. It's been what, two years since your last relationship?'

'Try four,' I correct, biting my lip. My words linger longer than I intended, but at least they get the message across.

Richard's eyes widen. He shoots a quick glance at the front door before leaning in a little closer.

'Tom... you're not saying?'

I narrow my eyes, answering with a single head nod.

'But that was four *years* ago? Christ, I don't even remember her name.'

Something snaps inside me.

'Rachel,' I yell, as conversations falter around us. 'You knew we were together. But that didn't exactly stop you, did it?'

'I thought you were just messing around! I didn't exactly think...'

'Of course you didn't – you *never* think! You cost me the love of my life and to you it's all just a joke.'

'*Love of your life?*' he says, glancing at his phone. 'You'd only known her four months!'

My fingers curl tight under the table.

'You really have no idea, do you? Well maybe you will, when you hear... what the *hell* do you keep looking at?'

'Sorry Tom,' he replies, glancing back from the window. 'Jenny really should have been here by now. She's never late for anything.'

His words catch me off guard.

He glances back at his mobile. 'She always has her phone with her; she always answers. I called twice on the way over and each time it just kept ringing.'

Dread runs cold across my back. Words sink into my throat and refuse to leave. I stand abruptly, tipping my chair. It crashes, splintering across the floor behind.

***

Turkish Delight

6th April 19:40

Satin white sheets, stained with perfume and sweat, cling to my face. Breath helplessly leaks from my lips. I open my eyes, revealing the muffled image of the ceiling light above. She shifts her weight, pulling the sheets from my eyes as the warmth from her naked body settles besides mine. Her golden curls tickle my chest, forcing my gaze upwards into her soulful mahogany eyes.

Abruptly, I turn, rolling onto my shoulder. A smile creeps tight across my face.

Finally, I have my revenge. Years of plotting, of putting up with Richard's arrogance and narcissism, culminate in just one primal act.

I sink my teeth into my lower lip.

But at what cost?

'What's wrong?' she whispers, words melting in my ears like butter.

'Nothing,' I say, meeting her eyes once more.

I didn't mean to fall for her. But how was I to resist? Such a tender soul with the charm and looks to match. She needed me; and I was more than willing to save her from his grasp. But it would break her heart if she ever discovered why it all started.

'Of course something's wrong,' she stammers. 'It's all wrong! What the hell are we doing?'

She turns her head away, but I can still feel her body tremble against me. Instinctively, I move to her, resting a hand on her shoulder. She grabs hold tight.

'What were we *thinking*?' Her words strain, creaking at their edges. 'Your friend; my *husband* – we've both betrayed him. The guilt – it's *unbearable*. He gave me everything and I...'

'Jenny,' I say, rubbing my other hand over her back. 'Richard doesn't deserve you. Remember?'

'Tom, I *love* him.'

206

'But does he love you?'

'He... he must do.'

'No Jenny,' I say, shaking my head. 'I'm so sorry. But to him, you're a prize, not a person.'

I turn her towards me, wiping the wet from her eyes. 'I made a commitment,' she continues; the resilience fading from her voice.

'He isn't the man you thought he was.' I glance across the length of their bedroom. 'Give it time. I understand how hard this can be, but he was using you. He *manipulated* you.'

She lowers her eyes with a hint of a nod.

'All that matters is that in a few days, the two of us will be together and we can put all of this behind us.'

She glances hesitantly towards her phone.

'You'll see.'

***

29th March 13:30

'Remember what we've talked about. Think back,' I say, watching the light trace her figure. Even from my chair, her sweet floral perfume draws me ever closer.

'I can't... I, I know he loves me. But I can't think of the last time he asked.'

'I'm sorry, Jenny,' I sigh, recalling the speech I'd prepared. 'This is difficult for me to say. Richard's a friend, but I have a professional responsibility to be completely honest with you.

'You came to me asking to get to the source of your depression; to help you feel whole again. But I can't do anything until you face reality.'

I watch her eyes fill as she swallows.

'I'm not saying Richard doesn't *want* to love you. But

maybe he's not physically capable. Maybe he can't show it. Either way, the reality is he can't be there for you in the way you need.

'He knows how ill you've been, yet he won't talk about it. He knows you need support and yet he's never there. If you can't think of a single time when he's even...'

'He saved me!' she interrupts.

I fall silent.

'He doesn't know it, but he's saved my life more than once.'

Her eyelashes flicker as she stares blank into the distance.

'A few months ago, I was at my worst. I felt completely useless. The guilt of being alive, nothing but a burden to anyone else; to Richard. I stopped eating; sleeping; doing much of anything at all. Eventually, I decided to start going for walks to pass the time...

'London has so many bridges; so mesmerising and beautiful. They would call to me; tempt me to climb up and peek out over the edge. The closer I walked, the more things started making sense again. It felt so... simple. Easy. Kind.

'I would stand there, gazing across the water. I'd feel the wind on my skin; I'd hear the call of the birds. But soon enough, all of that would go. I'd feel nothing. Hear nothing. I was free; staring into the endless blue below.

'But each time, before I could step any closer, Richard would call my phone, wondering where I'd got to and when I'd be home.

'That feeling. The feeling that someone still needed me – *wanted* me – was enough to keep me from taking that last step.'

Neither of us speak. The sound of the ticking clock echoes across my office. Anything I'd planned on saying seems irrelevant now.

I allow myself a measured breath.

'Jenny, if you ever feel that low again – if you ever feel yourself being drawn back to that bridge – please promise me you'll remember that feeling?'

She doesn't respond. My eyes wander, snagging on the shining blue cover of my smart phone on the desk.

'Promise me: you'll wait for that call?'

Valentine's Day – Jordan Ryder

"Are you going out with anyone tonight?" I asked the receiver.

"Nope."

"Do you have plans?"

"Nope."

I sat on the bed next to Vera as she flipped through the pages. *'Look for a list,'* I mouthed. To Al: "Have you already been out?"

"Nope."

"Huh."

"Yup." Talkative as ever.

There was a thud and I looked up. Vera had clapped the book shut, her eyes large.

"Al, I have to go."

"Sure, just tell mom I called."

"Kay."

"Bye."

"Yeah, bye," I said, though I'd already taken the phone away from my ear.

"What?" I asked Vera.

"We shouldn't be in here." She looked scared.

"What did you read?"

"I really don't think—."

"What is it, Vera?"

I remember thinking, quite clearly, that she didn't get to know something about my life that I didn't.

"Do you want to see it?" she asked, her eyes wide. I nodded and she opened the book, flipping pages until she got to one with a piece of paper stuck in-between.

I took the journal from her and, standing, read the note. It was a letter.

Dear Joanne,

I'm writing this to you because I need to be honest with you. In the program honesty and forgiveness are two steps...

The program?

...I am so sorry...

It was from months ago, I realized. And it was an apology letter.

So he had cheated on my mom, then. I'd known. It was clear from her voice when she'd told me they'd broken up. I'd had to ask, which had been unusual enough. What I hadn't known was that he was in a program. The only program I knew was for alcoholics, and Mark still drank. Often enough, but not too much.

I don't expect you to forgive me...

Damn right.

But of course she already had, hadn't she?

But I know I need to be honest with you. Anne came over to talk, I had no intention of...

Sure, you had no *intention* of anything. But you still did. Anne had been his girlfriend for 10 years before mom.

This is not an excuse...

It better not be.

But...

Yeah right.

I've been going to my SAA meetings every day since...

SAA?

Part of being a nymphomaniac is...

Nymphomaniac. Everything I knew about nymphos was from The Simpsons or South Park jokes.

...It's an illness, but one I thought I had better control over...

What the hell is going on?

"What's a nympho?" I asked.

"A sex addict," Vera breathed. Her eyes were wide, but her mouth curled. She didn't look scared anymore. She looked excited.

We'd been drunk that night. It was Valentine's day, we were 16, single, and home alone. My brother, Al, was in college, and Mom was out with Mark. Looking back, if Al hadn't called right then I would've been the one to open the journal. I would've flipped through the pages looking for the right one. *I* knew what I was looking for, and it wasn't that. And, if I hadn't been drunk I might've remembered the list wasn't *in* her journal. We wouldn't have picked it up to begin with. We never would've found that letter.

But we did.

You see, it had been over a year before that I'd stumbled onto a piece of paper jammed into a book. It had been an accident. A *true* accident. From the start.

Again, I'd been home alone. But I'd been looking for baby pictures of me and my brother. I was having a bad night and a bad year, and the photos were old, of my house the way it used to be. I'd pulled out the bottom drawer of my mother's dresser where she kept old prints and I'd knocked over a stack of books. Cleaning them up, I'd picked one up that had a pad of paper stuck inside, and it was while I was pushing the papers back in that I noticed the cover: "How to Save Your Marriage," a 7 step, how-to guide by Marianne Matthews. I stopped.

The book was sunny yellow and orange. Bright. Cheery.

"The 7-step program proven to save marriages like YOURS."

"Matthews's approach to 'troubled couples' is spot on."

"Don't wait till your marriage is in trouble. Read this book NOW."

I opened the book to the pad of paper. Wouldn't you have?

It was a list. It featured things like: *"Invite him inside in July. Talk about his emotions. Smile and empathize. Listen.,"* and *"Engage in a constructive dialogue about communication issues and strategies."* They weren't my mom's words, but I recognized her handwriting. The last item on the list was, *"Have him home by November."*

I closed the book and put it back on the pile. I shut the drawer with the photos still inside. I went downstairs and called Vera. Crying, I told her what had happened. How it'd been 7 months since my dad had moved out. How Al and I understood, they weren't happy together anymore, and we were trying to move on. He was 19 and I was 16. Mom was 54.

My dad didn't come home that November. Surprise. Dad had a new girlfriend by then, and they've bought a house now. She is lovely, and my dad is happy.

My mom didn't start dating again until over a year after I'd found the "How to Save Your Marriage" book and her list. It was October. Mark was the first, and they'd broken up and gotten back together once already before Christmas. I'd guessed why, and the letter had told me I'd been right.

So, a year later at 17 and with almost two full bottles of wine in us, I'd tried to show Vera that list, the one that had sent me sobbing to my cellphone and to her more than a year prior, and instead of the list we'd found the letter.

Almost a year after that Valentine's day, I looked at Mark's Christmas card to my mom.

Dear Joanne,

Look at how far we've come from one year ago...

And aren't you lucky that you have.

"She seems happy, at least," Vera had told me. My aunt had said the same.

I googled nymphomania once. One article suggested violent or cruel punishment from parents as a cause. Others were biologically based. I stopped after reading "a constant desire to have sex," and a man can have "sex an unlimited number of times without reaching an orgasm." I never googled it again. I

Turkish Delight

never could watch the movie Don Juan, either.

I could never sleep on the same floor of them in the house. Not because of any noise I ever heard, but because of the thought of it. Sometimes it was the wind sighing against the glass that sounded like an exhale from the next room. Or a creak in the floorboards that sounded like a bed moving, when it was just a footstep on its way to the bathroom. I wanted to be as far from their bedroom as I could get. I gave up a top floor room with a window alcove and a built-in shelf for my books. Instead, I slept in the room with an attached bathroom. It was bigger than hers, so every morning my mom came in before work to do her makeup and blow-dry her hair at 7 am.

And I never complained.

Four years after I found the letter, I found a book on the kitchen table from my mom's hen party. I was at her house picking up her jewellery. "Sex Games: *Wanna Play?*" it read. My brother thought it was hilarious, but I never laughed.

I stood next to two of them at the altar, listening as they said their vows. I watched them say "I do" and exchange their rings. My Mom cried. So did Mark.

I didn't give a speech. I let my brother speak for us, her children. I wrote it, but they were his words. *"Even though you don't like Supertramp, and you laugh louder than anyone at your own jokes, we couldn't be happier to be here today celebrating you both. Thank you for making our mom so happy, Mark. Welcome to the family."*

Later, Mark came up and gave me a hug.

"Thank you for coming. I'm so happy you could fly in to be here, I know it was a long way for a weekend." It was my Moms wedding. Of course I'd flown in. "I don't think she could've gone through with this if you hadn't made it. It means everything to your mom and I."

I nodded, silent. Swallowed.

He smiled.

I opened my mouth to speak:

"Me too. Congratulations."

Blind Date – Philip Pendered

Lottie came bursting into the house in her usual way, slamming the front door behind her.

"Hi, Mum," she called out as she pushed open the sitting room door, expecting to find her mother watching the TV. But her chair was empty and there was an empty glass on the coffee table. Lottie sniffed it. Wowee! Gin. Ah well, poor old Mum, she probably felt she needed something to cheer her up. After all, she doesn't have much fun. She doesn't go out enough, thought Lottie.

An appetising smell of fried bacon came from the kitchen. She made her way there, expecting to find her Mum busy over the stove, listening to classical music on Radio 3. But when she pushed open the door, there was no music to be heard, and no Mum to be seen either. So she looked in the oven, where she found a nice plate of mixed grill being kept warm for her. What a wonderful Mum she could be! Turning round she caught sight of a bottle of gin and, oh dear! it was nearly empty. Lottie began to feel seriously alarmed. "My God! She really has hit the bottle this time." She heard the door being closed upstairs and unsteady footsteps on the landing. Lottie rushed to the foot of the stairs wondering what she was going to see. Would her mother be staggering drunkenly with her stockings hanging down? Would she have to catch her? What she did see amazed her much more. An elegant woman was gliding gracefully down the stairs towards her.

"Mum," she gasped. "You've had your hair done, and you're wearing make-up."

The shy, hesitant smile that Lottie knew so well played round her lips, which seemed to be saying, "Well, what do you think? Do I look alright?"

"You look terrific, Mum," said Lottie. "But where are you going?"

"I'm going out."

" I gathered that. All on your own?"

"I'm going to meet someone."

"Someone?"

"He's called Patrick."

"But who is he?"

"That's what I'm hoping to find out. Your supper's in the oven, dear. Have a nice evening, and with that she sailed out of the front door, while Lottie stood staring open-mouthed.

At about the same time Patrick sat alone in front of a double whisky at a small table in a smart, modern, noisy bar. It was not the kind of place he normally frequented.

Why on earth had he chosen this place, he wondered. Well, he had felt so embarrassed talking to her; so when she asked "Where shall we meet?" this was the only place he could think of, and now he was wishing he had chosen somewhere cosy and quiet.

No. this was definitely not for him. He suddenly decided he couldn't go through with it, drank off his whisky and was about to go. But, he thought, it would be so unkind to make her come here for nothing, and she had sounded so nice on the phone. In any case he felt curious, curious to see what sort of a person could have thought up such an honest, natural ad.

He had been looking through the "soulmate" ads with a mixture of amusement, dismay and regret that romance seemed now beyond him. Why had he been reading those ridiculous ads he wondered. It wasn't out of idle curiosity. After all, Angela had died over four years ago, and though he didn't want to admit it, even to himself, there were times when life seemed empty. He couldn't deny that he'd been looking for someone to share his life with, what was left of it, and hoping to find that someone while there was still some life left in him. Their old friends had been good to him, of course, but they were all happily married. Then he had hoped to find the right sort of person at the evening activities he attended, yoga and creative writing classes, but he hadn't met anyone interesting enough to have a relationship with.

Turkish Delight

So there he had sat reading the soulmate ads, strange calls from bored or lonely women trying to attract an unattached male to their side, like the exotic animals to be seen on wildlife TV programmes, some rare species of frog perhaps, which during the mating season send their strange whoops echoing through the tropical night air in the hope that an available mate will hear it and respond.

Whatever the reason, he had found himself looking at that page. "**Women seeking men**" he had read. As he glanced down the columns, his eyes were caught by various desperate appeals to attract a mate: "Slim blonde 54, WLTM" "M" "for walks in wilderness." "Attractive shapely F, 50s, seeks rich gentleman, 60+ , who would enjoy spoiling this romantic petite F, who has a lot of love and care to give"; etc. And all of a sudden he'd spotted one that was quite different from the others: "A not particularly attractive woman of 56 hopes to find a nice man of similar age." That message had immediately appealed to him. She sounded so direct and sincere.

"Give it a go," he had said to himself. And now here he was, wondering what sort of person would turn up. He looked at his watch and saw there was still a quarter of an hour to go before the time they'd arranged. He decided to have another whisky, another double. To steady his nerves.

There were so many people crowded round the bar that it took him a while to attract the barman's attention. He was making his way back to his table and was about to sit down, when a woman approached him. She looked at him and smiled. So this was her? Wow! How could she describe herself as unattractive?

"Jenny?" he said.

"Hello," she replied.

"I'm Patrick," he said and held out his hand.

"Hello Patrick." She paused, and then said with a laugh: "Aren't we going to kiss?" And she put her face forward. He aimed his kiss at her cheek, but she turned her face so that the kiss landed on her lips.

"What would you like to drink?" he asked.

"The same as you."

"A double?"

"Why not? Is this your table? I'll keep the seat warm for us." And she went and sat on the bench seat he'd been sitting on.

When he came back with the whisky, "Come and sit next to me," she said, nice and close. Patrick took a good pull at his whisky, to give him time to think how he could start the conversation. They seemed already to be on more intimate terms than he had expected. As he put his glass down, she leaned towards him and said in a low voice: "What lovely eyes you have, Patrick! I love brown eyes. They really turn me on."

Patrick felt it would be rude not to respond, So he looked into her eyes and said, trying to make it sound as unromantic as possible: "Yours are nice too. I like blue eyes."

"Some people tell me they're grey."

"They look blue to me, Jenny."

"What a lovely man you are, Patrick! I think we could have a very nice time, just you and me together, don't you?"

"Ye-es," he replied cautiously. "But we hardly know each other yet, do we?"

"So let's get better acquainted, shall we?" she said, placing her hand on his thigh. "But not here," she added. "Come on, drink up."

"Yes, let's get out of this place," said Patrick, beginning to feel a little uncomfortable at the way things were going. It would perhaps change the atmosphere if they went out into the cool night air, he thought, and found a place where they could talk quietly. So, rather foolishly, he said: "Do you know somewhere quiet and cosy where we could carry on our conversation?"

"Yes, I know a very quiet, cosy place, and it's not far away."

"Alright. You lead the way then."

As they went out they passed a nicely dressed woman who gave Patrick a searching look, as if trying to catch his attention. But he was so anxious to escape from Scanio's that he didn't respond. There was something about the way this Jenny woman was behaving that had started to make him feel uneasy. It was all too good to be true, he felt, or rather, too sexy. She was trying to arouse him, he realised; what's more, she was beginning to succeed.. Could this be the woman who had written the ad that he had found so appealing?

They walked along together for a short way. Suddenly she stopped.

"Now let's get things straight," she said in a very different tone of voice.

"Yes," he agreed. "Let's get things straight. Look here. "Are you really Jenny?"

"What the hell does that matter? You can call me what you like, can't you? What difference does a name make?"

"I'm afraid there's been some mistake," he began. "I went in there to meet someone called Jenny."

"What are you complaining about?" she replied playfully. "You met me. We can have just as nice a time together, don't you think." She was speaking again in the sexy voice she had used in the bar, making a last desperate attempt not to let this potential client escape, he realised.

"I don't think you understand. Yes, it was a blind date. That's true. But it was a serious one. We wanted to see if we could get along together more or less permanently and..."

"In other words I've been wasting my bloody time, have I?"

"Yes, I suppose you have. I'm sorry, it was all a mistake. I mean, er, I didn't realise you were er, a...

" A prostitute? Is that what you were going to say?

"There's nothing wrong with prostitutes."

"Well then, what's holding you back? I could see you were enjoying it."

"I haven't got any money."

"Well, if that's all that's worrying you, my love, you can have it for free this time," she said, knowing perfectly well that that wasn't the reason he'd refused her. She just wanted to taunt him.

"No, really. That's very kind of you, but I didn't come here for sex, you see. I've got to go now. Can I give you this?" He held out a ten pound note.

"Ten pounds! Keep that for the collection bag next time you go to church. What a big baby you are! Frightened of a prostitute, huh! Ah well, lover boy, I'm always here if you need me. And she walked away with a smile of triumph on her face.

The following morning Jenny was sitting in the kitchen having breakfast. As she sipped her coffee, she thought about the previous evening. She was almost certain that the man she had seen leaving Scanio's with that woman had been Patrick. "I wonder what happened," she said to herself. "Ah well." And she went back to reading the paper. A little later later Lottie's head appeared round the door. "Well, Mum, how was your evening?"

"Interesting," replied Jenny slowly. "Yes, very interesting."

"What about Patrick? What was he like?"

"I'm not quite sure. I didn't get to speak to him."

"You mean he didn't show up?"

"Well, I think he did. At least, I saw a man wearing the sort of clothes he'd described to me, and hs face fitted the description he'd given too. But he was with another woman. She looked to me like a – how shall I put it? – woman of easy virtue."

"Do you mean to say he was going away with a prostitute? How hilarious! It sounds as if you've had a lucky escape."

"Well, I'm not sure. He looked so worried and embarrassed. I think it must have been a mistake. Anyway, I'll give him the benefit of the doubt. But somehow I don't expect to hear from

Turkish Delight

him again."

"So what did you do, Mum? Did you come straight home?"

"No. I stayed on in that bar for a time. It was, as I said, very interesting. Patrick's 'lady' wasn't the only one. I think it's a place for, er, lonely men. I was approached by several."

"You, Mum? Oh my God! What did you say?"

"The first time I was so surprised I didn't know what to say. So I mumbled something about waiting for my friend. It was an interesting experience, er, quite exciting in a way."

"Mum, you can't mean it."

"Alright, interesting."

Telephone rings. "Perhaps that's him," said Lottie as she went to answer the phone."

"I very much doubt it," said Jenny.

But a moment later Lottie came back. "A gentleman for you, Mum," she said, with a grin, and left the door open. This is what Jenny heard:

"Yes, this is Jenny. Who am I speaking to?"

"....."

"Patrick?"

".........."

" Patrick who was meant to meet me in that bar last night."

".............."

"Yes, I thought that was you, but you seemed engaged.

"............?"

"I hadn't realised it was that kind of bar."

".."

"No, she turned out to be a prostitute."

"

"................."

"I stayed on for a while, quite enjoying the atmosphere.

"............?"

"Perhaps. But not tonight. How about Tuesday?"

"..........."

"Yoga? What time does that finish?"

"..........."

"Alright then, half past eight on Tuesday. And you'll be calm and relaxed after the yoga. I look forward to meeting you then."

".......?"

"Yes, that's a good point. Where do you suggest?"

".............?"

" Why don't we go to the same place?

".........."

"Good. I'll meet you at Scanio's with a 'c' on Tuesday evening at 8.30. And this time don't let any other women grab you before I get there. Don't speak to anyone else. I'll say: 'You must be Patrick. I'm Jenny', and we'll go on from there. Bye."

"........."

At eight thirty on Tuesday evening Patrick walked into Scanio's. He spotted her almost immediately, sitting all alone at the very same table he had sat at. "I know you're Patrick," she said, "but you're not wearing the right clothes."

" These are my yoga clothes. There wasn't time to change. You must be Jenny, but you haven't said so yet." He smiled and held out his hand. She took it gently and looked at him, smiling.. He sat down opposite her, and didn't feel at all shy.

"I'm so sorry about Friday night," he began. "It was very stupid of me to be taken in like that. I don't know how she did it."

I guess neither of us is very streetwise. Was it a very distressing experience?"

"I wouldn't say 'distressing'. In fact, I have to admit that it was rather enjoyable to begin with, Until I suddenly realised what she was trying to do. "

"Come on, do tell me all about it, Patrick," said Jenny. Were you already sitting down when she started working on you?"

"Yes, exactly where you're sitting now."

"And she was sitting where you are, I suppose?"

"No, we were both sitting where you are, side by side."

"Golly!" she laughed. "It must have been a bit cramped."

"Yes, it was. And - er, intimate."

"And you were enjoying it?"

"To be honest with you, yes, I was. I feel so ashamed about it now." And he began to blush.

"Patrick," she said with a gentle smile. "There's nothing to be ashamed of. It's the most natural thing in the world. I'm glad to think that you can be aroused quite easily. I came in here as you were leaving, you know. I was pretty sure it was you, but just in case it wasn't, I stayed on here for a little while. And then, as I stayed on a little longer, do you know, I found that I was beginning to enjoy the warm, sexy atmosphere. I nearly got picked up too." They both laughed.

"I'm glad you weren't," he said, and gave her hand a little squeeze. " I wonder how I came to choose this place.

"Well, I'm glad you did, and I'm glad we've come here tonight."

"Why do you say that?"

She looked at him, smiling. "Well, look at us, Patrick. Here we are talking and laughing together, frankly and easily, as though we've known each other for years. If we hadn't come here and you hadn't had that, er, adventure, we would probably be wondering what on earth to say to each other. I'm usually quite shy, you know, and so are you, aren't you? Without your previous lady friend, we'd never have got round to talking so freely. I think we owe her a lot."

"Do you think I ought to come back here next Friday night

to pay her back?"

"You mustn't tease me like that, Patrick. I'm not used to it, and it makes me feel all funny." It was her turn to give his hand a squeeze. They looked at each other and smiled.

"You're quite right," he said, "sex is difficult to talk about. And it *is* important. But it's not the most important thing in a relationship, is it?"

"So what is, Patrick?"

"I don't know. Perhaps the most important thing is to be true to yourself."

"As you are, Patrick."

"It's what I most admire about you, Jenny." And he drew her gently towards him and kissed her on the lips."

Cleaning Up – Sandra Howell

The stench was so powerful, her diaphragm and abdomen rebounded squeezing her stomach. A sweet and sour tang of rotting food almost cut through the air. It was choked by the stink of an illegal abattoir.

An impasto of human waste decorated the wall. In places it was as if someone had used a palette knife to plaster the wall a dirty reddish-brown. She wiped the wall with the stringy rats' tails of the mop. At first she only succeeded in an uneven redistribution of texture and colour. After emptying the bucket several times, she could see the dove grey wall. Some of the waste had slid down onto the floor. It merged with what looked like lumps of cheese and carrots bobbing in a creamy broth.

In one of the cubicles, her cloth sopped up a burgundy molasses oozing from the toilet seat. The cloth had become a tie-dyed cherry red, transforming into a blush pink under the tap. She heard a groan. Not possible at 420am. Her t-shirt sucked the hollow at the base of her spine where her sweat had pooled. The water in the bucket was black again.

She pushed open the door of the fourth cubicle, leaving the wheeled bucket behind her. The searing whiteness made her squint. There were no smeared fingerprints on the door. The dark ring of scum at the water level was absent. There was no mahogany stain at the bottom. She couldn't see a drop of mustard yellow under the seat. Not even a watercolour red dribbling down the curve of porcelain. Not even an ochre puddle around the base. She couldn't smell anything either; not the eye-watering sting of ammonia, or the eco-cleaner they insisted she use, nor bleach which she knew was much better. Maybe she had cleaned it without thinking. At 4am she was on auto-pilot like everyone else. She was a good cleaner. But this was brilliant. It wasn't even squeaky clean. There was no sound, except for her breathing, which seemed to be getting faster? And that groan.

Less for her to do. She stripped a rubber glove from her right hand, skimming her forehead to stem the sting of perspiration in her eyes and tucked loose twists back into her headscarf. Mariama looked hard at the bloated image reflected in the metallic toilet lid. She was caught by; a hint of yellow in the creamy whites of her eyes, dew drops on her upper lip and her ashy grey knuckles.

She exhaled. She squirted the eco-cleaner into the bowl. Her re-gloved hand waved at the sensor. A red waterfall cascaded into the toilet, it was thicker than water. The pollution of the abattoir invaded the atmosphere. The groan swelled. She backed out of the cubicle catching her heel in the handle of the bucket. She managed to right herself.

"Mariama, you should of finished by now."

Mariama pivoted to see Donna standing on the threshold of the unisex toilets. Her long fine plaits, held back in a scrunchie, revealed a geometric face.

"It was disgustingly filthy," said Mariama.

"Why. Do. You. Think. You. Are. Here?" said Donna.

"Donna there's something wrong with that toilet." Mariama's chin lifted towards the fourth cubicle.

Donna's eyebrows dragged up to her hairline. Her heels tapped her way in. Donna looked back from the stall in a child-like state of wonder. Her silhouette was haloed in a bright light.

"Wow."

"Flush it...please," said Mariama.

Donna greeted the sensor. The groan howled. A torrent of red washed into the bowl.

"Need to get a plumber." Said Donna.

"Did you hear?" said Mariama.

"Noisy pipes."

"What about the smell?" said Mariama.

A smog of putrefying carcasses descended upon them.

"This building's always had bad drains, the plumber—"

"But this is horrific." Said Mariama.

"Your PhD, doesn't make you an expert," said Donna.

"It's not—"

"Just clean this up and do the next floor." The clack, clack of Donna's heels echoed after her.

Mariama swiped the foot prints left by Donna. Maybe she had been hallucinating due to a lack of sleep. She should go, but she could not leave that cubicle.

After the sixth time Mariama flushed the toilet, the water was the colour of a rosé. She took the cover off the cistern. At the bottom were a dark red organ, possibly a heart, and some entrails.

"Aargh." She stared at the tiny impressions her teeth left on the chewy rubber fist she had stuffed into her mouth.

A man with close cropped tight black curls, bulldozed into the toilets, "Sorry, Sorry, you always look so tired. Thought if I kept one cubicle really clean..."

"With blood pouring into the toilet bowl?" said Mariama.

"Aaah that. Graham always uses that cubicle, so I thought... didn't mean to get you into trouble. A prank. You know what us City chaps are like." He said.

Mariama looked from the man to the open cistern. The man offered her his hand.

"Steve. You found - they're from an old pig's carcass, hence the smell. Just a joke..." Steve's arm fell to his side.

She said, "What about the groaning?"

"Bit of a laugh. Recording on a loop. Moans every time it's flushed- and at random afterwards."

Mariama's lips flattened to thin lines. "It's not funny, it was terrifying."

"Graham usually starts early...Silly prank I admit—take you out for dinner as an apology?"

"No thank you." She said.

"Why not?"

"Did you?" Mariama nodded towards the dove grey walls and the floor.

"No that's revolting. Must have been an accident- after I set it up- the practical—you know what us City chaps are like."

Steve's voice went up an octave. "I'd be grateful if you didn't say anything."

Two parallel creases appeared between Mariama's brows. "You don't have to take me out."

"No. Please- let me make it up to you," said Steve.

"Another prank."

"No, honestly," he said.

Steve hooked his jacket on the door and rolled up his shirt sleeves. Snapping on latex gloves retrieved from his trouser pocket, he took a plastic sack from his inside jacket pocket. He entered the fourth cubicle, placed the open sack on the floor and plunged his hands into the cistern. Turning to face Mariama, the reek of decomposing flesh wafted over her, as Steve grappled with the organs. He tilted his head and smiled. A flash captured the heart swaddled in a nest of skinned snakes, writhing in diluted blood, dripping through his fingers into the sack.

Mariama reviewed the image on her phone. "Two thousand should be enough."

Available worldwide from

Amazon

———————

www.mtp.agency

www.facebook.com/mtp.agency

@mtp_agency

Printed in Great Britain
by Amazon